IN HIS SHADOW

SHE BELIEVES WHATEVER HE TELLS HER

MARIA FRANKLAND

AUTONOMY PRESS

First published by Autonomy Press 2022

Copyright © 2022 by Maria Frankland

This novel is entirely a work of fiction. The names, characters and incidents portrayed in it are the work of the author's imagination. Any resemblance to actual persons, living or dead, events or localities is entirely coincidental.

Maria Frankland asserts the moral right to be identified as the author of this work.

First edition

Cover art by Darran Holmes

I dedicate this book to my husband, Michael.

With thanks and appreciation for his amazing support.

JOIN MY 'KEEP IN TOUCH' LIST

If you'd like to be kept in the loop about new books
and special offers, join my 'keep in touch list' by visiting
www.autonomypress.co.uk

.

You will receive a free novella as a thank you for joining!

PROLOGUE

It takes between four and ten days after death for a body to reach putrefaction. In a cool cellar, I would expect things to be doing their worst towards the latter end of that spectrum. Today is day eight so hopefully my calculations are accurate.

The odour of death assaults me as soon as I step into the hallway. I reach forward for the light, which blows no sooner than I have touched the switch. No! The fuse box is in the cellar. I should have done this before it got dark, but I've been putting it off all day.

I edge through the kitchen, burying my nose and mouth into the neckline of my jumper. The smell is like nothing I've ever encountered – bad eggs, curdled milk, sewage, and decaying meat all rolled into one. As I reach the cellar door, I pause, trying to get some breath into my lungs without my senses connecting to my inhalations.

The walls between this house and the terrace it backs onto are so thin, they might as well be made from papier mâché. Once a shop downstairs and a large residential dwelling upstairs, it seems the developer took the cheapest option and built something barely stronger than a stud wall between the two resulting homes.

I listen for signs of life from the house behind. There shouldn't be any, but a slim chance exists that the last person I would want to run into could turn up there.

Nothing. Only the gasps of my own breath. Beads of sweat soak the skin beneath my jumper. Instinctively, I release my chin from it, inadvertently succumbing to the inevitable stench that now has its chance to launch its attack, causing my stomach to lurch and my mouth to fill with saliva. I swallow, hard. Although, I could get away with throwing up now, unlike a week or so ago. In fact, it could be viewed as an expected reaction.

I reach out for the door handle and slowly wrap my fingers around it, allowing the chill of the metal to cool my sweating palm. If only I could leave things as they are. But there's no way. I'll have to deal with this. Before long, passers-by will be able to smell what I can in here, as they walk along the street outside.I don't know how long I stand, rooted to the spot, steeling myself as I sway through indecision – do I throw the cellar door open, or edge it ajar an inch at a time?

Before I've even got it a quarter of the way open, a swarm of plump bluebottles fly into my face. I jump back, yelling, spitting them out and swiping at them. There's no way I can go down there. No chance. There's only one course of action I can take. The one we agreed on.

CHAPTER ONE

H ugh is distant. He won't make eye contact. He won't even make conversation. Perhaps it's nerves. What we're about to do is as colossal as it gets. As I shuffle from foot to foot, trying to get some blood pumping, my heels keep lodging between the cobbles. I drink in the chill of the sea air, and avert my gaze into the distance, hoping for distraction from watching the swoop of gulls.

"At least you'll get to keep your bouquet for yourself." The photographer, who I've never met before today, chuckles as he looks at me, then at his watch. He must have looked at it ten times in as many minutes. He's probably off to another one after this. "With no one to throw it to, I mean."

I try to smile. Really, I want to cry. Once again, I attempt to catch Hugh's attention.

"We'll need to be getting inside shortly, won't we?" The photographer blows on his hands then thrusts them deeper into his pockets.

"Like I said, the other witness will be here any minute." Hugh looks from left to right along the street. "We can't go ahead without two of you here. They made that very clear when we gave notice."

At least Hugh sounds as though he still wants to go through with it. I can't lie – I'm getting worried. I've no idea who the other witness is. Another unknown, I expect. All the romance has been sucked out of this day, in complete contrast to the day Hugh proposed to me. It's exactly a month since he whisked me here. Whisked is the only word for it.

He'd persuaded me to ring in sick, saying he had a surprise. I felt light-headed as we parked here, at Alnwick Registry Office, immediately suspecting what was coming next.

"But we've only been seeing each other for five weeks!" I turned to him once I regained my composure. "We're not even engaged."

He dropped onto one knee then. "Nicola Donnelly. I knew from the first moment I clapped eyes on you that I wanted nothing more than to make you my wife."

"Hugh!" Even in the blustery December air, my face was on fire. I looked up and down the street, hoping no one was watching us. I've never been one for public displays of affection, although admittedly, it had been the most romantic moment of my life.

"So, will you marry me, or what? We've come all this way to book it, after all." Then he opened a box containing a beautiful diamond solitaire. The logical side of me wanted to say, let's just wait a bit, but *how could I?* There was nothing else other than to allow myself to be swept up with his enthusiasm. I knew I could get used to the idea. Although my brother and my friends at work might have other ideas.

Hugh had grinned as he slid the ring onto my finger and got back to his feet. "I knew you'd say yes."

Hugh grins now as Gary strides towards us. *Great.* Bloody Gary. It seems as though Hugh's 'no family' regulation only applies in my case. Gary doesn't smile back. Dressed in black, he looks as though he's attending a funeral rather than a wedding. Hugh's dressed as though he's at one of his car showrooms, and as for me, well, it's not exactly the wedding I might have dreamed of. That said, it's not as if men have been queueing outside my door whilst I've been single. Nor am I getting any younger. I suppose I should count myself fortunate that someone still wants me at the grand old age of forty-five. When I went shopping for an outfit, the assistant had assumed I was going to be the mother of the bride and pointed me towards the fussy hats and the two-piece suits.

One of which I wear today. The only hint that I'm a bride is the posy which wobbles between my hands as I glance again at Hugh, wondering why on earth he won't meet my eye. I hope to goodness I'm doing the right thing here. His jaw is clenched as he tugs Gary to one side and mutters something into his ear. I'd love to know what he's saying to him. Judging by their expressions, it's nothing good.

It's the photographer's turn to hop from foot to foot now. "Shall we have one before we go in?"

"What?" Hugh and Gary turn to him.

"A photo, of course."

Without replying, Hugh turns on his heel and heads for the entrance. The photographer follows like an obedient dog. I'm just about to follow, when Gary catches my arm and tugs me back.

"Before you go in, Nicola, I've something I want to say to you."

He's tried to flatten his cowlick with gel and there are beads of sweat on his pointed chin, despite it being early January. He's red in the face as though he's either hungover or he's already been drinking today. But perhaps I'm being too hard on him. He's obviously been running and trying to get here on time.

"Yes?" Hopefully he's about to wish me well. I'm feeling so flat that it would perk me up to hear some kind words. Although on the brief occasions I've encountered Gary, I've had the impression that he far from approves of me. And something in the way he said my name makes me suspect his wishes will be far from 'well' ones.

"I don't agree with what either of you are doing. Getting married, I mean. It's far too soon for all this crap. Especially for you, from what Hugh's told me about you. Nor is it even necessary."

It seems I wasn't wrong. "Why? What's Hugh told you about me?"

"More than enough. I know all about what your father did, which makes me wonder about your state of mind."

A dustbin wagon rattles past us along the cobbles as Gary speaks and, for a moment, I wonder if I'm mishearing him. His eyes are as hard as pebbles. People wander past along the pavement, and I long for their ease and normality.

"Good luck," one woman says as she passes. It's all I can do not to burst into tears.

"Look. I don't want to think about all that today."

"Plus," he continues without looking at me. "I've been told about your ex upping and going. What was all that about? There must have been a reason for him to suddenly do one."

"Thanks for the reminder of all this Gary – right before my wedding." I stare at him in disbelief. Bastard.

"All I'm saying is if you cause any trouble for my brother, or try to come between me and him," he points at the registry office door, then back at himself. "You'll wish you hadn't. Have you got that?"

Oh my God. I can't believe he's speaking to me like this. "Look, Gary. Why don't you leave us to it? I really would prefer it if *you* did one, as you put it. If you can't be happy for us, I don't want you here." A couple slow down as they pass, seemingly aware of our altercation. Nosy sods.

"You need a witness, don't you?" Gary glances towards the door. "And besides, do you think Hugh would go through with this farce if you turfed me out of it? I'm the most important person in his life." He steps towards me. "Never forget that."

"Bloody come on, will you?" Hugh snaps from the doorway as he looks from Gary to me. I'm certain I can see a softening in his face. I just hope I'm doing the right thing.

I'm shaken to the core, but I mustn't let Gary have the power to ruin the day. Thank goodness Hugh isn't like his twin. He's not himself today, but he's the polar opposite of Gary. At least I hope he is.

CHAPTER TWO

It's a relief to exchange the street for the warmth of the foyer. My cheeks burn with the sudden change of temperature, or perhaps with the shame of how I've just allowed myself to be spoken to. I don't know what's happened to me.

Now ten minutes late, Hugh and I are ushered into a side room by a thin, dour-faced lady, whilst Gary and the photographer head silently into the ceremony suite. I'm abruptly aware that my instincts are screaming at me to run, but then something more powerful overrides them. My fear of being alone.

I shiver as Hugh drapes an arm around me for the first time today. His touch is comforting against the chill of my neck, though he doesn't pull me close like he usually would. How on earth can you miss someone when they're standing right next to you? Though, at least he's reaching out to me. I'm sure everything will be OK.

We're asked some questions and once again, we have to produce our identification. I guess she's making sure it's not a forced marriage or one merely of convenience. But whether love comes into it, suddenly, I'm not so sure.

"What entrance music are you having?" The registrar looks from Hugh back to me.

I shake my head. "None." We never discussed music. When I used to dream about which 'walking down the aisle music' I might have one day, it was always *Songbird.* Now I'm wondering which one of us is going to fly away.

"Right, let's get this show on the road." Hugh moves his arm from my shoulder and heads for the door. I follow him, fighting my sense of deflation. This is our wedding day, and a far cry from anything I would have expected for myself. I stare at the back of Hugh's head, silently willing him to snap out of the mood he's in.

Gary and the photographer stand on either side of the carpeted aisle. Both of them face forward and don't turn towards us as we enter the room, like I would have expected. Hugh strides in front and I walk side by side with the registrar. I bet I'm the first 'bride' she's walked down the aisle. Surely Hugh and I should walk together? Or he should already be at the front, waiting for me.

My father's face flashes into my mind. I always imagined that when I got married, he would be beside me, linking my arm, proud and emotional. This time, a year ago, he would have been. I blink back tears as I wonder what he'd have made of all this. He'd have expected me to be walking down the aisle to meet Jason, not Hugh, who I've only known for a matter of weeks. Dad would probably have tried to talk me into waiting until I knew him better. However, Jason showed me what he was made of, upping and leaving before Dad's funeral had even taken place.

As I stand before Hugh, I search his face for signs that he'll make me happy. That he won't rip my heart out like Jason did. I keep telling myself that his behaviour is pure nervousness. Up until today, everything has been perfect between us. Our eyes briefly meet before his gaze flits towards the registrar. She's assembling her documents on the desk in front of us. If Hugh turns out to be a cad, I guess we can always get divorced. Bloody hell. I'm about to be married, and I'm thinking of getting divorced. Really, I should get out of here. I know I should. This is the first time I've seen Hugh in this sort of mood – it must be something to do with Gary being here, or something he's said.

"Please be seated." The registrar nods in turn to Gary and to the photographer who drop obediently onto their chairs. There's seating for thirty in here. I'd love to have filled this room with people today. My brother and sister-in-law, my work colleagues, friends from the gym, and of course, my parents, if they were still here.

My eyes sweep across the opulent cream wallcoverings, which contrast with the crimson seats. This is a place of happiness and for looking to the future. Hugh's really just overcome with the enormity of it all, that's what it will be. As soon as we've got this official bit out of the way, he'll be back to his usual wonderful and attentive self, and we'll go for a slap-up meal to celebrate. We'll be unable to stop staring at our own and each other's wedding rings, and the waiter will bring us a bottle of champagne. People will smile at how *loved up* we are.

I'm not sure what Gary will do after this though. *Why has Hugh even asked him to come?* I'd have much preferred him to have plucked a second witness from the street, a complete stranger, especially after what Gary's just said to me outside. Perhaps it's jealousy he's harbouring or maybe it's something deeper. Whatever it is, I hate the thought that Hugh's been discussing my past with him.

Gary's face darkens as the ceremony goes on. I try not to take any notice or let it bother me, but it's impossible not to. To say he and Hugh are twins, they're like Laurel and Hardy in looks and stature. Gary is Hardy to Hugh's Laurel. That's where the humour ends though. There's certainly not a lot of that here today.

"I now have pleasure in pronouncing you husband and wife." The registrar smiles at us, although she looks as puzzled as I feel. Given the atmosphere in here, I'm surprised she hasn't taken us to one side to make sure this is what we want. "You may kiss your new wife."

Hugh leans towards me, but for the first time since we met, I sense a reluctance from him to be anywhere near me. I'm gob smacked as he pecks me on the cheek like a boy forced to greet a dreaded auntie. Perhaps it's because we're in front of his brother. The heat of tears prickles behind my eyes. I'm not going to be able to fight them for much longer. I've had over two months without so much as a tear. Why on earth am I being forced to feel like this on my wedding day?

"Now my duties are over, I'll take one last photo before I leave you all to celebrate." Relief is etched across the photographer's face as though he can't get away from us fast enough. I don't blame him. Hopefully, Gary will follow suit. I could perhaps stomach one drink with him, so long as he's civil to me. Just for Hugh's sake, I suppose. As long as I know he's leaving then. Hugh and I are booked into a hotel near the seafront. Somehow, I'll get Gary to make himself scarce. I only hope the hotel is fully booked. The last thing I want is Gary checking in. In fact, if he does, I'm going home on my own. As if I'm even having to contemplate this scenario. This is happening a lot lately – visualising negative possibilities, always imagining the worst that could happen. I suppose it's only natural after all my recent losses.

The registrar's voice sounds behind me, making me jump.

"Congratulations." She thrusts some papers at me. "There are two copies of the certificate, as requested. Now, if you don't mind, we need to clear the room for the next ceremony. With you being a little late, and all."

Despite my best efforts to hold them in, the tears that have threatened to erupt for the last hour spill from my eyes as we weave through the throng of the next wedding party waiting outside. Joy and a sense of occasion radiate through each and every one of the people gathered, and the groom can't take his eyes away from his wife-to-be. Why couldn't my wedding have been like theirs? Nothing is ever as it's supposed to be in my life.

My thoughts waver again to Jason, my former partner of twelve years, the man to whom I gave the best years of my life. He insisted from the start of our relationship that he would never want marriage or children. We had some tough conversations, but I eventually accepted his wishes. It was him I wanted, after all. Then, literally a week after Dad died, Jason confessed that he'd been with another woman for the past eighteen months. *Eighteen months.* How had I not realised? Not only that, but she was pregnant. After depriving me of that possibility, the news was like being booted in the stomach. Then the triple whammy came when I later found out they were getting married. I didn't even get out of bed that day. I bet they had a better wedding day than the one I'm having.

Gary and Hugh stride ahead of me, deep in conversation again. We've just got married. Hugh should be walking with me, holding my hand. We have to get rid of Gary.

"So what's the plan?" Trying to pull myself together and load a false lightness into my voice, I catch up to them as we reach the car, still trying to give Hugh the benefit of the doubt.

"I'm going to drop you at the hotel for half an hour Nicola. I'll have a quick drink with Gary, then I'll see him to the train station."

"You're kidding me." I slam the passenger door as I get in. "We've only just got married Hugh. You can't just dump me at the hotel."

The door behind me slams. I didn't know Gary was getting in the car with us.

"It will only be for half an hour Nicola. You can get unpacked. Make a brew." Hugh glances at me – at least he has the grace to look slightly apologetic.

I don't want to make a scene in front of Gary, so I decide to accept things as they are. Same old, same old. Put up and shut up. As soon as Gary's gone, we'll make up for this. "So, you'll come back for me in half an hour?" I reach for his hand as he changes gear. "Do you promise?"

"Half an hour." He tugs his hand away. I always thought it was me that was less comfortable with public displays of affection.

As we pull up outside The Red Lion Inn, Hugh presses the button that pops the boot. He's driving my Audi, which I suppose is half his. Now we're married. It suddenly dawns on me that everything I've got, including all my parents worked for, could half belong to him. I was so swept up in the romance and the excitement of our relationship that I hardly considered a pre-nup to protect it all. And on the fleeting occasion that a pre-nup entered my mind, something stopped me from mentioning it to Hugh. I suppose I was worried about upsetting him and spoiling things. If I'd been allowed to tell my brother what I was doing, he'd have made me consider it. Or stopped me from getting married altogether.

But now, as I drag my case from the boot, I wish I'd had more of a backbone.

CHAPTER THREE

"We've booked a room in the name of Wainwright." It's officially my name now. I can't quite believe what I've done. But until today, I thought Hugh was madly in love with me. Now I'm not so sure. The feeling of dread in the pit of my stomach is intensifying by the minute.

"Ah yes, the newlyweds." The receptionist's smile is as radiant as the rock on her ring finger. She's at least twenty years younger than me and will certainly have no trouble being recognised as the bride when she goes to find her dress. "Is Mr Wainwright on his way in?" She glances towards the door.

"Erm, he's just dropping someone off at the station, then we're going out to celebrate." I force a smile and put my hand out for the key.

"There's a little surprise in your room to get you started," she calls after me as I tug my case to the foot of the stairs.

It's a pleasant enough room, too basic to be classed as a honeymoon suite, but it'll have to do. There's a bottle of champagne on the dresser with two glasses and a card propped in front. Mr and Mrs Wainwright. With a sigh, I slump onto the bed and tug the clip from my hair. I feel like opening the bottle and downing it, but instead, I fill the kettle from the sink in the en-suite. I'll be sensible. Besides, I'd rather share it with Hugh.

If only I could share our wedding pictures on social media. Not that I go on there much, but I could do with some likes and comments right now. The hair and make-up lady started work on me at seven this morning so I'm looking my absolute best. I've put ten times more effort into my appearance than Hugh has. He hasn't even commented on how I look today. The photographer said he'd have some editing to do on the few photos he took, and would send the pictures along in a couple of weeks. What he probably meant is that he'd need to airbrush my wrinkles and my scraggy neck.

Only a handful of people knew I was getting married. Because we've just had the Christmas and New Year break, the other lecturers never had a chance to get any sort of fanfare together for me. There would have been a night out, at the very least. And Hugh wanted me to keep the wedding from my brother. I haven't quite got to the bottom of that. Especially since his own brother was invited to attend in the end.

"But Kieren and Claire would want to know," I'd tried to argue. "They'd want to be there, especially since Dad can't be. Kieren will be gutted at not having the chance to give me away."

"It's more romantic this way, Nicola. Just me, you and two witnesses. We can throw a party when we get back if it means so much to you. We can invite everyone we know then."

At that, I'd relented, crossing my fingers that Kieren and Claire would understand. Hugh led me to believe that the witnesses were going to be people we didn't know. But then his bloody brother showed up. And I've been abandoned here whilst they go for a drink together. Well, sod them. I reach for the champagne bottle. I'll have a drink on my own. Normally, I'd have rung down for an ice bucket, but I'm not waiting for that. Even warm champagne contains alcohol. Besides, a drink might settle my jangling nerves. I'm feeling them more now than I was before the ceremony. And the weight dragging at my belly is growing heavier all the time.

The pop of the cork serves to depress me more. It's a sound of joy and celebration. Not a bride, alone on a winter's afternoon in a gloomy hotel room.

The first glass doesn't touch the sides. After pouring another, I lean back against the pillows, mindlessly scrolling through my phone for several minutes, looking at happy pictures of people for whom life still goes on. I drain glass two and reach for my case. I'd better hang the dresses I've packed, so they're not too creased when Hugh and I finally get the chance to go out together. That's if I'm not too sozzled by then.

I shuffle to the window and watch as the world continues to live life beneath it. I've never been lonelier. Even in the aftermath of each of my parents dying, I still had Kieren. The street below is a flurry of activity, as it would be on a Monday afternoon. Between the buildings in front, the sea is just about visible. I look left, then right, longing to see the return of my silver Audi and with it, my new husband, but there's no sign whatsoever. I imagine him and Gary sitting across from one another in a pub and wonder what on earth they could be talking about. There's only one place Hugh should be right now, and that's with me.

I've eaten nothing since a tiny breakfast before we left Leeds.- So I rip open the Shrewsbury biscuits, usually my favourite, and nibble at them. I'm lightheaded after two glasses of fizz on an empty stomach. Glancing at the clock beside the bed, I notice it's already been an hour since Hugh dropped me off. He promised me half an hour. I pour glass number three and swipe up my phone to call him. The way I'm going, I'll be neither use nor ornament when he finally gets here. Still, it's

14

his fault. Hopefully, one day, today will be something we joke about. Though right now, I can't imagine it.

His phone goes straight to voicemail. I down my drink in one and drain the bottle. What sort of man does this to his new wife straight after his wedding?

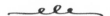

As I open my eyes and squint in the fading daylight, I wonder where I am for a moment. Then it hits me like a truck. I reach to my left and smooth my palm across the duvet, hoping to find the warmth of Hugh lying beside me. Nothing. I reach for my phone, expecting a stream of missed calls and messages from him. Nothing. I've been asleep for nearly two hours. My head is thick with the alcohol I drank as once again, I press the call button next to Hugh's name and raise the phone to my ear.

It's still switched off. Maybe his battery has died. What if he's had an accident? I can't think of any other reason why he'd just abandon me on our wedding day. Perhaps I should call the police station and the local hospital. I'll give it a bit longer, then I'll have to.

Undoing the buttons on my blouse, I wrench it off. Then I scrunch my clothes into a compartment in my case and zip it up. I don't want to see this outfit ever again. I slide my legs into jeans and pull on a jumper, deciding to get some fresh air. Try and straighten my head out. When I get back, Hugh will be here.

"Is everything OK?" The receptionist frowns as I try to sneak past the front desk. "Still no Mr Wainwright?"

I'm longing to tell someone, have someone reassure me, but obviously, I can't. They'd probably tell me how stupid I've been. And I have. All the signs were there earlier today. I just ignored them.

"He's been held up." I stride towards the door without looking at her and nestle my misery deeper into my scarf. I bet she won't be deserted on her wedding day.

As I pound along the seafront, tears freeze onto my face. Idiot. Idiot. Idiot. I repeat the word in time to my footfall. And what an absolute idiot I've been. At this moment, I could wade into that inky-black sea and never look back. It can't be any deadlier than the misery I'm drowning in.

Then I think of Dad and the thoughts that might have passed through his mind at the very end. Clearly heartbroken after losing Mum to cancer the previous Christmas, it seems Kieren and I weren't enough for him to want to continue living. He still had a good life; his home and car were his pride and joy. He had plenty of friends on the golf course and a hefty bank balance. He and Mum had bought a campervan two years before for all their retirement adventures. They'd planned to travel all over the place. But the locked garage, and the hosepipe rigged through the window of his campervan told us another story.

I try to force a deep breath in, though it's difficult in the sea breeze when I can't stop crying. Too busy with closing the house up and sorting Dad's affairs along with Kieren, I never gave myself a chance to properly grieve for my parents. But since Hugh and I arranged to get married a month ago, I haven't been able to stop thinking about them. And today, I need them more than ever.

I trudge along the edge of the waves, eventually lulled by their rhythm and the velvet black of the sky. I'll walk a bit further, then when I get back to where we're staying, Hugh will be there. He might moan at me for drinking all the bubbles, but it's not as if we're short of money. Dad might have departed from our lives, but he left Kieren and me very well provided for. Not that I needed it of course. I might not have made a success of my personal life, but I certainly have with my career. Kieren's made a success of both – his wife Claire is lovely. The only cloud in their vista is that she hasn't fallen pregnant.

I don't think for a moment that Hugh was ever interested in my money. In fact, he was the only date I had whose eyes didn't widen when I answered his question about what I did for a living. I hardly think my head of department salary would rival his as the owner of several car showrooms.

I'd done online dating for a laugh. Fascinated at watching a colleague playing 'human snap' on a rare evening out last year, a few of them had downloaded the app onto my phone and got it set up. I'd watched them, amused, whilst promising myself I'd delete it the next day. Then, as we spent the next hour swiping left and right, I found it almost addictive. Suddenly, from being dumped by Jason from the highest height possible, I was getting messages left, right and centre from a variety of men. Some were just 'hey,' 'hi,' or 'how you doing?' but the one I received within two hours of getting on the app from Hugh really stood out. 'Happy to have matched,' it read. 'I really hope I can get to know you better – you look and sound too good to be true.' I kept looking at his profile and his pictures, hoping he was for real, and knowing I'd absolutely have to meet him.

The next day I deleted the app. But only because, by then, Hugh and I had met. Literally twenty-four hours after matching. By the end of our first date, he knew all about what had happened with my parents and with Jason. I felt so comfortable in his presence. I even told him I'd left it too late to have kids, but yet wanted to get married one day. His exact words had been, "so what are your thoughts on getting married?"

I nearly choked on my wine. "Don't worry, I'm not proposing... yet." He flashed that grin at me, and I fell for him in that moment. By the end of that date, he knew pretty much everything about me – I'm not sure whether I divulged my bank balance and knicker size, but I came close. However, I found out very little of significance about him, only surface level stuff like his showrooms, and that he was a twin, and that he was temporarily living at his brother's following the break-up of his previous relationship. When I had tried to get him to open up, he said he was more interested in talking about me. He added that we had lots of previous years when we hadn't known each other to make up for. The evening flew by and as we stood up to leave, I knew we were going somewhere.

Then his card was declined when he tried to pay the bar tab. Normally this would have been a big, red flag, but I happily paid it instead. I had no reason to doubt him when he said he'd brought his expired card by mistake.

We met every single day in that first week. On day three, I got drunk and slept with him – something I immediately regretted.- All the women's magazines warn you not to play your best card too quickly, but with Hugh, it only made him more attentive and wonderful towards me.

However, by day seven, I felt slightly suffocated and wanted to drive over to see Kieran. Hugh had flown into a huff and eventually stormed off when I wouldn't ask him into the house.- By the time he had left, I was no longer in the mood to bother going to see my brother. Afterwards, he bombarded me with calls and texts. It had been nice to be so wanted, so needed, but it was all happening too quickly.

When he returned the next day with a bouquet of flowers, he had never returned to Gary's again, apart from the occasional night. This is possibly one reason Gary is so hostile towards me. He must see me as a threat.

The receptionist has left for the evening by the time I get back to the hotel. There's no sign of my Audi along the street, and our room is in darkness as I let myself in. He hasn't been back. I sink to the bed and the tears reappear. We'll never get our wedding day again – he's ruined every minute. I feel like packing up and returning home, but he's got my car. What the hell have I done? And more to the point, what am I going to do? I lay on the bed and curl into the foetal position. I can't believe how naïve I've been. Five hours have passed since he dumped me here. Something awful must have happened. There's no other explanation. I reach for my bag and tug out my phone.

"I'm looking for my husband." The word husband feels uneasy. I twirl the word around in my mouth until I want to spit it out. Husbands don't treat their wives like this.

"I'm sorry. We're not allowed to confirm hospital admissions. It's data protection."

"But I'm worried he's had an accident. He's been gone for hours. We only got married today."

"Like I said, I'm really sorry." The woman's voice softens, and I half expect her to congratulate me. "Perhaps you could try the local police station. Would you like the number?"

It's the same story with the police. They won't tell me a thing.- Nor will they let me report Hugh missing. He's not been 'gone' for long enough and sounds to have left me here of his own volition. The police officer's words, not mine. I'm told to call back tomorrow if he still hasn't turned up.

Tomorrow. How will I even be able to sleep tonight? I can't just wait here. I'll go insane. Perhaps if I look around the pubs, I'll find him.

If my work colleagues could see me now, they'd have me sectioned. Until my parents dying and Jason leaving me, I was a confident, forty-something woman. I would never have allowed myself to be reduced to this kind of behaviour, certainly not for a man. I deliver talks to hundreds of students in lecture theatres and keynote speeches to dozens of colleagues. Yet here I am, trudging from pub to pub, looking for someone who seemingly doesn't want to be found.

I try to blend in amongst everyone else as I nonchalantly perform a sweep of each pub, searching for the husband who's cast me aside like a toy he's grown bored with. I've only known the man for two months and can hardly believe what I'm doing.

After combing the local area and probably a dozen pubs, I've had enough. I sink to a stool at the bar in the Black Swan and order a large wine and a sandwich. If I don't get some food down, I'll be ill. I pretend to be immersed in my phone and hope nobody will try to make conversation with me.

CHAPTER FOUR

I don't sleep well in strange beds at the best of times. But this is one of the longest nights of my life. Longer, in some ways, than the night that Kieren and I sat outside intensive care a year ago, as we willed Dad to pull through. It was a miracle that I'd found him still alive. I'd taken some shopping up and heard the rumble of the engine behind the garage door as soon as I'd got out of my car. I scrunch my eyes against the memory – I'm low enough tonight without allowing myself to sink into thoughts of last year.

Passing car headlights occasionally illuminate the ceiling, then I listen as the engines die away. Sometimes, the lights linger for more than a moment, and my heart rate quickens each time. I imagine the engine I hear is my Audi, so I leap from where I'm lying and look up and down the street.

Wherever Hugh is tonight, his reason for doing this to me is going to have to be out of this world. He's got until half-past five to show up, or I'm out of here. I've repacked my dresses and plotted my route to the station. The first train home is at ten past six. I've also been searching online about annulling the marriage and it seems I'd be able to – we haven't consummated it, therefore I've got an escape. If I struggle to get my car from him, then so be it, it's not as if I can't afford another one. I'll just change the locks on the house and dump his stuff at his brothers. Then I'll throw myself back into my job. They've had to cut me some slack at work over the last year or so, what with Mum, then Dad, then Jason – I've been all over the place.

I hate Hugh for what he's put me through over the last twenty-four hours. He knows what I've already been through.- And tonight, I've experienced every emotion from fearing he might be dead, to wishing he was dead, to wanting to kill him myself. I must have tried ringing him over a hundred times, to no avail. He's not been active on social media, but all the messages I've sent are saying they've been delivered. Only the earlier ones, until about seven yesterday evening have actually been read though. I feel like some sort of stalker. Yet we're married. We're bloody married now. What the hell have I done?

Perhaps he's lying in bed with another woman, but what man would do that on their wedding day? I'm worried, I'm angry, but most of all I'm baffled. He led me to believe that I was everything he wanted in his life. Why the hell would he have married me if he didn't really want to?

As I walk towards our street, part of me wonders if I might find him here. But home is exactly as we left it twenty-four hours ago. Our breakfast pots from yesterday are stacked on the draining board; the laundry has dried on the airer, and the house has a faint smell of coffee, combined with the lavender oil that I use in my diffuser. When I closed the door behind me yesterday, I thought we were starting a new adventure and that I was embarking on the happiest day of my life.

Now I'm here, back to where I started after Jason left me, but this time, I've got a marriage to wriggle out of and God knows what else to face. What happens next all depends on what reason Hugh comes up with for how he's behaved. There

22

is, of course, the possibility that something's happened to him. Legally, I'm his next of kin now, so at some point, someone will have to let me know if he's lying in a hospital bed or a morgue somewhere. Ours will be the shortest and unhappiest marriage in history.

Thankfully, I'm not due back at work until Thursday – I shifted my lectures around this week. So, I don't know what the hell I'm going to do with myself today. Pace the house until I wear out the carpets, I expect. It's not even nine o'clock and I feel as though I've done a day's work already. I should be exhausted after being awake for most of the night, but mostly, I feel sick. I've got moths, never mind butterflies flapping around my stomach, and I feel as though I've aged twenty years in twenty hours. A soak in the bath is in order. Plus, it will kill an hour and it might stop me opening a bottle of wine.

As the bubbles pop around my ears, tears leak from my eyes. I can't help but recall the baths Hugh and I have taken in here together. We can just about fit in as long as he drapes one of his long legs over the edge and I rest my feet against the tiles.

Once, when I'd had a heavy day at the university, I returned home to candles, Hugh preparing a meal and a trail of rose petals leading from the front door, up the stairs into here. Jason would never have done anything like that for me. After so many years together, we'd been living almost like brother and sister.- Admittedly, things had become too comfortable - bills and bins had taken over as our go-to topics of conversation. And I'd been blind to the warning signs that he was betraying me.

Hugh, in contrast, has only ever made me feel wanted, desirable, feminine, important, just everything I'd hoped a man would. I realise that I'm thinking about him in the past tense.- That's because I know, I really know, that unless he's got the most amazing excuse on the planet, he's history after ghosting me so spectacularly. This is the kind of story that makes it into the women's magazines whose advice about relationships I've taken no notice of.

I'm drying myself in front of the radiator, when the front door bangs and my heart nearly jumps out of my chest. With shaking hands, I tug on my dressing gown and dart to the top of the stairs. Hugh is already on the second step, still wearing the outfit he married me in, and sporting a day of beard growth. It makes his eyes look bluer and I hate myself for making such an observation.

"Where the hell have you been?" It's as though we've been married for years, instead of less than twenty-four hours. Him, the errant, dishevelled husband and me, the nagging wife. I should be at the back of the door with a rolling pin.

"I could ask the same thing of you." He stops where he is. It still feels strange, there being a different man in the house after twelve years with Jason. "When I got back to the hotel, I was told you'd gone."

"Well pardon me for not hanging around." I lower myself to the top step of the staircase, taking care to ensure he can't see up my dressing gown. Who knows whose other naked body he's been enjoying since he left me yesterday? "It's not much fun staying in a hotel on your own. Especially when you're supposed to be a newlywed."

"Yeah well. If you hadn't been such a miserable cow when my brother turned up yesterday." He leans against the wall. "I might have wanted to get back to you sooner. He wasn't impressed. And neither was I."

"What?" My voice is a screech. I can't believe he's just said that to me. He should beg for forgiveness after what he's done. "You should have heard what your brother said to me yesterday!"

"You had a right face on the minute he walked up the street.- So what I've done last night is totally your fault." He grasps the banister as though he's going to come towards me, but then stays where he is.

"What is? What's my fault?" Oh God. What's he done last night? What is he about to tell me?

"You've clearly had a lifetime of your own way, Nicola. With Mummy and Daddy. Perhaps you need bringing down into the real world."

Tears spring to my eyes as I get to my feet. I don't know what to do with myself at the moment. I can't keep still.

"Was it too much to want to be with my new husband on our wedding day?" My voice rises a notch as I tug my dressing gown more tightly around me. The thought of him seeing me naked turns my stomach. "How could you be so cruel Hugh?"

"Oh, that's right. Turn on the waterworks." His face twists into a sneer. It's strange how someone can be so good looking and so ugly at the same time. "That sort of thing might work with some men. In fact, it's probably why Jason put up with you for so long, but it certainly doesn't work with me. Especially after the night I've had."

Something shifts within me as I hurtle down the stairs, stopping at two steps above him so our faces are almost level. "After the night you've had." I'm shrieking at him now. The walls are so thin, the neighbour behind can probably hear me. Though hopefully she'll be at work at this time on a Tuesday morning. "I've been ringing police stations and hospitals. I thought you were dead."

"You'll wish you were if you don't stop squawking at me."

That comment certainly stops me in my tracks. "What did you say?" The breath catches in my throat. "Was that supposed to be a threat?"

"If you must know," his voice levels out. "I've been locked in a cell all night."

"Why? What have you done?" It occurs to me then, just how little I know this man. Never mind what he's done – what the hell have I done?

I'm not sure if I believe a word that's leaving his mouth. After all, I rang the local police station. Surely they'd have told me if he was in custody. Besides, he could have rung me. He would have been allowed to make one phone call.

"I was three times over the limit, wasn't I? I didn't want to go back to the hotel and face your miserable mug, so I carried on drinking. It'll be down to you when I lose my licence."

I dig my fingernails into my palm. "So why the hell did you marry me then? If I'm that miserable?"

"Perhaps I came to my senses too late Nicola. Yesterday morning, all you could go on about was your brother not being there, and your bloody dad. How depressing can you be?"

As his sentence goes on, Hugh's voice rises. I can't believe what I'm hearing. What woman wouldn't be sad about her dad not being around to give her away on her wedding day?

"You keep my dad out of this!" I shout back at him. "He's got nothing to do with you."

"Don't you raise your voice at me."

"Or else?" I look around for something in case I need to defend myself. I've never felt so vulnerable.

"Then when Gary turned up," he goes on, his voice still elevated, "you had a face like a smacked arse." He is shouting into my face now. "Even the photographer and the registrar felt uncomfortable around you. They couldn't get away from you fast enough."

"How do you work that one out?" I've never yelled at anyone like this. My throat feels strained, and tears of frustrated anger are sliding down my face. I just want to curl up into a ball somewhere and die.

"You give off a negative vibe Nicola. You're an utter depressive. Just like your father was."

I sink to the stair where I'm standing. I can't take much more of this. His eyes bore into me for a few moments. We're opponents, two steps apart. Then suddenly I remember my get out of jail free card and my resolve fires again. "You might as well get your things together Hugh. I'm going to have our marriage annulled."

"What? You - you can't do that."

"I think you'll find I can." My voice has lowered again, and I smile through my tears. At last. I've regained some control. "A marriage can be annulled if it hasn't been consummated. I've looked into it."

"Oh, you have, have you?" Then an arrogant shadow crosses his face. "So how are you going to prove that we have not consummated it? It would be your word against mine."

"I'd have the word of the receptionist at the hotel to verify that you didn't show up yesterday, and that you were looking for me this morning. As long as I see a solicitor today, you're history." Thank God I've seen the light.

"They locked me in a prison cell Nicola." He leans towards me. "What the hell was I supposed to do?" I feel his spittle in my face as he leans forward.

"You could have let me know." Though if I'm honest, even if I'd known he was locked up, it would have made little difference to me deciding to get our marriage annulled. Not that I'm going to tell him this.

"I was ashamed of myself." The sudden desperation on his face tells me I've rattled him with my threat of annulment. "Don't you get it dammit? Three times over the limit. I'm in deep shit. I need my licence."

"Do you expect me to feel sorry for you? Especially when you're blaming me for it. Anyone would think I'd poured that drink down your throat and forced you to drive."

"The longer I stayed out, the worse I knew you'd be with me. I couldn't face it Nicola."

"So you carried on drinking, and then you drove my car. I mean it, Hugh, this sham of a marriage is over before it's started. I've already made an appointment with my solicitor." It's a complete lie, but I need to show him he can't get away with treating me like this. This is the first time we've ever argued and by the looks of it, it may well be the last. But I'm so grateful that I've found some fight whilst I've still got the chance to escape.

"I'm sorry." All bravado seems to seep from him. "Please let's get through this."

"I don't know if I can. We can never regain what should have been our wedding day. You ruined everything." I lean against the staircase wall.

"How about if we start again? We could go back to Northumberland. What about next Monday? I promise you Nicola, we can make up for it all." He barely pauses for breath.

"I'll be working next Monday." I continue down the steps and slide past him, careful to not brush against him as I go. *What the hell am I on about?* Never mind me saying I'll be working, I should be saying, *I'll no longer be married to you.*

"I love you Nicola."

I march into the kitchen and click the switch on the kettle. "Yeah, course you do."

"I'll have one of those if you don't mind." Hugh sidles up behind me and rests his hands on either side of my waist. He turns me to face him, but I step to the side. "Look Nicola. Gary's told me to piss off now that I've gone through with the wedding. I'm also going to lose my driving licence. I can't lose you as well."

"What was Gary even doing at the wedding? You wouldn't let me invite Kieren."

"We're twins. I couldn't expect you to understand the bond we've got. It's like he knew something was going on with me when we were planning it all. He wouldn't let it go until I told him."

"He's jealous of me. It's written all over him."

"Of course he is." Hugh steps forward again and for the second time, I duck whatever embrace he's trying to catch me in. "He's jealous because he knows how much I love you."

"So why couldn't you have said that to me yesterday?" Shit. I'm mellowing. I can feel it. After the twenty-four hours I've just gone through, I'm letting him talk me around. What a pushover. I fill the cafetiere with water and watch as he takes a seat at the kitchen table and drops his head into his hands. I know he needs his driving licence for work. It's a good job he's in charge of the showrooms. In different circumstances, he might have lost his job. But I'm certainly not accepting any responsibility for it.

He turns to look at me and the sadness in his eyes softens me some more. Idiot. Idiot. But I can tell he regrets what happened yesterday. And if I'm honest, I don't want to lose him. As I found out from my brief spell of being single, at my age, men tend to be married, gay, or have enough emotional baggage to ground a plane.

I guess what Hugh's done to me isn't as bad as what Jason did. For eighteen months as well! Then to go all out with the marriage and baby thing for himself, after denying me for so many years. Maybe Hugh and I can come back from all this. I really don't want to be on my own again. The weeks and months after Dad died and Jason left were the loneliest and darkest I've ever known.

With a lot of talking, I might understand why Hugh abandoned me. If he tells me exactly what was going on in his head.

"I had every intention of coming back to the hotel Nicola.-Really, I did. But after the fight I had with Gary, I carried on drinking and..." His voice trails off. "I'm sorry. I've been so stupid."

"What did you two fall out about?"

"Look – it was all about you. He was saying things that... well, I'm not going to go into that with you."

"I want to know." Or do I? I'm probably best not knowing, especially with my self-esteem being where it is.

"Look, I'm back, aren't I? We're back. We're married. You're my wife. Surely all that matters now is going forward and living happily ever after." He holds his hand out to me and I sit on the chair next to him without taking it. I hate myself for yielding to him, but it feels better than the alternative.

"I don't know Hugh. You've no idea what you've put me through." I look up at the ceiling. Before all this, we'd promised each other we were going to paint the whole house. Top to bottom. Hugh said he wanted to put his own stamp on the place.

He touches my arm. "Please Nicola. I tell you what. Why don't I have a shower and a shave, then I'll take you out for lunch. Anywhere you like. Let's make up for yesterday."

"I suppose that would be a start." Something lifts inside me.-We've married too quickly, that's all. We need to just step back a bit and take some time to get to know each other properly. And maybe I need some counselling or something. I lost my parents within months of each other, and then Jason. The last thing I want is for my past to get in the way of my future. And I want me and Hugh to work out more than anything I've ever wanted.

"Then, when we get back, we can think about consummating this marriage, as you so sexily put it." He rises from his chair and pours us both a coffee.

"Believe me," I take a cup from him, "the last twenty-four hours have been far from sexy. Certainly not how I expected to be spending our wedding night."

"Try being locked in a cell." He rubs his fingers over the bristles on his chin. "Nothing too sexy about that either."

"What's happening there then?"

"I'm in court in two months. So I need to get a decent solicitor. Three times over the limit is going to be tricky to get leniency with."

What a start to married life, I think to myself. I'm probably going to have to ferry him around everywhere.

"I'll make sure it doesn't impinge on you," he says, as though reading my mind. "Until I get my licence back, I'll have to take taxis. It's not as though we can't afford them."

It's interesting how he uses the word *we*. He's got enough of his own money, or he should have. I can't remember whether he told me it was four or five car showrooms that he owns.

"I'll take my cuppa upstairs whilst I get a shower." He takes hold of my chin with gentle fingers. "I promise you Nicola." He tilts my face upwards, so I'm forced to look him in the eye. His gaze is unwavering. "If I have to spend the rest of my life making it up to you, then I will."

"Let's just see, shall we? You've certainly got a lot of making up to do."

He pauses in the doorway. "I've missed you Nicola."

CHAPTER FIVE

I hurtle down the stairs and swipe my phone from the kitchen counter just before it rings off.

"Kieren. I'm glad you've called." The sound of my brother's voice makes me smile. "I've got something to tell you." Pulling a chair out with a scrape, I sit, feeling the chill of the wood against my skin. I turn to glance at the window. Hopefully, the blinds are tilted far enough that passers-by won't be able to see in and get an eyeful of me with no clothes on. Thankfully, the yoga I do and the gym mean I'm not in bad shape to say I'm in my mid-forties.

"You sound out of breath sis."

"Yeah, I've just run downstairs to the phone." I'm always warmed when he calls me sis. It makes me feel as though I belong somewhere. Especially now, after the last day or so. Thank God things seem to be OK now.

"In that case, you should increase your gym classes. Out of breath at your age!"

"I know." I think of Hugh lying upstairs in my bed. Despite my misgivings, I'm relieved we've sorted it all out. Going for lunch together was really nice, apart from one or two iffy moments, and getting back here cemented everything. Well, kind of. I think the drink drive situation must be playing on his mind.

"So, what have you got to tell me?"

"Right, well, I'll just come out and say it." I pause, praying he'll be happy for me and not mad that we didn't invite him. "I only went and got married."

He's silent for a moment. "You did *what?* When?" His voice goes up a few notches. I hold the phone away from my ear. "To who?" He doesn't sound happy, more confused.

I laugh at what could just be his concern. He's the only family I've got left. Well, apart from Hugh now. "Don't worry – I'm going to introduce you to him."

"When?"

"As soon as we can get it arranged."

"It would have been better to have met him beforehand. Or to have been invited. Who is he, anyway? I didn't realise you were that serious with anyone."

I'm about to reply, but he continues, barely pausing for breath. "You must have only known him five minutes Nicola. It's literally only been a few months since you and Jason parted company."

He actually sounds annoyed with me. I try to think how I'd have felt if roles were reversed. He and Claire had a traditional wedding, and I was a big part of their day. Still, if they'd wanted to go off and do their own thing, I would have respected that.

"I know, but these things happen. Sometimes you meet someone and you just know..." Who am I trying to convince here – my brother or myself? "Anyway, his name's Hugh. He's a few years younger than me and well, you'll have to meet him. See him for yourself. I'm sure you'll get on great."

"How much younger than you?" Annoyance seems to have turned into suspicion.

"Only five years." At times, I feel this age gap keenly.- Especially since I've entered the menopause and gained a few extra lines around my eyes. Particularly over the last year.

"So what does Hugh do?" It's the sort of question Dad would ask. Kieren's like a younger version of Dad. I picture him now at the other end of the phone, his eyebrows knitted in concern.

"He owns a few car showrooms around Yorkshire."

"Owns, or manages?"

"Owns." I should have known this would be one of Kieren's lines of enquiry. "Don't worry Kieren. He's not after my money. He's got enough of his own." He'll be asking me next if Hugh's intentions are honourable. Judging by his lacklustre performance in the bedroom just now, who knows...

"What are the showrooms called?"

"I don't know."

We fall silent as it dawns on me that Hugh's never mentioned the name of his company.

"So when did you do it?" Kieren's voice snaps me back into the present. "Get married I mean? I have to say, it's come as a bit of a shock."

"Yesterday." It was the worst day of my life, I refrain from adding.

"Why didn't you tell us? Me and Claire would have loved to have been there. We should have been there."

"It was all a bit spur of the moment to be honest. We didn't want to make a big deal."

"It can't have been a spur of the moment. I do remember getting married, you know. You'll have had to have given notice. Had marriage banns read out and all that." I detect more suspicion in his voice. Kieren and I know each other well. Too well. Even when we haven't seen each other for a while. But he'll always have my back, no matter what. If only I could confide in him the inauspicious start of our married life, but obviously I can't. I can't say anything that could risk him and Hugh getting off on the wrong foot. He and Kieren are the two most significant people in my life. Plus, Hugh is only upstairs so I've to be guarded in what I say.

It's bad enough that Gary dislikes me so much, and makes it even more important that Hugh and Kieren get along when they meet. I've suggested to Hugh on several occasions that we arrange something with Kieren and Claire, but he's always come up with a reason not to. Usually some lame excuse to do with work.

"OK. Look, if I'm to be perfectly honest, Kieren, Hugh wanted it to be just me and him."

"So it was all about what Hugh wanted, then?"

Kieren's right, I know he is.

"No. I'd have liked you to have been there. Of course I would, but anyway, he said we might have a party." It dawns on me then that there'd be hardly anyone for me to ask. Other than my work colleagues and people from the gym. I've always kept my circle small, but after the drama of the last year and then with Hugh and I monopolising one another since we met in November, there hasn't been the room for anything or anyone else, so my circle has shrunk even more.

"I have to say Nicola. You don't sound very happy at all."

"I am happy. I'm fine." It's a good thing he didn't ring me at nine o'clock this morning, that's all I can say. I don't think I'd have been able to hold it all in.

"Shall I come across?"

"What for?"

"*What for?* I haven't seen you since last year."

"I'm sorry. It's just..."

"And I'd like to meet this husband of yours, obviously. Someone who thinks it's acceptable to keep your only family away from your big day."

"I'm sorry Kieren. Really, I am." I must make sure he never finds out that Gary was there. He'd have a fit. When those photographs turn up, I'll have to hide them away. I'm not sure I'll want to look at them anyway – they'd only bring back what I went through yesterday. What should have been the happiest day of my life turned into one of the most miserable. It's definitely up there with some days I've recently lived through.

"I should have given you away Nicola." Kieren's not letting this go. Prior to losing our parents, we'd go months without getting in touch, and as far as I could see, we were slipping back to that again. But it seems I was wrong. I feel awful now for not standing my ground and insisting to Hugh that my brother and sister-in-law got an invitation. Maybe yesterday would have turned out differently if they had. I can't imagine Hugh or Gary acting in the way they had if my brother had been around.

"It's what Dad would have wanted, you know," he continues, his voice lowering. "For me to have given you away."

"I know. I really am sorry Kieren. We'll make up for it."

"We haven't got together since October, you know. To say we're only thirty miles apart, that's ridiculous."

"We'll get something sorted soon."

"We didn't even see you over Christmas. You said you wouldn't be much company." He pauses. "Was that because of him? What's going on sis?"

"Nothing, I promise."

I sense a shadow in the doorway of the kitchen, so turn and notice as it shifts from right to left. I realise then that Hugh's listening in to my conversation. How long has he been standing there? Why doesn't he just come in? He doesn't need to lurk out there.

"Never mind soon Nicola. Soon never comes. Let's get something sorted now. I'm free on Friday evening if you are?"

"I'll have to check with Hugh."

"Since when is it necessary to check with someone else whether you can see your own brother?"

"I thought you wanted to meet him? So, I need to make sure he'll be around. I'll ask him now if you want." My anxiety levels shoot up. We've only just got ourselves sorted out. I hope he'll be OK with this. My gut instinct tells me he won't.

"Is he there? Maybe I should have a word with him."

The shadow shifts again. The house is so quiet that Hugh will be able to hear what Kieren's saying from where he's standing.- Though why he still doesn't come into the kitchen, I've no idea. I stride over to the door. "Hang on Kieren."

Hugh's face is bright red, and he does cut throat signals as I thrust the phone towards him. Then he turns on his heel into the lounge and slams the door behind him.

"What the hell was that?"

"Erm, I'm sorry. Hugh's just gone out. Look, I'll check about Friday night. Then I'll ring you back."

"Is everything OK sis? That was one hell of a bang."

"Yeah. Of course it is. Don't worry. I'll speak to you again soon."

"What the hell was your brother enquiring into my work and financial situation for? Who does he think he is?" Hugh slams himself onto the sofa. Great. As if things have gone sour again. Already.

"Kieren's just interested to find out who his sister has married, that's all. He's never met you, has he? He doesn't know you like I do."

"And you, with your grovelling." Hugh springs back to his feet and I take a step back from him. This side of him is horrendous. I never saw even a hint before we were married. "How many times did you tell him you were sorry? What are you sorry for?" He flings his arms out. "What sort of hold has he got over you? It's bloody odd if you ask me."

"You're one to talk." I sidestep him and perch on the edge of one of the armchairs. "If it wasn't for *your* brother, our wedding day might not have been ruined." I glance at the clock on the mantlepiece. It used to be Mum's and comforts me every time I look at it. However, there is little that feels of comfort right at this moment.

Then I recall how, this time yesterday I was beside myself with misery. I sink into the chair. After lunch and some time together in the bedroom, I thought everything was normal again between us. But Hugh seems to be in a similar mood to the one he was in this morning. Maybe it's because our time in the bedroom wasn't exactly a success.

"It was *you* who ruined our wedding day Nicola. Not me. Not Gary. You." He jabs an accusing finger in my direction. "You, and your whining voice and your face like a bag of spanners. It's about time you sorted yourself out. You do know you'll end up like your father if you don't do something drastic."

"What's that supposed to mean?" I reach for a cushion and hold it protectively against myself. It must be the third time he's said this to me.

"It's a slippery slope, is misery. Maybe you should see about getting yourself on some tablets."

"I don't need tablets. I just need things to be like they were before. Between us I mean." Hysteria is rising in me like the bubbles in yesterday's lonely champagne. "What the hell's got into you Hugh – I thought we'd sorted things out." I can't deny I was considering counselling earlier. But I'll keep that to myself.- I'm not going to add more fuel to his fire.

"You just make sure you keep your brother out of my face, do you hear me? I don't want him here, sniffing around and poking his nose into my business." Hugh paces around as he rants. Maybe it's the drink drive thing that's making it difficult for him to get back to himself. That must be preying on his mind.

"He just wants to meet you, that's all." I stare at the carpet, wondering how everything could have gone so horribly wrong again. To be honest, if Kieren had any inkling about what has been going on for me over the last two days, he'd be over here and bundling me into his car.

"What if I don't want to meet him?" His face is twisted into the same sneer it was earlier.

"I've had to meet your brother." Gary's fat face swims into my brain. As the weeks go on, I'm getting the gist of the strange bond that exists between them. It's a kind of love and hate relationship, fuelled by jealousy and possessiveness but yet, they can't go more than five minutes without seeing each other. I keep telling myself it must be a twin thing.

"And look at the trouble you meeting Gary caused."

"None of that was my doing." Although I'm wondering if there's any truth about what Hugh has said about me spoiling yesterday. I was missing my parents, that's all. And Kieren. But maybe I was acting too needy, wanting Hugh to myself. Men always find that a turn off.

"Like I said earlier Nicola, I want us to keep our lives to ourselves." He sits beside me. "We don't need anyone else. We've got each other, haven't we?"

"But what am I supposed to tell my brother?" I wouldn't put it past Kieren to turn up on Friday regardless of what I tell him. He'll see it as 'protecting my interests.'

"You'll think of something."

At least Hugh has mellowed slightly. If I were to carry on arguing my case, he might up and leave me again. I couldn't bear it. I somehow managed to put my resentment towards him over yesterday to one side when he took me out for lunch, and we had a long discussion about the future.

"What would you do Nicola..." As the waitress had taken our order, Hugh had looked at me with the intensity that's become like a drug, "if you could do anything you wanted with your life? Anything at all."

"I'd have a baby," I replied, without hesitation.

I don't know if I'll ever truly forgive Jason for depriving me of that. It's too late now, though. Perhaps if I hadn't gone into early menopause, there'd still be a chance.

"Premature Ovarian Failure," the GP had called it when he telephoned with the results of yet another blood test. "We can put you on HRT if you like." And that was it. No sympathy and no apology for snatching my chance of being a mother away forever.

"I mean, something that's attainable. We both know you can't have that." Hugh laughed as he lifted his glass to his lips. "Even if it were still physically possible, it would hardly be fair for a kid to have a mother who might drop dead by the time it's a teenager."

"I thought you were supposed to be making things up to me." I'd raised my voice to such a level that half the restaurant turned to stare at us. There was a few seconds hush, whilst I buried my burning face in the wine list, waiting until previous levels of conversation returned.

I wondered if Hugh knew how callous he sounded, or whether he was just being insensitive. Whatever it was, these last two days have been the first sign of it.

Then he reached for my hand. It felt like coming home. After a day of being starved of affection, I was craving it like a junkie would crave a shot. "So, what would you really do Nicola?" His voice returned to normal.

"I don't know. I love my job. The students and my colleagues. I'm good at what I do. I don't want to do anything else."

"I never had you down as the arrogant type Nicola. *I'm good at what I do.*" He gave me a funny look. "Anyway, I'm not sure I like you working there. There are too many men for my liking."

"Give over. Of course there are men. It's a university." I realised my voice was elevated again, so I glanced around to make sure I hadn't disturbed anyone. People at the other tables seemed relaxed and happy. I envied their ease and their normality. "There are far more female lecturers and students than males. Anyway, you trust me, don't you?"

"I don't know sometimes. You've barely shut up about that Jason since we got together. I worry that somehow, I'm going to be the one punished for his mistakes."

"Of course you're not." Did I talk about Jason all the time? I didn't think so. I'd have to watch that.

"Anyway, we're digressing here. You still haven't answered my question. You're good at that, too."

"What question?"

He sighed. "What would you do if you could do anything you wanted?"

I thought for a moment. Clearly, he wanted some kind of answer. "I don't know. Write a novel, I suppose." It's true. I've often fancied the idea of having a writing retreat overlooking a lake, somewhere to escape to, something to escape into.

He grinned then and looked as though he was formulating a plan. I decided not to press him on it. It was just a relief to see him smile.

"What about you?" At least this question might encourage him to reveal something of himself for a change. "What would you do if money was no object and you could do anything you wanted?"

"We'll find out, won't we?" His face bore an expression I couldn't read. "As from this day on, money really is no object. I really can do anything I want."

CHAPTER SIX

I pull up after my trip to the supermarket, behind an office furniture van.

"Cheers mate," Hugh calls after a man as he leaves my house, well, our house now.

"What's going on?" Forgetting about the shopping in the boot, I stare at him. "Who was that?"

"I've got a surprise for you. Come on." He takes me by the hand and leads me through the open door into the hallway. He's been more like himself over the last couple of days, and I definitely feel more relaxed around him. I don't know what got into him on our wedding day, or the day after, but hopefully things are back to normal now.

"What surprise?"

"Follow me." I walk behind him up the stairs, and instead of turning left into my bedroom, we turn right into the spare room. He flicks the light on. Whilst I've been at work this morning, he's turned it into a study. There's a desk and swivel chair, bookcase, comfy chair; he's even bought a rug and a wastepaper bin.

I stare into all four corners of the room and then back towards him.

"Now you can get on with your novel like we agreed."

"Did we?"

"Obviously you'll want to make this room your own, pictures, cushions, and all that. But I've got a new desktop computer on order for you."

"But I don't need a desktop. I'm happy with my laptop."

"You need complete peace to work on your novel, so you should be here, at home." He smooths his hand over the desk. "You don't want to be lugging a laptop here, there and everywhere."

"But when I said I wanted to write a novel, well, it was only a thought. I wouldn't have a clue where to start. It's something for the future, maybe."

"You're head of English at a university, aren't you? Well, not for too much longer. If anyone can work out how to write a novel, surely you can. You may not have too much common sense, but you've certainly got brains."

I open my mouth to defend myself, then immediately decide not to respond to his last comment. I'm puzzled by the other comment though. "What do you mean, *not for too much longer?*"

"You're giving a term's notice, remember. You'll be finished there by June."

"But..." I feel dazed. "I love my job. I never said I'd leave it. Where have you got that idea from?"

"You only had one glass of wine last night Nicola." He laughs. "Surely, you must remember what we talked about." His expression is a cross between amusement and sympathy. "This is your big chance. A brand-new start. No more dancing to the tune of an employer. You'll be your own boss, same as I am."

I really don't remember what I said last night. But evidently, I've somehow led Hugh to believe I want to be a stay-at-home novelist. "Hugh. You might have misunderstood me. Look, the office, study, or whatever you want to call it, is great, and we'll definitely use it, but..."

I can tell by the look on his face that I'm saying the wrong thing. And I'm touched that he's gone to all this trouble to help me with something he believed I wanted, but...

"I don't understand. What's changed your mind in less than twenty-four hours?"

"I will write a novel one day." I walk across to the desk and rest my hand over his. "But not just yet. Maybe when I've retired or something."

"Last night, you told me you couldn't wait to get on with it." He yanks his hand away. "You said you were grateful for my belief in you." His jaw tightens and the anger that I've grown fearful of flashes in his eyes. "Don't you dare go shoving that back down my throat now."

"I am grateful. Really, I am. Maybe I could write a novel alongside my job. That's how lots of writers start out. I don't even know if I'll be any good at it."

"Rubbish. You said yourself that it's time you did something different."

"Did I?" It must be an age thing because half of what he's going on about, I don't even remember. I've read about menopausal 'brain fog.' Maybe it's that.

"Besides, it's not as if you haven't got enough money put by if you need it." He pauses. "Which reminds me, we should get on with all the official stuff this afternoon. Now you're home."

"Like what?"

"You know, sorting the accounts so they're in joint names, changing insurances, your passport, all that sort of thing." His previous irritation has become something else – it's as though he's trying to convince me of something.

"Do you mean like the utility bills?" I don't like where this conversation is going. Still, it's better than him trying to railroad my career.

44

"We could sort them too, I suppose. I guess I need my name on at least one of them if I need any finance for anything. But I was thinking more about current and savings accounts."

More than ever now, I wish I'd insisted on a pre-nup. "I don't mind opening a joint account that we both pay into each month," I begin, "or a new savings account that we both start paying into from now." His face hardens. "But I think we should keep our personal savings and current accounts as they are."

"We're married now Nicola," His voice hardens too. He lowers himself onto the chair and clasps his hands in his lap. "Doesn't that mean anything to you?" I hate the way he glares at me when I've said or done the wrong thing.

"Of course it does, it's just..."

"What?"

"Nothing." How can I say that I'm not certain enough to give him access to my money? Jason and I were together for twelve years, and we always kept our finances separate and pooled for the bills and holidays. It's better that way.

"I get it. I support you whilst you write your novel, but you're not willing to support me? Is that it?"

"You've led me to believe since we met that you don't need supporting." I want to argue that I'm not asking for support whilst I write any novel, but I won't go back there for the moment.

"Nicola. We're either married, or we're not. If you were to die, I'd get the lot, anyway."

"What a peculiar thing to come out with." I try to lighten my voice, but hearing his words evokes a strange fear deep at my core. I search his face for a sign that he is joking, but I don't find it.

"And we'll need to sort wills too," he goes on. "Just to firm everything up."

My head's spinning. "I need to bring the shopping in." One minute he's talking about if I was to die, the next he's mentioning wills. Maybe I should warn someone who to point the finger at if I suddenly get bumped off.

"I'll give you a hand." The chair creaks as he stands.

Really, I wish he'd leave me alone for five minutes. I need to think. I need to work out what to do. Suddenly, it doesn't feel as though my life is my own – it's as though he's taking it over.

"They go in there." I pass him some cereal boxes, as I wonder what on earth I'm going to do about this novel and my work.- Could I really stay at home and write a novel? Perhaps I could try it to keep the peace. I'd miss my friends at work and my students, but it's not as if I'm on my own anymore. I'd get used to it.

Maybe I could ask work for a sabbatical – it would only be the same as if I'd ever needed maternity leave. Yes, that's probably my way around this one. I can easily afford a year off work. And that way, I keep my options open.

"By the way, I take it you remembered to tell your brother not to turn up here tonight?" Hugh fills the caddy with tea bags.

"No. I was going to mention that to you, actually." Without looking at him, I stack the fruit bowl. "I really want to see him, if I'm honest Hugh."

"Why?" He swings around from the cupboard. "I thought we'd already talked about this."

"Kieren's my brother. And the only family I've got left." As I say it, I feel sad, although it's not completely true. I get on well with Claire too.

Hugh points at himself. "I'm your family now. And you're mine. I've moved in with you, haven't I? And put you above my brother, and he's my twin."

"Yes, but you're still seeing him."

"Only because he puts the pressure on if I don't. He relies on me. Too much, if the truth be known."

"I've gathered that." It's the first time Hugh's said anything remotely negative against Gary, so I'm jumping on it. "He doesn't seem to want to let you go. It's probably why he had such a go at me outside the registry office."

Hugh slams a jar in the cupboard. "I can say what I want about my brother. But you can't, so watch it, eh?"

"But it's alright for you to come between me and Kieren?"

"You don't need him. You're just trying to live in the past and it's not healthy."

"Of course I need him." I shove all the shopping bags inside one another. "Look, if you just met Kieren, you'd get on really well." Even as I say this, I'm not too sure. Not with the moods Hugh's been displaying this week. And Kieren would say what he thinks. It could be ugly.

"If he comes around here, I'm clearing off. I mean it." Hugh slams the cupboard door. I can't understand why he won't meet Kieren.

"What do you mean, clearing off? How long for?"

"For as long as I see fit."

That look again. That tone of voice. I'm going to have to lie to Kieren. Tell him I've got a migraine. "I'm off to hang the washing out." I keep my voice even. "It's not often we get a sunny day."

I want these stupid arguments to stop. And I don't want Hugh to go. I can't face being left alone again. It was hell on the night of the wedding. I've got used to having him around now. I really don't want him to go.

Grabbing the laundry basket, I head into the yard at the front of our house. Thankfully, he doesn't follow me. I'm in the middle of pegging things out when a voice makes me jump.

"Nicola. How's things?"

"Yeah. Good, thanks." I load as much enthusiasm as possible into my voice as I smile at Julie. She lives in the adjoining terrace, backing onto mine. She's always seemed a bit off with me whenever we've passed in the street, but was friendlier when I was delivering a Christmas card for her last month. That was the first time we introduced ourselves properly.

I think she lives there alone – I've never heard any voices through the walls, apart from the low drone of the TV. We only usually say hello in passing, so I expect she will now make some comment or other about the weather and then clear off. I hope so. The mood Hugh's in, he probably wouldn't be very friendly if he were to come out here.

Julie doesn't smile back, but instead frowns as she leans over the wall. "It's just, I've heard one or two things – from your house, I mean."

"Like what?" I place a jumper back into the basket and step closer to her. Oh no – this is so embarrassing.

"Over the last day or two. Raised voices. You sounding as though you're crying." She glances towards my front door with what looks like caution etched over her face. "I don't want to speak out of turn, and you can tell me to mind my own business, but are you OK?"

"It must have been the TV you heard. I often hear yours too." I try to smile. "I'm fine. Honestly."

"It sounded as though you went through enough with the last one you lived with." She hasn't taken her eyes off my door for the last few moments, but now shifts her gaze to me. "Are you really sure you're alright?" This is the most we've ever spoken to each other, and I can't believe how the conversation is shaping up. Particularly with Hugh just inside. At least it's winter and all the windows are closed.

I wish I'd waited five minutes before hanging this washing out. Julie probably heard the occasion when I was literally begging Jason not to leave me last year, and the time I'd lost it when he confessed his bit on the side was pregnant. "I'm fine." My voice is a mumble. "Honestly."

"You know where I am Nicola. I've been thinking for ages that we should have a cuppa sometime. Or a glass of wine. Get to know each other better. I've lived here for nearly a year now."

"Gosh. That's gone quick." I'm pleased to change the subject. "And yes, a drink would be good. Wine definitely sounds preferable." Something within me lifts. It's the first time she's shown friendliness towards me and it's what I need right now.

She smiles back at me this time and nods towards Hugh's trousers pegged on the line - the ones he wore for the wedding. "I see things have changed for you."

I hold out my ring finger, trying to look happy. "Yes. I got married. Four days ago."

"Oh, er, right. Congratulations. Maybe that's whose voice I've been hearing through the back wall."

I can feel myself colouring up. "I'm sorry if we've disturbed you."

"It's not your fault the builders didn't build proper walls. I've forgotten how thin they are until the last couple of days. With us both living on our own, I hardly heard you before now."

"I'll make sure we keep things down in the future."

"Don't leave it too long before we have that drink." She gives me a strange look and I wonder what she's thinking about me.

"I'll look forward to it," I call after her as she walks away.

"I bet you will." Hugh is framed in the doorway as I swing around. "Who was she?"

"Julie. She lives in the house behind us." I wonder then how much he heard. Whether he heard her asking me if I'm OK. God, I hope not.

"She looks like a bloke, if you ask me. I wouldn't want to get on the wrong side of her. Perhaps she fancies you." His voice rises and I hope against hope that she's already gone inside.

"Of course not, and no, she doesn't." Granted, she's tall and well-built, but she looks nothing like a bloke. In fact, there's a familiarity about her that I can't quite put my finger on. I'll have to find out if we attended the same primary school or something. As I look at Hugh, I can't believe he's being so nasty. And they say women are bitchy.

"When are you having a drink with her, then?" He steps into the yard, ducking below one of my hanging baskets.

"It was just a loose arrangement. We didn't fix a time."

"Before long, you'll be going to another neighbour and then another neighbour. Particularly when you start working from home. Then the whole street will be gossiping."

"About what?"

"They'll always find something. I'd much prefer us to keep ourselves to ourselves. So don't get into the habit of making these arrangements with anybody else."

"But it's good to have friends. Other couples we can go out with perhaps?" I'm really hoping I'll be able to persuade him to go out with Kieren and Claire, eventually.

"Like I keep saying. We've got each other now." He rests his hand on my shoulder as I pick up the laundry basket. "Here – I'll take that. You don't need anybody else."

His words warm me and chill me at the same time. Much as I want to live happily ever after with Hugh, I do need other people in my life. And I always will.

"Anyway, hurry up with that." His tone changes. "We've got all this official stuff to sort out, haven't we?" His head knocks into the hanging basket as he turns back to the house. "I think we'll have to go into the bank with the marriage certificate to get these accounts open."

I was hoping he wouldn't push that. I don't mind opening joint accounts, but if he thinks I'm transferring all my money in, he can think again. Somehow, I'll wriggle out of it.

"Before we do that though, you've got a letter of resignation to write." He drops the basket in front of the freezer and heads towards the lounge. "Where's your laptop?"

"I'll sort it on Monday whilst I'm at work."

"You'll sort it now." He calls back.

"I was thinking of just taking a sabbatical, rather than all out resigning. I love my job."

He reappears in the doorway. "I don't think it's your job you love, Nicola. It's something else. What is it, all those younger men? Fresh meat?"

I stare at him. How do I respond to that one? There's nothing I can say. "I think my laptop is in the bedroom."

"I'll get it. We can send your resignation by email - then it's done. I'll give you a hand."

"I'm quite capable of writing an email Hugh."

"I'm not saying you're not. But I'll make sure it's worded right. I know from your messages to me that you go all around the houses. You're lucky that you've got me to keep an eye on you now."

Do I need an eye on me? Anyway, I decide to go along with what he says. Keeping the peace is the most important thing. I'll speak to Tom at work on Monday. Ask him face-to-face to turn my resignation request into a sabbatical request. There is, of course, always the chance that I'll make a success of my writing and not want to return to lecturing. But that will be my decision, not Hugh's. But first, whilst Hugh is upstairs, I need to text Kieren.

Sorry bro. I'm going to have to cancel this eve. Migraine.
I'm shocked when he texts straight back. Normally I'm lucky to ever get a reply. *Really? You've still got a few hours to get rid of it. And we don't have to stay long.*
No really. I'm in bed with it. I feel shocking.

He's straight back again. *I hope you're telling the truth. I've got a bad feeling about you at the moment.* I glance behind. There's no sign of Hugh – he must be in the bathroom.

Don't be daft. I'm fine. Honestly.

Apart from the migraine, you mean? Normally he'd put a smiley face on his texts too, but there's none of that this time.

Yes. Apart from the migraine. Look we'll sort something else out soon, I promise.

No worries. Catch you later.

"Who the hell are you texting?" I jump as Hugh appears behind me. He plucks the phone from my grip before I have the chance to tighten it. He touches the screen. "What does your brother mean? I've got a bad feeling?"

"I don't know. Probably that he doesn't believe I'm unwell."

"You could have come up with something more inventive than migraine. Anyway... we've stuff to be getting on with." He tosses the phone onto the kitchen counter. "Like I said, all that matters is me and you."

Try telling that to Gary, I want to say, his words before the wedding returning to me. But obviously, I keep quiet.

CHAPTER SEVEN

I 've always loved Tom's office. The smell, the feel, the easy chairs - it's lined floor to ceiling with books, of which he claims to have read every one. It's how my new office at home is going to look. I do have an office here, but it's more like a broom cupboard.

"So Nicola. Obviously, I've called you in after getting your email on Friday." The lines in his brow deepen. "I even tried ringing you."

I feel the heat in my cheeks. There was no way I was taking a call from Tom in front of Hugh. In any case, I'd put my phone on silent after my text exchange with Kieren.- I'm head of department but as the vice chancellor, Professor Tom Hayward is my line manager. Though, after many years of working together, we've also become firm friends.

"Yes. I was coming in to see you at lunchtime about it."

"It's all a bit sudden, isn't it? I see from the email that you've changed your surname as well."

I nod.

"Gosh, the rumours were true then? You got married? I didn't believe a word of it when I heard."

I nod again, feeling somewhat sheepish.

He strokes at his beard whilst not taking his eyes off me. "You don't look very happy about it. If you don't mind me saying Nicola."

"It's just all, taking some getting used to, that's all."

"What is?"

"You know. Being married. Moving in with someone. Sharing my life again."

"Do you think it could be a bit soon, after your dad, and... dare I say it, Jason?"

"If it is, it's too late now." I twizzle my newly gained rings around on my finger. They're feeling more like symbols of captivity than of love.

"Have you been together long?"

"Long enough."

"Well, speaking as your friend here, rather than your manager, I hope you know what you're doing."

"I've already gone and done it." I try to laugh, but it sounds hollow.

Tom must sense this, as the troubled look in his eyes intensifies. "Why do you want to leave Nicola? You're great at your job, well respected by staff and your students year on year. Not to mention your impressive salary, and even more impressive pension package – I have to say – you'd be nuts to give it up."

"I know, and I don't want to leave completely. Just for a year. I want to write a novel."

Amusement crosses his face. "Since when?"

"I've told you before, haven't I?"

"I don't recall you ever mentioning it. Anyway, isn't it something you could do alongside your work here? Perhaps we could reduce your hours slightly? It seems a bit drastic to leave your job, if you don't mind me saying so."

That would be the perfect solution, but Hugh will kill me if I go for it. He's already bulldozed me into so much. We're now joint account holders of a new current account, savings account, and joint pension plan. But what he doesn't know is that I've only transferred about a third of my money out of my personal accounts. The rest is safe, and it's staying that way – I just have to make sure he never gets hold of my statements.

He's even made a will-writing appointment, where our life insurance is also going to be discussed. I can't shake the feeling that he's planning to do me in or something – why else would he be in so much of a rush to sort a will and the life insurance.- Maybe I will make a good novelist, with thoughts like these feeding my imagination. Perhaps they could be the premise of the novel it seems I'm destined to write. Then if he finishes me off, my novel will lead people to him...

"Earth calling Nicola."

"Sorry. I was miles away." If only I could be completely honest about the predicament I've put myself in. I really could do with talking to somebody. But Tom, and anyone else would think I'm crazy for allowing all this to proceed so quickly. And they'd think I was even crazier for accepting the treatment I've received recently.

"About reducing your hours. What do you think?" He glances at a timetable on the wall in front of him as he speaks. "The last thing we want is to lose you, obviously. We could say four days instead of five."

"Thanks Tom. That means a lot." I'm horrified to feel the familiar stab of tears at the back of my eyes. It feels wonderful to experience some genuine kindness and respect from someone after the last week. But until recently, Hugh had seemed genuinely kind and respectful too. He never seemed to tire of telling me how he couldn't wait until we could start having adventures together, and he talked of us building our own house, acquiring a holiday retreat, and doing all the things on a 'living bucket list' we had drawn up together. *The world is our lobster,* became one of his favourite sayings. He's not said it once since last Monday, though.

Everything has changed since then. All the previous warmth towards me has left his face and his voice. We made love on Tuesday afternoon, after we'd been out for lunch – in fact, that's the only time since we've been married. However, when I think back, it was soulless and perfunctory, totally different from how it used to be between us. I can't shake the feeling that it only happened at all because I'd made the threat of annulment.

"Are you OK Nicola?" Tom reaches over the desk and touches my arm. Then he presses a button on his phone. "Sam. Would you mind doing two coffees, for me and Nicola, when you get a moment please?"

"Yeah. Honestly, I'm fine Tom." I blink away the tears again. I'll miss him, and my other colleagues – even if I'm only away for a year. It will be a long one.

"You don't look fine to me."

"What if I pursue this idea of writing a novel full time – just for a year?" I daren't go home and tell Hugh that I've decided on something else.

"I'm not sure you've really thought this through at all." He shakes his head. I think the world of Tom. Maybe in another life. Like I often say, lots of the best men turn out to be gay.

"Hugh, that's my new husband. Well, he's really set on me doing this novel thing, and he's bought furniture for a home office and everything." I'm gabbling, but it's better than bursting into tears. I don't know what's up with me lately. "He's even ordered a new computer. And he reckons I need to focus. Just on the novel – nothing else."

"You're the Head of our English faculty Nicola." Tom frowns at me over the top of his glasses, as though I'm one of the students.

"Surely you're not going to allow a man to be in charge of your life and dictate what you do?"

"I'm not. I know it sounds daft, but really, I want to do it – besides I've promised him now. So I was wondering about a sabbatical, rather than a permanent resignation?"

He sighs. "I guess I can put that to the senior management team." He pauses, as if choosing his words. "But Nicola, you know, and I'm not trying to flatten your ambition here, that the chances of you making it big with a first novel are pretty slender. You'd be as well keeping your income steady in the meantime. Again, I'm speaking as a friend."

"It's not about the money Tom. I've got my parent's money now, haven't I?" Though I'd give anything for them still to be here, with me – I don't let myself go there though. "I could choose never to work again if I felt so inclined."

"You're in a very fortunate position – well you are in terms of your career and finances anyway. Just promise me you'll be careful."

I thought I was in a fortunate position with my new relationship too. I can't talk to anyone about it though. I just need to wait for the dust to settle and for everything to find a new normal. It's a huge change for both of us.

"Thanks Sam." Tom smiles at his assistant as she places two cups on his desk in front of us.

"I hear congratulations are in order," Sam flicks her dark hair behind one shoulder, and smiles at me. "Be warned, I think a celebratory evening out is in the offing. I heard something in the staff room. And it's sure to be a messy one!"

"Thank you." I try to smile back whilst immediately worrying about the night out. Will they expect Hugh to go? And if not, what will Hugh say about me going? Bloody hell. This is going to take some getting used to. I haven't had to answer to anyone since I was a teenager. And in my most recent relationship, Jason always let me do my own thing and vice versa. But look where that got me...

"Your chariot awaits." Hugh grins widely at me as I hurry through the rain across the university car park, and towards the red Porsche he's sitting in.

"Whose is this?" I climb into the passenger side. It's got that lovely new car smell and cream leather seats. "This is seriously some car." He must be test driving it for a client or something.

"Heated seats as well." He presses a button. "And it's automatic. Not that I'll be letting you drive it, of course. Women shouldn't be trusted with a piece of machinery such as this."

"What – you mean it's yours?"

"Fresh from the showroom. Obviously not one of my showrooms." He laughs. "So, what do you think? Shall we take her for a spin?"

Without waiting for an answer, he revs the engine and dashes towards the exit. I'm thrown back in my seat as he swerves out of the university car park. Hugh's grinning from ear to ear as he races the car through the surrounding streets. As we pass people, they turn to stare. I suppose they would at a brand new, bright red Porsche.

I'm not going to risk his wrath by asking how he's paid for it. That he's soon going to be banned from driving is also puzzling. I'd like to see some evidence of that. He must have some papers from the police station. Next time he goes out, I'll have to look for them. I tug out my phone and open my banking app. I've got an awful feeling.

Sure enough, in our new joint account, there's been a debit earlier today for £82,950. Oh. My God. He's not even paid anything into the account yet. This is my money. At the time of opening the account, I got some tale from him about having to give notice before being able to instigate a large transfer.

"I can't wait to show this motor to Gary. He'll be drooling with envy." To my horror, I realise we're heading towards the motorway. He only lives a couple of exits along it, so the way Hugh's driving, we'll be there in ten minutes. "You don't mind, do you?"

I mind very much. "Can you pull over please?"

"What's up with you now?" He brings the car to a halt at the side of the road. We sit in silence for a moment, watching as raindrops pelt the windscreen.

"You've used my money to pay for this Hugh." My voice is flat, and I keep my gaze forwards. But I've got to say something. It's not exactly a small amount of money. If it were a few thousand, I could overlook it, but eighty-two?

"You said I could. Oh no." He chuckles. "Don't you remember? Don't say the menopause brain is back again."

"I said nothing of the sort." But with my lack of sleep this week, who knows. I've never known insomnia like it. My mind won't stop whirring to the point where I could throw my head repeatedly against a wall to find some peace.

"You really did Nicola. Blimey, do I have to record the conversations we have? Or get you to sign something?" He slaps his hand against the steering wheel. "Anyway, it'll be fine once they have transferred my money in. I'm not expecting you to pay for all of it."

"I'm not paying for any of it. You've said absolutely nothing about buying a car. I'd hardly forget agreeing to buy a Porsche."

"I'm wondering if you should see a doctor, Nicola. Your memory really seems to be slipping."

"There's nothing wrong with my memory."

"Maybe it's depression. Like I said the other day, you're as miserable as a funeral most of the time."

It's on the tip of my tongue to remind him of his face on our wedding day, but I hold back. Never would I have held back with Jason to this extent. At least with Jason, I felt comfortable enough to speak my mind. But then, he left me in the end. Everyone leaves me. I can recall threats made by even my parents to throw me out when I was a pain in the arse teenager.

"Perhaps you need some happy pills," Hugh continues as he glances into his rear-view mirror.

I ignore his last comment. "There's no point in buying a car like this if you're about to be banned from driving."

"What? What on earth are you on about?" He grins as he notices people staring at the car.

"You being three times over the limit, that's what I'm on about."

"Who on earth told you that?"

I stare at him, and my voice rises. "You did, of course."

"I told you nothing of the sort."

"On the night of our wedding, you reckoned to have been locked up all night for drink driving." I turn to him. My brain feels like mush. Maybe he's right. Perhaps the menopause, or something else is addling my brain.

"I honestly don't know where you've got that from Nicola."

"You bloody told me." My voice is a shriek. Either I'm going mad or he's a lying bastard. It's got to be the latter.

"Nicola." His voice drips with sarcasm. It's a far cry from the voice that's whispered how much he loves me in the thick of the night. A million miles from the voice that's said he's waited all his life for me and will now make up for his thirty-nine years of lost time. "You're right about one thing."

"What's that?"

"Why on earth would I buy a car like this if I was about to get banned for drink driving?"

"So where were you last Monday, then? If they did not lock you up for drink driving, I mean."

"When?" He presses a button, which makes the windscreen wipers speed up.

"The night of our so-called wedding."

"Why *so-called* wedding? It couldn't have been any more legitimate. Particularly now that we've consummated it." He makes a sign at someone who beeps at us. "Although I won't be doing that so often."

"Doing what?" Surely he doesn't mean what he's saying. All thoughts of money fly out of the rain smattered windows. How can he be so cruel?

"A menopausal woman that can't recall what she's said, or agreed to, isn't exactly attractive. Not to me, anyway."

My fists bunch in my lap. "How dare you treat me like this?" I yell. Finally, I'm feeling some fight against him. About bloody time. "I want you out of my house and I want the money back for this car."

"I'm going nowhere." The evenness of his voice makes me want to swing for him. "We're married Nicola. I've got rights. Anyway, never mind wanting me out of the house. I want you out of my car. Go on. Do one. I can't cope with being yelled at like this."

"Your car! Pay for it then." Nevertheless, I grab my bag and slam the door after myself with all my might. He drives away with a spinning of wheels, and I furiously swipe away my tears with the back of my hand. Tom, Kieren and even my neighbour, Julie, who barely knows me, seem to have sensed something 'off' about Hugh. They don't know him at all. And I don't either.

Chapter Eight

I 'm drenched by the time I find somewhere to shelter. Although I'm so upset that I've barely felt the rain.

I seem to be making a habit of going to pubs by myself lately. Normally, I wouldn't. In my experience, they're full of men that think I'm ripe for being chatted up. That's the last thing I need right now.

I take my wine and crisps and feel beyond grateful for the vacant seat facing the open fire. Hugh throwing me out of the car was most certainly for the best. I don't want to be within spitting distance of bloody Gary. Plus, I need to think. Get this stupid head of mine straight. I don't know what I'm doing anymore. I can't seem to recollect conversations I've had or things I've supposedly agreed to, which is worrying. Mum was showing traits of dementia before her cancer diagnosis and Dad, well, he wasn't exactly thinking straight to do what he did to himself.- These things run in families, as Hugh has already pointed out to me on several occasions.

I'm certain, absolutely certain, of the drink drive thing though. Hugh definitely told me he was three times over the limit that night. I heard him with my own ears. I'm sure I did.

Or could I have just heard what I wanted to hear? Perhaps he was with another woman that night. Or maybe he just cooked up an elaborate excuse so it would be easier to win me round and get me into bed. That way, I couldn't follow through with my threat of annulment.

He must have looked up what I'd threatened him with for himself and realised I really could annul our marriage. How the hell did I fall for that? Why didn't I keep my big mouth shut? Probably because I was chasing the pre-marriage Hugh. The one who was attentive, complimentary and affectionate. What on earth has got into him this week? I sip my wine. My brain feels like it's swathed in a dense fog and what I can't believe is how much he's changed towards me.

Now, because of my naivety, if things get to a point where I want him out of my life, I'll have to prove unreasonable behaviour, or adultery. And I'll be at risk of him demanding a divorce settlement. Surely not, though, not when he's got enough money of his own. He bought all that office furniture and ordered a computer the other day. Then I realise. The credit card I keep in my laptop case. I only use it when I'm ordering things I want buyer protection for. I hold my thumb over the button of my phone and wait for my credit card app to load. Sure enough, he's spent half the credit limit. Two days ago. What am I going to do? A message flashes up on my phone.

I'm going to have a drink with my brother. I'll probably stay at his house tonight. Hope we can sort things out tomorrow. X

I sink inside as I read it. Things have been awful over the last few days, but surely it's just a blip. There must be a reason he's been so different with me. But until I get to the bottom of it, how can we go forwards? He's put a kiss on the end of his message. He's saying that he hopes we can sort things out. But being around his brother might just poison his mind towards me even more. Besides, I can't bear the thought of all night alone, tormented by him really being with another woman or imagining what Gary might fill his head with.

Please come home, I type back. Have a drink with me. We can sort things out tonight. X

Even though I'm worried, I do still love him. This week, he's not been the Hugh I know. But we can get through this. And he has promised to transfer all the money back, so it will be fine.

He doesn't reply. I stare at my phone screen for a long time.- Resisting the urge to order another wine, I instead order a taxi. I'm going to have a long soak in the bath, then put my head under the covers. Get rid of this crappy day. I only hope that sleep will rescue me for a change.

The sat nav in the taxi directs the driver to pull up outside Julie's house rather than mine. As I pay him, I notice Julie pull back her curtain, presumably to see who's outside. I wave at her and before I've hooked my bag onto my shoulder, she's flung her front door open.

"Do you fancy that glass of wine Nicola? I've just opened a bottle."

"I erm, I don't know." Can I trust myself not to spill my whole miserable tale? And Hugh's already said something about not wanting neighbours to know about our business.

"Come on. You're not in a rush, are you? Without you, I'll end up drinking it all by myself." She stands with her hand on her hip and her blonde hair piled on top of her head. It nearly touches the top of the doorframe.

From the message he sent, Hugh is very unlikely to come back tonight. The prospect of my empty house and the void of a lonely evening ahead doesn't exactly fill me with glee.

"Thanks. That would be really nice." I stride up the path to meet her.

"You look like a drowned rat," she says as I reach the door. "I'll get you a towel."

"I'm not as bad now. Compared to what I was an hour or so ago." I follow her in and glance around at her house. As I stand in the hallway, I can hear her bustling around in the kitchen. It's exactly the same layout as mine. Right to the kitchen, left to the lounge. A spacious three up, two down with cardboard walls. I can always hear her hoover and her washing machine. But at least she's a quiet neighbour. It would have annoyed me to high heaven if she had screaming kids or a yapping dog.

I've been racking my brains to work out exactly what she may have heard between me and Jason last year. And I'll have to make sure that there's nothing else to hear between me and Hugh.

"There you go." She gives me a towel, which I wrap around my shoulders with a shiver. It's fresh out of the dryer or off a heater, and feels like a hug, which I badly need at the moment. "Come through." She then hands me a glass of red wine and I follow her gratefully into her cosy lounge.

"You've got it nice in here." I sink into the armchair that instantly cocoons itself around me. It's one of the comfiest chairs I've ever sat in. "I'm going to get a fire put in my house like yours. After Jason left, I wasn't sure if I was going to stay there, but for the time being, I probably will."

"I'll let you have the number of the guy who put it in, if you like?"

"Thanks." Although I'm sure Hugh will have something to say about workmen in the house. Especially if he's at work. Plus, he's also made noises about us building an eco-house in the middle of nowhere. I'm not sure that would suit me though. As if I'm not isolated enough.

"Cheers." She holds her glass in the air. "Here's to getting to know our neighbours."

"Cheers. And thanks for this. It's just what the doctor ordered." I sink further back into the cushions. And it is. Though I'm curious why she's suddenly befriended me after looking the other way for nearly a year.

"Tell me. How's married life going?"

It could be my hesitancy, it could be the wobble of my lip, or the darkness she might see in my eyes that answers her question without me saying a word.

"That good, eh? I thought as much when I heard you both shouting the other day. What's that saying, marry in haste..."

"Repent at leisure. I know. Hugh was so lovely before we married. It's like a switch has been flipped."

"How long have you known him? It can't be that long."

She must have spotted Jason coming and going when she first moved in. Then, amidst the rows, she will have seen me dragging my sorry self around, and even more so after he left me. I'd start crying in the middle of the street, at work and in the supermarket. All of it was too much, and I was a mess. Mum's death last Christmas, Dad ending it all, and then Jason leaving me only a week later. It's no wonder I took a stab at securing happiness with Hugh. The entire sorry story comes pouring out as I sip at my wine. Which was what I was worried about, but talking to her makes me feel better. I haven't got too many friends around right now and she doesn't interrupt, as many others would. She just listens with an expression that's difficult to decipher. As I finish my glass, and my tale, Julie sits next to me on the arm of my chair and drapes an arm around my shoulders. She smells of Pears soap.

After a moment of quiet, she takes my glass. "I'll get you a refill."

"I probably shouldn't. This will be my third tonight. I've got work tomorrow. Oh, what the hell."

Julie returns to the room and re-perches herself on the arm of the chair. It feels strange being so close to her. After all, we barely know each other, but the wine has certainly taken the edge off things. And now, she practically knows my life story. I know very little about her though. This is becoming a common theme.

"Tell me what's good in your life right now Nicola." She pauses. "You certainly seem to have plenty of money."

I fall silent again to think. "I've got my brother, and I guess I'm financially stable, like you say. I've got a good job, and I got a decent inheritance."

She stays sitting on the arm of my chair. "I bet you did. Some people get nothing. Some people don't even have any parents."

"Are yours still alive?"

She shakes her head vehemently. Too vehemently. There's definitely a story there. "Everything they left you, was it split with your brother then?"

"Yeah. But I'd rather be stony broke and still have them here."

"Close then, were you?"

I'm sure I pick up a hint of bitterness in her voice, but I can't be sure. I nod. "Yes. I can't believe they've gone."

"So, do you reckon you'll leave him?" she asks. I'm surprised at her directness. Maybe it's just her way.

"Hugh?" I shrug. "I hope it doesn't come to that. I can't stand being on my own." It's true. I had enough of it last year. Night after night after night of closing the door after work, drawing the curtains, and then not speaking to a soul until the following day.

"You get used to it. Anyway, you don't have to be on your own." She squeezes my shoulder and returns to her own chair. "You've got me now. And it's not as if I live a million miles away."

I'm warmed, yet confused by her friendliness. But I'll take it. It's come at a good time. "Let's talk about something else," I say. "All we've talked about is my crap since I arrived. Let's talk about you now. Tell me how you ended up here."

"I'll open another bottle, shall I?"

I probably shouldn't have anymore. But Hugh's not coming back tonight. He hasn't even had the decency to reply to my text.

"Here we are." Julie strides into the lounge and places the bottle on the table before sitting on the sofa. "So about me then. Not much to tell, really. Self-employed. I'm not exactly raking it in, but it pays enough to cover the bills."

It's strange that her first go to when conversing is money, but I suppose some people are driven by that, and measure others in the same way.

"Have you lost your parents too?" I'm unsure whether to bring this up, but it's probably a more beneficial conversation than money – it might help us both.

"Yeah. My mum killed herself when I was a baby."

"Oh no. I'm so sorry." What a grim conversation. And what a thing to have in common.

"At least you knew your dad."

That's a peculiar thing to say. Surely it must make it harder to have actually spent your life with a parent who died in such awful circumstances as mine. But I don't say my thoughts out loud.

"What about *your* dad?"

Her face clouds over and I realise it's a question I shouldn't have asked. "Waste of space. He never wanted to know me."

"I'm sorry." And I am. "My parents weren't perfect. They would veer between being too strict and seeming not to give a damn, but we never wanted for anything. We always had the best of things, holidays, bikes, school, our home..."

Judging by her expression, I should really shut up. Wine always loosens my tongue and I've certainly had enough. I'm drinking too fast.

"Another?" Julie glances at my nearly empty glass and reaches towards the bottle.

I'm warm and safe in front of this fire and don't feel like shifting. I wish I didn't have to go home. Then my phone flashes on the table.

Where are you?

Why is he asking that? He said he was staying with Gary tonight, so surely he'll think I'm at home. Having said that, he did dump me in the middle of town. Perhaps he'll think I've gone to visit Kieren, or one of my friends from work. Perhaps he could even be concerned about me.

Julie is watching me. "Is it him?" She fills her glass, then points the bottle towards mine.

I rest my hand over the top of my glass. "I'd better not. He's asking where I am. Plus I've got work in the morning."

"It's not as though you're doing anything wrong here." She sits forward in her seat and slides her feet back into the slippers she came to the door in.

I sigh. "The thing is, he's supposed to be at his brother's."

"What's his brother like?" She cocks her head to one side as though she is really interested. Perhaps she's wondering if he's single.

"Awful. No, worse than awful."

"Really? Why?"

"I wouldn't trust him as far as I could throw him. He seems really jealous of me, but I can't work out why."

"Do you think you'll tell your husband you've been round here?"

"I might tell a white lie. Just so I don't upset things."

Julie pulls a face. "It doesn't sound like a good start to married life."

"I know."

"Why can't you tell him you're here?" Her tone of voice says it all, and I don't blame her.

"Just a sec, I'd better reply to him." I type back. *Going to bed soon. Why?* That's not exactly a lie. I will be going to bed soon. *So you're at home then?*

Where else would I be?

You tell me.

Shit. I've got an awful feeling he's turned up. But he said he was having a drink tonight so presumably he can't drive. Though after the wedding night, who knows? "Julie. Would you do me a favour?"

"Sure." She lets her hair out of its band so it falls around her shoulders as she looks at me.

"Just take a look around the corner and see if there's a red Porsche outside my house."

"A red Porsche." She raises an eyebrow as she gets to her feet. "It must have really been some inheritance."

"No. Look. Don't even go there." I keep telling myself it's only money, but my gut is saying something else.

As she leaves the house, I lean forward in the chair and wrap my arms around myself. Please God, don't let him have come home.

"No red Porsche." She comes back into the room, shaking her head.

"I'd better be getting home." I haul myself to the front of the chair. "Thanks so much for inviting me in. It's been lovely." It was until that text anyway – now I've got nerves jangling around inside me.

"Anytime." She takes my glass. "I'm glad of the company. I should have invited you around sooner."

I want to ask her about how she copes with living alone, and how she has got used to it. After Jason walked out, I had eight long months alone before meeting Hugh. I just worked and worked to fill the void and wherever possible, I'd stay at Kieren's or with a friend. I don't think I could have ever got used to it. But if things continue as they are with Hugh, I might have to.

As I leave, Julie calls after me, "I hope everything's OK – with Hugh, I mean."

"Thanks," I call back as I reach her gate. "So do I," I whisper to myself.

"You know where I am." The door clicks behind her.

I'm warmed by her words. I heave a sigh of relief as I push my own garden gate open. The house is in darkness and there's no sign of Hugh having returned. I'm too tired for a bath now. And a bit tipsy. I'm going to get myself to bed, where I might manage a chapter of the book I've been reading. Hopefully the wine will send me to sleep. The thought of going to bed without Hugh is almost unbearable. It's strange how quickly I've got used to having him sleep beside me.

Tomorrow's another day. He'll transfer the money back into the joint account and then really be able to enjoy his Porsche.- This will keep him in a decent mood and he'll be back to his usual self.

CHAPTER NINE

As I put my key in the door, it's yanked open with such force it takes my breath with it. "Where the hell have you been?" Even in the darkness, I can see the anger etched across Hugh's face. He must have got a taxi back.

"Just round at Julie's." I brush past him and flick the stairs light on. "We had a drink, that's all. I thought you were staying at Gary's?"

"He was doing my head in."

"Why?"

"I don't want to talk about it. How come you're so late back, anyway?" I can sense him behind me on the stairs and I wonder for the millionth time how I can have gone from being the happiest woman on the planet to... this.

I swing around and face him. "We had a couple of drinks that's all. It's not as if I were a million miles away."

"So you're going round there for cosy drinks now?"

I turn my back and continue up the stairs. "She invited me. Look, you'd cleared off for the night Hugh as far as I knew. Was I just supposed to sit here on my own?"

"You were fine doing that before you met me." The sneer I've grown to dread has returned to his voice. "You and your sad

72

life. You're lucky I came along when I did. No one else would have taken you on."

I raise my voice without planning to. All this arguing, all this drama over nothing – it isn't me. I just want a quiet life. But the wine must be giving me a false bravado. "Where do you get off, talking to me like this Hugh, making me feel like you do? My life feels sadder now, if you must know. Since I married you." Now at the top of the stairs, I turn and jab my finger at him as I say the word you. He's two steps below me.

"What did you say?" He bounds to the top in one step and slams me into the landing wall. The force of the movement as my back connects with the wall winds me. He grabs one of my wrists so tightly I know it will be bruised tomorrow. "Answer me!"

"Get off me," I screech as his other hand grabs at my throat. I push him backwards, surprised at my own strength, as he steadies himself at the top of the stairs. By the way he stumbles, it's clear that he's also had a few drinks. Which would explain the absence of the Porsche. In that moment, I realise just how easy it would be to push him down my steep staircase. I could make it look like an accident. I'd be free again. Free to look for someone who wants to make me happy. Then I recoil at myself. How could I allow such a thought? And like Hugh has just said, no one else would want me anyway.

"If it's no big deal, why did you lie to me when you texted me back?" He follows me into the bedroom. "If it's one thing I can't stand, it's liars."

"I didn't lie."

"You made out like you were at home."

"I didn't. I said I was going to bed soon, that's all."

"You lied to me!" He's shouting again. I bet Julie can hear him. It occurs to me then that we haven't swapped phone numbers. Maybe we should. I need someone in my corner more than ever.

"Look. I'm sorry." I sink to the bed. "I just want things back to how they were between us. In fact, I'd give anything for that. Whatever I've done Hugh, I'm sorry." And at this moment, I am. From November until last week, I've been deliriously happy with him. We've done so much together in such a short time. As well as that, he's unknowingly helped with my recovery from the events of last year. I just want things to stay the same.

"It's OK." He sits beside me on the bed. Despite everything, he's such an attractive man. If I don't get myself right, he'll go off with someone else. "We'll get you right, whatever it takes. I can see how depressed you are. How little confidence you've got in yourself. I'm here for you, you know that, don't you?" He tilts my face towards his, in the way that always melts any doubt I have towards him.

Is that how I'm coming across to him? Depressed? Lacking in confidence? Maybe all that's what's putting him off me. Whatever it is, I've got to work on it. From tomorrow, no matter how I'm feeling inside, the outwardly facing Nicola is going to be happy and badass. I'm not going to drive him away like I did with Jason. As Hugh was on about the other day, men at our age are mainly looking for younger and more energetic women, and men in the age group above ours are basically just looking for someone to cook, clean and keep them company until they pop their clogs.

"I think we should make a day of it." Hugh stretches his feet from under the covers and turns to me, smiling.

Despite the wine I drank last night, my head is remarkably clear. The sun is seeping around the blind, and I have every reason to hope that today will be a good day. He seems to be acting like yesterday never happened and I'm certainly not going to mention it. "What do you mean? Are you suggesting we go off somewhere?"

"You'd have to ring in sick, obviously."

"I can't. I'm giving a lecture this morning."

"Ooooh. A lecture." He loads a snobbish tone into his voice and pushes the tip of his nose towards the ceiling.

I look at him, unsure whether he's joking or just making fun of me. "Well, what else would you call it? It's what I do."

"Not for much longer. I forgot to ask with the excitement of the new car yesterday - were they alright about you leaving?"

I certainly wouldn't use the word excitement in relation to yesterday, but decide just to answer his question. "Of course. They haven't got a lot of choice, have they?" I'm not telling Hugh I've asked Tom for a sabbatical – he'd have a fit. It's not worth it, especially at the moment. "Where is the car, anyway?"

"I left it outside the pub near Gary's."

"How come?"

"Like I said, we'd had words."

"About what?"

"I was sticking up for you, if you must know. Even if what he was saying was right, he's got no business saying it."

"What was he saying? No, forget I asked that question. I don't want to know."

"I'll tell you if you really want me to."

My self-esteem is already in tatters, but I'm not going to tell Hugh that. He'll think I'm even more pathetic than he already does. Instead, I try to change the subject. "I'm surprised you left the car there overnight. Gary doesn't exactly live in the most salubrious of areas, does he?"

"Get you. Miss Middle Class, silver spoon in her gob."

"Mrs now," I retort, which surprisingly raises a smile from him. They've been in short supply this last week.

"Are you going to ring in work, or what?"

"I've never pulled a sickie in my life."

And I don't want to start now. I've only got a term left with my students and I'll miss each one of them when I take my sabbatical. I feel sure the management team will grant permission for it. If I were still single, there's no way on this earth that I would take a year out, but now I'm married, and I've decided to write a novel, or at least, I'm told I have, things are different. There's a small part of me that's looking forward to it. I won't miss all the assignment marking, that's for sure. And Julie works from home, so I'm sure I'd have company through the day. She did say *you know where I am* to me last night.

"No time like the present, then." Hugh smiles again. We're back to being Nicola and Hugh again. And it's the Hugh that loves me and wants to spend time with me. He's worth taking the day off for.

"OK." I reach for my phone. "I'll go downstairs to make the call. I'll feel like an idiot faking a pathetic, ill-sounding voice in front of you."

He laughs. "A coffee would be good whilst you're down there."

"What's the plan then?"

"How about you take me to pick up the car and then we'll go for some breakfast. After you've made yourself look a bit more presentable, that is."

It's the first time he's ever criticised my appearance. I know I look a mess this morning after not sleeping well. It's little wonder after the drama of yesterday and the wine I drank. I haven't even brushed my hair yet. It's probably a good idea to make an extra special effort today. Remind him of what he saw in me when we first met. "OK. As long as we're going out of town. I don't want one of my students seeing me."

"What does it matter? You're leaving the place, anyway. Which reminds me. We'll have to wait in this afternoon. The new computer is being delivered."

"Oh right." I'm disappointed. After a rubbish time lately, I was suddenly looking forward to going off somewhere together. "How about I ask Julie to take the delivery? She works from home, so I'm sure she won't mind if I leave a note on our door."

His face darkens as we walk to the gate. "Stop arguing back. I said we're waiting in."

"Fine," I say, noticing the drop in his voice again. "We'll come back and wait. Maybe we can go off somewhere afterwards."

"You've got a novel to be starting once that computer arrives. Like we agreed. It won't write itself."

I follow him to the Audi, feeling deflated. I thought I'd thrown a sickie at work for us to be doing something together. And I don't know why he keeps saying I agreed to have a go at a novel. I only ever expressed an interest. It's weird.

After having no dinner last night, I fill my plate up at the 'all you can eat' breakfast buffet. Hugh eyes my plate as I sit down.

"You'll be needing a wardrobe full of new clothes as well if you're going to carry on like that."

I laugh at his dig, that's not quite a dig, yet I could take it as one if I were so inclined. "I'd better get my sorry arse to the gym more often hadn't I? It's been a couple of weeks since I've been."

"I thought you preferred doing yoga at home?" He pours tea into both of our cups. If only he was doing this at a breakfast table in a lovely hotel, miles away from here.

"I do enjoy yoga. When I'm pushed for time. But it's not the same as doing a class and being amongst people."

"Why not? You can go walking or running as well, can't you? Plus, these things don't cost a fortune in unused gym memberships, do they?"

"Says he who's just bought a Porsche. Anyway, I like the gym when I can motivate myself to go. Besides, I've got friends there."

"You've got me now. We could go running together. I'd be up for that."

I follow his gaze to the door and then to Gary as he heads to our table. At first I think I'm seeing things.

"Grab a plate bro. This one's on us."

"You never said we were meeting Gary," I hiss at Hugh as I slam my fork down. My appetite has suddenly vanished. After what Gary said to me before the wedding ceremony, I really don't want to sit across a table from him. And Hugh made out like they'd fallen out last night, anyway. With me at the centre of it.

As Gary sits, he smiles at me, but the smile goes nowhere near his eyes. Great. This is absolutely all I need.

"Is the car still in one piece?" Hugh asks.

Gary stabs at a sausage with his fork and brings the whole thing to his mouth without cutting it. "Sure is. I think everyone in the pub knows it's yours, so obviously, they won't touch it."

"We'll collect it after we've eaten," Hugh says.

"It was good of you to buy him that Nicola. Wedding present, was it?" Gary shovels beans into his mouth. "I'd have married you myself if I'd known there was a Porsche involved."

"No... I..." I wince as Hugh nudges me sharply under the table, which I take to mean, *don't you dare discuss our business with my brother.*

78

"What are you up to today, then?" Gary's eating habits remind me of a cement mixer. This puts me off my breakfast even more than I was already.

"Nothing exciting," Hugh replies. "Just waiting in for the delivery of a computer. Nicola's writing a novel."

Gary appears to choke. He's laughing at me. "Oh... right. What sort of novel?"

I display my sweetest smile. "One where someone gets murdered."

He laughs louder.

I glare at him. "I'm going to wait in the car. Suddenly I'm not hungry." People on the tables beside us are staring as I throw my chair back with a scrape and snatch the keys from where they sit in front of Hugh. I march towards the door. No way can I share a table with that man. There's something about him. Besides, Hugh won't even meet my brother. Why should I try to get along with his?

CHAPTER TEN

I should drive away, but it's a couple of miles between here and the Porsche, and I don't want to make things any worse. I try to distract myself with an eBook on my phone, but I can't focus. Normally I love reading but all the enjoyment seems to have gone out of everything lately. I don't even do yoga any more. I take a deep breath in and let a jagged one out in the car's silence. Then close my eyes. Why the hell didn't I just go to work? If I'd have known what I was letting myself in for, I wouldn't have thought twice about it.

I jump as there's a tapping on the window at the side of my head. It's sodding Gary. Much as I want to ignore him, I probably shouldn't. I've got myself into enough hot water as it is. I open the door and look beyond him to see if Hugh's followed him out. He hasn't. Whether this is good or bad, I don't know.

"What's your problem with me Nicola?" Gary stands with his thumbs hooked into the waistband of his grubby jeans. The shadow of a blonde beard makes him look like he needs a good wash, and his hair is on end. He surveys me with the same air of distaste as he did last week. He really is someone I want to keep my distance from. Mum always used to tell me to trust my instincts with people.

"I don't know what you mean?" If I play dumb, maybe he'll go away.

"Like I've said to you before, if you try to come between me and my brother, you'll regret it."

"I'm not trying to do anything of the sort." The man's a nightmare, and once again, he's threatening me.

"You don't need to try. You're coming between us whether you try or not."

"Look. Why don't we start again?" I can't believe I'm making such a suggestion to this creep, but falling out with him will surely only make things more difficult for me.

"I can see right through you, Ni-co-la." The way he elongates my name makes me wonder if he's wired right. "I know exactly who you are. What you are."

"I've no idea what you're talking about." My temper is rising. I didn't have much confidence in myself before, but this is getting beyond the joke. "Enlighten me then. Who and what am I?"

He smiles. I hate him.

"You're a leech Nicola. An emotional leech. You're sucking the life out of my brother right under my nose and I'm not going to stand by and let you."

I don't know if my jaw has dropped open, but it feels as though it might have done. A leech! I've literally paid for everything since Hugh came along. If this pillock does not get away from me, I fear I may well start the engine of this car and run him over. If I could get away with it, maybe I would.

"Just because you were dumped, and your old man topped himself, does not give you the right to drag my brother down to where you are."

"But I haven't. We were happy..." My voice trails off. Why am I even bothering to explain myself to him? And how dare he bring my dad into this? I slam the car door.

He rams his fist into the window.

81

"Go away!" I shout, fighting back the tears again. "Leave me alone."

Hugh and I make the journey to the pub where he was last night in near silence. I don't know what's worse. His anger, his mistrust, or the cold shoulder. What I do know is that I'm extremely unnerved by it all. As soon as I can, I'm going to talk to Kieren. Sometimes I think he only ever seems to bother with me on his own terms. When he needs me for something. Well, maybe it's time I needed him for something. That's if he's speaking to me after cancelling last week.

I drop Hugh at the pub's entrance. He gets out of the car without saying a word and I drive away. I really wish I'd gone to work. Given the atmosphere between us, I don't really want to go home, but in the absence of any other purpose, I find myself pulling up outside the house anyway. I switch the engine off and close my eyes.

Minutes later, Hugh pulls up behind me. I can see his face in my rear-view mirror and it's clear he's in the same mood as the one I dropped him off at the pub in.

We get out of our cars at the same time and Hugh slams his door. After my altercation with Gary, I'm fit to blow.

"When you've paid for that car, you can slam its doors. Have you got that Hugh?" I then stride towards the front door. I realise as soon as I've got inside what a mistake I've made. I should have walked in the opposite direction, gone to Julie's house, gone anywhere...

Hugh slams me against the hallway wall in a similar way to how he did on the landing last night. "If you ever make a show of me either outside my home, or in front of my brother like you have today again, I'll..."

"You'll what?" My words pump out in gasps as he's got me around the throat again. He doesn't press hard enough to leave a mark, so I guess it would be my word against his if I were to make a complaint. I notice how he uses the term *my home*. There can be no denying how quickly he's got his feet under the table. He lets me go and I rub at my neck, trying not to show that he's hurt me.

"Go on. You'll what?" I follow him into the lounge. "No! Please! Not that!"

I've told him how precious the carriage clock is to me and now, as he holds it aloft with a crazed look in his eye, I feel my heart break some more. Moments after it shatters at my feet, I drop to my knees, not caring if I'm cut to ribbons by shards of glass. "How could you? How could you?" I don't think I've ever cried so much in my life as I have lately.

"I'm sorry." Suddenly, he looks distressed and crouches beside me. "It's you." He points at me. "You make me act like this. You bring out the worst in me. What is it about you?"

Fresh tears tumble down my cheeks. "What's happened to us Hugh? I was so excited about marrying you. Call me gullible, but I thought we were going to live happily ever after."

"You wouldn't know happily ever after if it bit you on your cellulite covered arse."

Another insult. He rises back to his feet and marches into the kitchen. I wait for a few moments, trying to come to terms with the wreckage of Mum's beloved clock. *It's only a clock*, I try to tell myself. Yet, I know that's not true. I have to get to the root of what's got into Hugh. Maybe he's ill or something. Finally, I gather enough courage to follow him into the kitchen.

He's standing with his back to me, resting his elbows on the kitchen counter. "My brother's right about you," he says. "You're nothing but a depressive. You're dragging me down to your level, and I don't know what to do for the best." He leans closer to the counter and drags his fingers through his fringe.

"I'm sorry. Really I am Hugh." I know I sound pitiful, but what choice have I got here? One thing he's said is right. No one else will want me now. I admit I'm a mess at times, and it's not as if I'm young anymore. "Look," I go on, "I know that occasionally I let things get to me. My dad's death hit me hard. But I'll get some counselling, I promise. I don't want to lose you Hugh. Please, let's just sort this out."

What am I saying? They're both right – Hugh and Gary. Perhaps I have sunk lower than I'm accepting. Here I am, begging my new husband to be nice to me.

He straightens himself up slowly and turns to face me. "You promise me you'll get some help?"

"Yes. I should have done it last year." Hope lifts within me at the change in his voice and facial expression.

"Right. Get an appointment for as soon as you can, and I'll come with you."

"There's no need for you to come with me." Shaking my head, I say, "I'm a big girl, you know." I can't think of anything worse that discussing my woes with a doctor in front of Hugh.

His tone becomes more aggressive. "If you won't let me take care of you, perhaps we should part company. There are plenty of other women who'd be grateful to have me around."

"What! No! I didn't mean..."

"Look Nicola. I only want to make sure you don't get fobbed off by the doctor. You need to be on some antidepressants... as well as some pills to help you sleep."

"I don't want sleeping tablets. They'll turn me into a zombie."

"But it's fine to force me into a zombie when you keep me awake half the night with your tossing and turning."

"I'm sorry."

"I've still got to go to work every morning. We haven't all got the choice to laze around writing stories."

"I thought that's what you wanted me to do?" Bloody hell. It's hard work, this being married business. But whatever it is, it's still preferable to the life I was living pre-November. I'm cut out to be with someone and I hate being by myself – it seems to add to the depression. Maybe Hugh's right about the antidepressants. And maybe the sleeping pills too. Once I get those into my system, everything will get better. But can I wait that long?

The truth is that I haven't slept properly since cancer robbed me of my mum. Why does death always choose Christmas? At that time, I could sense something was off with Jason towards me too. Rather than being supportive of my grief, he seemed irritated by it. And he was never at home. Ever. At least I know why now. At the time, I blamed myself, and was baffled by his absence. He was never there for me when I needed him the most.

I was also worrying about my dad who wasn't coping with Mum's death. It turns out he was coping even worse than I thought. After he committed suicide, followed by Jason walking out, I don't know how I'd have got through without the support of my work colleagues – and Kieren to a lesser extent. I could tell that he was making as much time as he could for me for a change. But my sleeping habits have never recovered. It's as though the events from last year are still haunting me. So perhaps I should be grateful that at least Hugh's showing some concern. At least he cares.

"I'll ask the doctor about the counselling whilst I'm there. I got offered some last year but couldn't face talking about everything then. It was too soon."

"What do you want counselling for?"

"You said yourself that I need tablets. But they only mask what's going on – they don't get to the root cause of it all."

"Yeah, you need tablets, I agree, but you don't need to go talking to some stranger. You've got me to talk to now."

"Well, let's see what the doctor says, shall we?"

"I mean it Nicola. I'd rather you discussed things with me. Tablets, yes, counselling no." He puts his arm around me. "Thank goodness I came along when I did. How did you ever survive without me?"

Chapter Eleven

"These tablets aren't helping me one bit." I can barely lift my head off the pillow as I look up at Hugh through the haze in my eyes. "How am I going to get back to work today? I can't drive in this state."

"We'd better get you back to the doctor." Hugh strokes my hair. "Get you signed off for longer whilst these tablets properly kick in."

"But it's been nearly a week already. They're making me feel worse, not better."

"The doctor said that might be the case, didn't he? The fact that they're making you feel rough means they'll soon start working." Hugh passes me a glass of water and the antidepressant I'm supposed to take on an empty stomach. Every morning, they make me feel sick, whilst the sleeping tablets I'm taking on a night make my brain foggy. It's an horrendous combination. In my more lucid moments, I feel like arguing again for counselling as opposed to medication, but Hugh has been so nice to me over the last week that it seems stupid to spoil things between us. More than ever, I need him right now and can't risk him deserting me.

"I'm not being dramatic, Hugh, but I feel ten times worse than I did before I started on these things." As I swallow the tablet, the chill of the water slides all the way into my belly. I'd give anything to feel better.

"Look, I'll ring my work and let them know I'm staying at home with you today. Then I'll call your work and tell them we're going to get you another sick note." There's warmth and sympathy in Hugh's face. It feels good, despite how rotten I'm feeling. "Then I'll get you another appointment at the doctors."

"But I don't want another sick note. I want to get back to work."

"You could always start writing your novel. That'll take your mind off things, won't it?"

Though I feel terrible crushing the enthusiasm I see in his face, I can't even think straight, let alone write. "I'm in no fit state. I'm sorry."

"To be honest," he continues, "it's likely that you'll have to keep getting sick notes right up until your notice period is over at the university. You're neither use nor ornament to them now, are you?"

I search his face for signs that he meant that last comment as an insult, but he doesn't seem to have done. I lie back down. Perhaps he was joking, or maybe he's just being cruel to be kind, as Mum used to say. Tears slide down the sides of my head and soak into the pillow. "Are you sure you're alright not to go in today Hugh?" I'm not going to tell him, but I'm beyond grateful that he's staying with me. Over the last three weeks, it's like I've hit a brick wall in life. And it's all changed so fast.

"One perk of being a business owner." He kisses my forehead, then heads towards the bedroom door. I envy his strength and vitality. I let the kiss linger on my skin. They are few and far between these days. It's no wonder really – I'm a shadow of who I was when he met me and I'm probably slowly driving him away.

I stare into the space he's left, then avert my attention in an attempt to enjoy the birdsong and sunlight drifting through the open window. Both things are totally at odds with how I'm feeling. I need to get myself sorted out. Back to work. Or on with this novel.

I also need to muster some courage to broach the subject of the financial and legal stuff with Hugh. I can't seem to log into any of the new accounts we opened just after the wedding. It still irks me to call it 'the wedding,' I feel heavy when I recall how miserable I was that day. And I've never really got beyond it.

I need to check that Hugh's paid into the accounts what he promised to. I'm scared to ask him outright in case he thinks I don't trust him. And I haven't got the strength for a confrontation right now. Taking these tablets has meant I've taken my eye completely off the ball.

If I don't feel any better in a few more days, I'm going to have to accept that they aren't doing me any favours and come off them. Personally, I really believe that I need counselling more than medication. Hugh has said I can talk to him rather than to a stranger, but I feel like a right misery going on about my parents to him. And clearly, I can't talk about Jason either.

Plus, I can't tell him the truth about how much I need to be at work. I know Hugh loves me, but I've always had wonderful support from my colleagues. I still haven't seen Kieren either. Hugh's apparently explained to him that I'm not well and says Kieren has agreed to stay away until I'm feeling better. It's strange that he's not texted or rung me though – I know Kieren can be self-centred at times, but if Hugh's been honest about me being poorly, I'd have thought he'd be concerned.

"Right, that's both places of work rung, and a doctor's appointment made." Hugh strides into the bedroom and thrusts a cup of tea at me.

I haul myself into a sitting position. "Thank you. And I'm sorry." I start crying again and wipe frantically at my tears. I'm sick of crying. "We're supposed to be newlyweds. We should be at it like rabbits. Look at the state of me."

"In sickness and in health." Hugh pushes back the strands of wet hair which are clinging to the sides of my face like seaweed.

I can't remember the last time I even brushed my hair or put any make up on.

"What did my work say? Who did you speak to?"

"Some man. Your manager, I think. He said to take as much time as you need and not to be rushing back before you're ready."

Tom. He must mean Tom. "Did he say anything else?

"Just that he hopes you're feeling better soon. We all want that for you."

"Not as much as I do." I put my cup to the side of the bed and close my eyes. I'm exhausted. Whenever I close my eyes, I see images of Dad, sitting in his beloved campervan in the darkness of his garage. When they found him, no one was in any doubt of what he had intended to do. It's no wonder I'm shattered all the time - I can't seem to stop these dark thoughts.

I open my eyes again and reach for my tea. Hugh is sitting in the chair next to my dresser, watching me. Goodness knows what he'll be thinking.

"Drink it up," he says. "It will do you good. You need to make sure you eat something as well."

I sigh. He's right. I've got to get myself better. When I see the doctor, I'm going to ask about reducing these tablets. I'm also going to get my hair done and put some makeup on. Nicola Donnelly, sorry, Wainwright is going to fight back. Whatever has got into me lately, I've had enough of it.

I swing my legs over the edge of the bed. "I'm going to get a shower."

Hugh frowns. "Are you sure you're up to it?"

Before we married, I'd have made some quip about him joining me in there, but we've made love once since we married and that was a near-disaster. I can hardly believe how things are turning out and I can't help but worry that his attraction towards me has waned. Who could blame him?

"I'll leave you to it then."

I watch as he leaves the room, then feeling too sick to drink it, pour my tea down the sink in the en-suite. I'll pretend I've drunk it, so he doesn't think I'm being ungrateful.

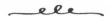

"You're looking better than you did earlier." As Hugh eases out of the surgery car park, he glances sideways at me. "You were knackered before – what's brought you around?" There's a hint of suspicion in his voice and I worry for a moment that he's about to accuse me of fancying the good-looking doctor I've just seen.

"I suppose I just feel better now I'm doing something about it all. The doctor said I can reduce my dosages if I want to," I reply. "But I'm not sure how I feel about being signed off for an entire month."

"It's for the best." Hugh squeezes my arm. "You went through a lot last year, especially with your dad. Finding him like you did must haunt you."

"Yeah." The vision of him slumped forwards in his seat, grey and almost lifeless will never leave me.

"So, it's time to let someone else look after you for a change. Namely, me."

"Thanks." The tears burn at the back of my eyes again. Hugh being nice to me feels good. I haven't seen another soul for well over a week, so no one else has had the chance to be. I've had a couple of get-well cards from some of the other lecturers at work, but no human contact.

"Your brother obviously isn't too bothered, is he?" Hugh pulls up at the lights. "Has he messaged or rung at all?"

I shake my head, hoping he'll change the subject. He probably won't like it if I voice my disappointment at Kieren not getting in touch when he knows I'm not too well. If only I knew exactly what Hugh had said to him. "Perhaps I'll have a go at starting that novel of mine today." I try to inject some enthusiasm into my voice. "Now that I'm feeling better. I'll start planning it out. It will do me some good to get into something."

"That's my girl." He slaps me playfully on the thigh and smiles. "Once you start it, you won't be able to stop."

"And I was thinking of maybe getting a dog to keep me company." I smile as I recall Zoey, the German Shepherd I grew up with. "I can't write a novel without a dog curled at my feet."

"A dog?" He sets off from the lights.

"Yes. It wouldn't just be for company, it would get me out of the house for a walk a couple of times a day for fresh air." Now I've voiced what I'm thinking out loud, I'm even more enthused about the idea. In my more lucid moments over the last week, when I've been less entrenched in a tablet-induced stupor, I've been thinking about how a dog could fill the baby-shaped void I have in my life. I continue. "Other dog owners are usually friendly, so at least I'd talk to some other humans whilst you're working. It's going to get lonely just working on a novel day after day."

"How will it? You'll have me coming and going. You're not taking these marriage vows seriously at all, are you? To the exclusion of all others, isn't that what we promised each other?"

"But I've wanted another dog for ages. I've got the time and space for one now." I don't tell him that Jason was allergic to them. The mere mention of Jason's name seems to upset Hugh.

"I don't like dogs, actually." Then his tone changes. "And besides, you can barely look after yourself, let alone a dog. Look at the state of you."

The sting of his words stays with me all the way home. *Look at the state of you.* The subject, it would seem, is well and truly closed.

CHAPTER TWELVE

I absently flick through a book I've had delivered on how to write a novel, which I'm struggling to muster much interest in.

Meanwhile, Hugh's restless. He's pacing around the lounge and checking his phone every five seconds. There's something about how he is with his phone which always makes me wary. I don't know if it's to do with Gary or suspicion about another woman.

"Will you sit down for goodness sake?" I squint at the sunlight behind him as he stands in front of the window. "You're making me nervous." I can't concentrate as it is. Not with the effects of these rotten tablets. I really don't think I want to continue taking them.

"I need to get out of here." He looks at his watch. "I'm going into work for a bit. Then I might meet Gary for a pint."

"But you said you'd stay at home with me today." Maybe I sound needy, but that's how I feel. I've gone from disliking being on my own to *fearing* being alone. I never used to be this bad.

"I can't hang around here with you all day." He seems to look straight through me. "Have you taken a good look at yourself lately? Go on, look in a mirror." He yanks the mirror I use for my make-up from the drawer in the sideboard and thrusts it at me. "Go on."

Oh God. Here we go again. I should have known that him being nice to me could only last for so long. I do as instructed, recoiling at my piggy eyes, sallow skin, and lank hair. No wonder he doesn't want to be around me.

"You're lucky I stick around." He snatches the mirror back. "Most men would be off like a shot."

"Please Hugh, please don't be like this again." I pull a tissue from the box beside me.

"Oh God. Don't start bloody crying again. You should be upping those tablets, never mind reducing them." He steps towards me, his voice bordering on being a snarl. "I've never felt so miserable in my life. You're an utter depressant Nicola."

"Please Hugh. Please." I reach out for him, grabbing a fistful of his jumper. "Stop it."

"Get off me." He yanks his jumper from my clutches and strides towards the door without looking back.

As the gate slams, I literally howl into the silence. Then the car door bangs, and the engine starts up. I slump to the floor and thump the cushions on the sofa for all I'm worth. "I've had enough." My voice sounds alien. "I've. Fucking. Had. Enough."

In the corner of my eye, I notice movement outside as I sit up again. Hugh has got back out of his car and is saying something to Julie. She appears to ignore him and carries on walking. Perhaps he's said something about me to her. Maybe she was on her way here and he's stopped her. I rest my head back onto the cushions. I've no energy anymore. I'm done.

Around ten minutes later, the doorbell echoes through the house. I raise my head from the sofa, wiping tears and snot with my sleeve as I get to my feet, my head swooning with the effort. Hopefully I can get to the door without passing out. I haven't even eaten yet today.

"Nicola. Are you OK? I could hear you from outside. God, you look bloody awful."

"Thanks." I try to smile. "I've had better days, I guess." As if she could hear me sounding off before. How embarrassing.

Julie steps towards me. "Can I come in?"

I widen the door, inviting her entry. "Did Hugh tell you to come?"

I'm pathetic, rooting for crumbs that he still cares about me.

"No. I've just seen him outside actually. Well, a few minutes ago."

"I know. I saw him talking to you. What did he say?"

"He said you were ill and to leave you alone. So, I pretended to walk on. When I saw him drive off, I've come to the door."

"I've just been a bit down, but I'm glad you've come." I sniff as she follows me into the kitchen. It's good to be in the presence of another human for a change.

"I've called round a couple of times," she tells me. "You sit down. I'll make us a brew."

"Have you? When?" Whilst I've been laid in bed over the last week, I've often heard the doorbell, but because Hugh tells me no one has been, I've explained it away by telling myself I've imagined it. Once I thought I heard Kieren's voice – that's how bad the tablets are affecting me. I'm hearing things. There's no way Kieren would have gone away if he'd have come to the door. My phone has been constantly ringing from inside my bag, or at least I think it has. It's gone silent over the last day or two and I haven't had the energy to check it.

"I've heard some crying and carrying on here over the last few days again." Julie fills the kettle with water. "I've tried to come round through the day - thinking you might be on your own, in case you might want some company."

"That's nice of you. I've often heard the door, but the tablets have made me too tired to get up. And I'm sorry if you've been disturbed by any noise."

"Your husband has always answered when I call."

It still feels weird hearing Hugh referred to as my *husband*. And our marriage couldn't have got off to a worse start.

"You're best calling when he's out to be honest."

"Why's that then?" She pours water into two mugs.

"He can be a bit possessive, that's all. I think it's because we've only just got married." I'm probably speaking out of turn, but it's not as if she'll go reporting back to him. She's made it clear who's side she's on.

Julie pulls a face but says nothing. She doesn't need to.

"If the Porsche is outside, he's here," I continue. "Only he sometimes parks it further up the street if there isn't space right outside."

"So now you've treated him to a Porsche, what are you going to do with the rest of your money? What's next? A swimming pool?"

"I hadn't exactly planned to buy him a Porsche." I wish I could tell her about the money situation. "Anyway, having money means nothing when you haven't got your health. So, which days have you been around? I'm trying to get my bearings with things."

"I can't remember. One day blends into another when you work from home. Though, every time I've been, your husband's said you're ill, or sleeping, like I just said." She opens and closes a couple of cupboard doors.

"What are you looking for?"

"Some sweeteners."

I point at the cupboard. "They're in there. It's true, what Hugh's told you. I haven't been too good at all. The doctor's put me on tablets. Tablets I really want to come off." My skin feels clammy and my stomach's churning again. I tug a banana from

97

the bowl in front of me. "I really don't think they're going to help me."

"Look Nicola, I know we don't know each other too well..." Julie sits facing me at the table and slides a mug towards me.- "But I feel as though I do know you, to some extent, with all I've heard since I moved in behind you."

"I'm sorry. I really haven't meant to disturb you." This is so humiliating. I peel the skin back on the banana.

"If the doctor has prescribed tablets for you, you probably need them – you shouldn't even be *thinking* about coming off them. Look at the state you're in."

"Don't you start." I take a large slurp of tea, then a bite of the banana, fighting the urge to wretch. I must get this down me.

"Are you OK?"

"Yeah." I put the banana down and wash the bit I've been trying to chew down with tea. "I've just had Hugh saying *look at the state of you.*" Fresh tears spring to my eyes at the memory of the anger in his face.

"I don't mean anything bad by it." She shakes her head. "Only, it's not even a fortnight since we had a glass of wine together. You seemed OK then. Well, OK-ish."

"Is it really that long ago? *A fortnight?*"

"Yes, and you've certainly got much, much worse since I saw you then. Maybe you should be taking more of your tablets, rather than thinking of cutting them back."

"It's my own fault I've got worse. And I wasn't far off in this state, as you put it. Only I'm good at putting a brave face on things." I bristle at the memory of when I was around at Julie's that night. Hugh and I had only been married for a week or so then. Right now, it feels as though we've been married forever. It's been a dreadful start to married life, and they call this the honeymoon period. I only wish I knew what's gone wrong so I could begin to put it right.

"I want to help, if I can."

"You can't." Misery claws at me as I drain what's left in my cup. "No one can." I feel utterly exhausted again, and it's not even lunchtime.

"Maybe it's what happened to your dad that's at the root of things?"

"It's everything. But I'll just keep taking the tablets, like you said. I'm sorting it out."

"I'm not sure it's only tablets you need," she says. "It seems deeper than that. Maybe you should talk to me."

"To be honest." I look at her. "I can barely keep my eyes open. It's the tablets. Do you mind if we do this another time? I need to lie down."

"Of course not. I've lots to be getting on with anyway." She gets to her feet and rests her hand on my arm. "I'll let myself out. You take care."

As she opens the door, I hear a familiar voice. "I'm just dropping these off for Nicola. Is she in?"

I try to raise my head from where it's resting on my arms on the table. Who is it? I look terrible. I feel terrible. I can't see anyone else. "No." I call weakly. But as Julie's footsteps fade towards the gate, Natasha from work appears in my kitchen doorway. She's around the same age as me, but looks ten years younger. Especially now. I'm too exhausted to be irritated by Julie letting her in.

"Oh my God. Nicola!" She drops the flowers onto the kitchen counter and rushes towards me. "You look dreadful."

"So you're a doctor, are you?" I jump as Hugh appears behind her in the doorway. He's really good at sneaking up on conversations. I force myself to sit up straight and try to focus. Damn tablets.

"Where did you come from Hugh?" I look at him, wondering how my voice sounds. I don't feel myself at all. "I thought you'd

99

gone to work." Even through my blurry eyes, I see that the blue of his work shirt makes his eyes look bluer, miserably reminding me that other women would be only too happy to take him off my hands. Especially after what I saw of myself in the mirror before.

"Evidently." Hugh steps into the kitchen and looks from Natasha to me as he folds his arms across his wide chest. "Who are you then?" He turns to her.

"I'm a friend from Nicola's work."

"And to what do we owe this pleasure?" He leans back against the counter.

"I came round to see Nicola, actually." She rests her hand on the chair opposite me.

It feels strange seeing Natasha here, in my kitchen. It's almost as though I'm hallucinating.

I notice she maintains eye contact with him. Though she's probably getting a sense that she's not welcome here, she doesn't seem perturbed in the slightest.

"I've told your place several times that Nicola isn't up to seeing visitors." He steps closer to us. I want to bolt from the room. If I had the strength and energy, that is. The last thing I need is a confrontation between Hugh and Natasha. I don't want Hugh to drive my friends away.

"It's not exactly a long way for me to come, even if I was to be turned away." Natasha laughs. "I only work at the university."

Hugh laughs back, but it's more forced than the canned laughter in old sitcoms. "I know exactly where you work. Do you think I'm not taking care of my wife properly?"

"Of course that's not what I think. I thought Nicola could maybe use some company..."

"She's covered by a sick note. She shouldn't be getting harassed by her place of work."

"Look here - I'm her friend. I don't know what your problem is but..."

I see anger flame in Natasha's eyes and I hope she keeps a lid on it, for my sake. But she's standing firm. Part of me wishes I could defend myself against Hugh like she seems to be able to. To have a fraction of her confidence right now would be a blessing. And I can't understand why he's being so unpleasant to her. He seems to have something against *anyone* who wants to spend time with me.

"Nicola, would you like to go somewhere else?" Natasha's voice is gentle, as she walks around to the back of my chair. I feel the weight of her hand on my shoulder. "I've got the car outside. We could go to my house or for a coffee somewhere."

"No, she would not."

"I was speaking to Nicola, not you."

"You don't get to come into my house and disrespect me. I'd like you to leave. Now."

"I'll leave when Nicola asks me to leave *her* house." I turn to look at her, and if I'm not mistaken, her nostrils appear to be flaring. I can't imagine Natasha losing her temper. She's so easy-going and so... nice.

"I think you should go Natasha. I'm really sorry." What else can I do or say with Hugh towering over me?

"It's him who should apologise, not you." She points at Hugh.- "Are you really sure you want me to go Nicola? I can help if you want me to."

"Get out." Hugh's voice wobbles with anger, but I know for a fact that he won't dare give Natasha any of the treatment he's been giving me. She can walk away from here. She won't find herself walled up or be forced to watch her belongings get smashed. Though in some ways, that sort of thing is easier. If he actually turns physical, he always calms down quickly and begs for my forgiveness. Then he's overly nice for at least an hour.

No, it's the way he makes me feel within myself that I can't cope with. Ugly, useless and mental. I wasn't ready to get into another relationship last year. I should have waited. But it's too late now. For the millionth time I ask myself, *what have I done?*

Chapter Thirteen

It's the same routine as yesterday. And the day before. And the day before that. Hugh brings me a glass of water, along with my tablet, and sits beside me as I place it on my tongue. Instead of swallowing it, I push it to the top of my gum, as I did with last night's sleeping tablet. Already, I feel better. It's not as if I actually wanted to take tablets, and only went on them to appease Hugh, and show him I was prepared to take action to sort myself out. I'll keep on pretending to take them for now, just to keep the peace, and I'll see how I go without them.

And I'm taking more action than that, unbeknown to Hugh. As soon as he goes off to work, I'm going to make plans to see Kieren. Then if there's time after that, I'll call at the gym for a swim. Hopefully one or two of the ladies I know will be there – and they'll stop for a coffee too. And I'm going to take Natasha a bottle of wine to apologise for the way Hugh spoke to her the other day. It's bad enough how he treats me at times, but then to know she's come into my home and been subjected to his hostility, well... a bottle of wine may go some way towards an apology.

"Right, I'd better get going sweetheart. I've made you some tea." He places a mug on the bedside table. I love it when he calls me sweetheart. He called me it more than *Nicola* in the weeks leading up to us getting married. I wish I'd have waited to get married – kept the magic alive for a while longer. The whole time, I suspected we were rushing into things. Though hopefully, we won't have done too much damage to one another and will get through this, stronger as individuals, and stronger as a couple too. *For better or worse.*

"Have a lovely day." I smile and blow a kiss at him.

He pauses in the doorway, looking puzzled to the point of distrustful. "You're looking brighter. What are *your* plans for today?"

"Well, I've a novel to be writing, haven't I?" I won't mention getting back to work. I'll see how I feel in a day or two. And there's no way I'll tell him the truth about how I'm going to spend my day whilst he's at work. Some women might feel as though they're being controlled, having to lie like this, but I'm sure he's only being this way because he's trying to wrap me up in cotton wool.

He blows me a kiss back from the doorway as he leaves.

I sigh as I listen to his footsteps drum down the stairs, then to the bang of the front door. Not so long ago, we'd have had to drag ourselves away from one another before heading out to work. We were always kissing, always ending up in bed. I can't believe how much my unresolved grief has come between us. It has bubbled up from nowhere at the worst possible time. I try to push it to the back of my mind and reach for my phone to ring Kieren.

Where's his name gone? He's no longer in my contacts. Bloody phone. I notice there are a few other contacts missing too. It must be something to do with my surname change. Perhaps I've revoked an old memory setting. I can't remember where I've changed my name and where I haven't. Maybe I should have just stayed as Donnelly. I don't feel like a Wainwright. Not yet, and I'm certain I never will.

I go to my old messages – I can get Kieren's number there.- They've all been wiped. Very odd. WhatsApp has completely vanished from my phone, and I'm logged out of Facebook. Weird. Perhaps my phone has installed a new update overnight and gone a bit crazy. I enter my username and password for Facebook so I can call Kieren through Messenger. Error message. I try again. Same.

I fiddle about for ages trying to do a password reset until I'm eventually locked out of Facebook. When I try to reinstall WhatsApp, I face the same password issues. Instagram and Twitter have locked me out too. Not that I can remember whether Kieren is even on any of them. But Claire, his wife, might be.

"Bloody hell." I throw my phone onto the bed. I stare at it for a few minutes, trying to work out what to do next. Then I pick it up again. I suddenly have a terrible inkling that all this is nothing whatsoever to do with my name change.

"What have you done to my phone?" I don't even say hello when Hugh answers.

"What the hell are you on about?"

"All my numbers have gone, and I can't get onto social media either."

"What numbers?"

"Everyone's. Even my brother's." I catch my reflection in the mirror. Pallid skin, chapped lips, hair like rat's tails. Hugh's right. I'm an absolute state.

"Who've you being trying to call?" His voice takes on its accusatory edge.

"No one. I just noticed they'd been deleted."

"I feel like you're blaming me for something here." He's in silence wherever he is. In a car showroom, I'd expect to hear some hustle and bustle behind him. Voices, car doors, engines. "And I don't like it."

"I'm not accusing you of anything, Hugh. It's just I can't even get onto Facebook."

"Why would you want to waste your time on that load of rubbish? I thought you were working on your novel today. That's what we agreed on when I set off."

"I wanted to get hold of my brother, that's all."

"Why?" His voice hardens again, and I imagine his jaw tightening.

"Why not? Do I stop you from ringing your brother?"

"Don't bloody start again..." he begins. "I've just about had enough of your attitude towards Gary. And I've just about had enough of you as well. Accusing me of tampering with your phone. You still haven't answered my question. What you were ringing your brother for? I bet it was to slag me off."

"Since when do I have to answer to you!" I yell into the phone before ending the call. This time, I hurl the phone to the wooden floor. If it had hit the rug, it would have been fine, but I can tell from the sound of its landing that I've cracked something. I drop to my knees at the side of the bed and repeatedly thump on the mattress. "What have I done?" I cry to the silence of the house. "What the hell have I done?" I feel maddened with tiredness, grief, and regret and can't believe how wrong everything has gone. Never, ever, have I felt this low. And I don't know what to do about it.

Before I know it, the doorbell is echoing through the house again. It's like groundhog day as I open the door to Julie.

"I thought I'd better come and see if you're OK." She smiles through what looks like a concerned expression and heads straight for the kettle. "You sit yourself down."

I scuttle to the table, beyond thankful she's appeared. More than ever before, I need company. After yesterday. I should call Natasha as well. Then I remember the cracked screen on my phone. I need to get hold of her, at least to apologise. I might see what she's doing at lunch time. No way can I stay trapped in here all day.

"Have you got your phone with you Julie?"

"Yes. Why?" She twists around to look at me.

"My colleague, Natasha, who turned up as you were leaving yesterday. Hugh was really rude to her."

"Why? What did he say?"

"He practically threw her out of the house. Can you Google the switchboard number for Leeds University for me?"

Julie's blonde hair drapes forward as she does as I asked. Then she thrusts the phone at me. "It's ringing for you."

"Yes, can I speak to Natasha Kershaw please? In the English Department. It's Nicola Donnelly here. Head of English."

Julie gives me a funny look. I'm not sure she knows how high up I am, *or was*, in the University. She can't be giving me a funny look because I've used my maiden name. There's no way she could know either of my names. It certainly wouldn't feel right using Wainwright. I don't even feel married.

"Thank you. I'm just putting you through to the lecture theatre."

"Nicola," Natasha whispers into the phone. "Are you OK, after yesterday, I mean? I've been really worried about you."

"You haven't said anything to anyone, have you?"

"No, of course not."

"Why are you whispering?"

"I've got a theatre-full of students. Can I ring you back?"

"Erm no. My phone's not working properly. I'm on my neighbour's. Listen, are you free at lunchtime? For a coffee perhaps?" I recall the case of wine down in the cellar. I can take a bottle from there as my apology gift.

"Yes. I'll be done in here at twelve. Shall I pick you up?"

"That would be great."

"I'll sound the horn. I won't come to the door this time. Got to go."

Then with a click. She's gone. But I feel brighter knowing I'll see her at lunchtime and for now, I've got Julie for company. Things are looking up. I pass the phone back to her. "Thanks."

"You're welcome. I take it you're meeting your friend then?" There's a note of something in Julie's voice. Jealousy, perhaps. I can't put my finger on it. My mind snaps back to Hugh and the mood he's likely to be in when he returns later. In the meantime, I need to keep myself strong and together.

Julie stirs the drinks and puts the sweeteners back in the cupboard.

I really don't know what I'm doing anymore. If Hugh thinks he can control whose phone numbers I have, and my access to social media, he can think again. I'll just get another phone and sort new passwords out. Then I'll keep my phone well away from him.

That's if it was him. He hasn't admitted to anything yet. He seems to have something in his head about protecting me from the world lately, but what he needs to remember is that I'm tougher than I look.

I sigh as I stare at a photograph of my parents on the wall. It was taken two years ago when they thought they had their whole retirement to look forward to. I knew I'd miss them when they started gallivanting around in their campervan, but I never could have imagined that I'd be missing them because they were both dead just a short time later. The empty space next to their picture also strikes me. It's where a lovely holiday photo of Jason and me once hung. Before I got rid of every trace of him. *He's dead to me too.*

"You've gone quiet." Julie slides a mug in front of me. "Get that down you. Have you eaten yet this morning?"

I shake my head. Julie returns to the other side of the kitchen and places some bread into the toaster. "Are they your parents?" She follows my gaze to the photograph.

"Yes. I can hardly believe they've gone sometimes."

"At least you had them." She tucks a thick wedge of her long hair behind her ear. "It must be better having parents who've died than never having had them at all." Her voice is flat, and it's difficult to gauge whether it contains bitterness or sorrow. Probably a combination of the two.

"I'm sorry that happened to you." What else can I say?

"You told me your dad took his own life, but not how."

I can't believe she's pushing this conversation, really. She knows I'm being treated for depression. I decide to answer, nonetheless. Perhaps what I've been through will help her as well. "With a hosepipe. In his garage. I found him."

"Was he already...." She doesn't say the word dead, which I'm thankful for.

I shake my head. "He lived for another ten hours in intensive care. It was last March." It might not be the cheeriest conversation, but I suppose I need to talk about it from time to time. I can't talk to Hugh, no matter what he says. "He didn't want to live without my mum who'd died from cancer at Christmas."

"It's no wonder you're on tablets. Shit! The toast." She dashes to the toaster and pulls two black slices from it. "I'll try again."

"Thanks for all this." I smile at her through the smoke. The smell burns into the back of my nose.

"What — for burning your toast?"

"Just... for being here. It means a lot."

"Blame these walls," she laughs. "There's not much I don't hear through them."

If I was having an active sex life with Hugh, I might feel embarrassed at this point, but since it's become non-existent... However, I wish things were different.

"You're actually looking a lot better than you did yesterday. What's changed?"

"I haven't taken my tablets. Hugh thinks I have, but I don't need them." As I look at her, I hope she'll be able to advise me either way. It's as though I can't rely on my own judgement right now. I hate how pathetic I've become. Reliant on others, incapable of making the simplest of decisions, unable to think straight, not able to string a coherent sentence together half the time.

"Have you spoken to your doctor about it? You probably should before coming off them."

"They were supposed to be making me feel better." I shudder at how rough I felt twenty-four hours ago. "But you're right. I'll have a word with him."

"Maybe just stay on them until after that. And you should tell your husband if you've decided to come off them."

I shake my head. "He doesn't understand how ill they're making me."

Julie falls silent for a moment, then suddenly says, "can I join you when you go out with your friend? I could do with a change of scenery."

"Erm, yeah, if you want to." I'd be lying if I said I'm not a little taken aback at her request but hopefully Natasha won't mind. "But what about your work?"

"One advantage of being self-employed. I've only a couple of orders to get through today."

I noticed a rack of cellophane-wrapped garments when I was recently round there. Sometimes I hear the hum of her sewing machine through the kitchen wall. It's been a comforting sound over the last year when I've been here alone. A reminder that someone is co-existing close by.

She slides the plate of toast in front of me. "Why don't you get yourself sorted, then I'll come back at twelve when your friend gets here?"

Glancing down at my dressing gown, I say, "I haven't even had a shower yet. I'm not even sure I've got the energy to go out anymore." Even though I haven't taken my tablets last night or this morning, a wave of tiredness blindsides me.

"Go on then." She nudges me towards the door, and it feels good to have some purpose in my day. I just wish I didn't feel so exhausted.

Picking the shampoo bottle up from the floor is an effort as I shower. Even the soap feels heavy. Then, through my fog, I stare into the wardrobe for what feels like forever, trying to choose something to wear but not able to think straight.

As if washing my hair wasn't hard enough work, lifting a hair dryer to it is like lifting a weight in one of my gym classes. Luckily, my hair doesn't take as long to dry since I had it cut above my shoulders. Because it's dark, it's showing flecks of grey, reminding me of the necessity to make a hair appointment. As I poke earrings into my ears and smooth some blusher over my cheeks, I notice my phone, cracked screen and all, flashing on the floor. I step over it and reach for my handbag. There's only one person who'd be ringing me now. Well, it could be Natasha or Julie, calling to cancel. However, I don't think Julie knows my number. I hope they don't cancel.

111

The prospect of spending an entire day alone within these four walls is not a happy one.

I blink at myself in the mirror and slap the sides of my face.- "Wake up Nicola," I snap at myself. I'll just have to get a strong coffee.

I wander from the kitchen to the lounge, then back again. If I sit down, I'm certain that I'll fall asleep. I notice Natasha as she pulls up outside and honks her horn. She looks nervous as she spots me in the window.

I grab a bottle of wine and close the door behind me. "It's OK," I call as I lock the door. "Hugh's at work."

"We'll go somewhere out of the way, shall we? Roundhay Lake, maybe?"

"Sounds good. There's a nice café there too." I don't blame her for not wanting to hang around here in case Hugh comes back in the same mood as yesterday.

"We could have some lunch. I'm OK until two o'clock." She moves her car into gear as Julie rounds the corner.

"Just hang on a sec. My neighbour's coming too. I nearly forgot."

"Oh. Is she? OK then." She looks taken aback as I wave at Julie. "Julie – Natasha. Natasha – Julie."

Natasha twists in her seat as Julie slides in the back and they smile politely at each other.

"What's with the wine?" Natasha glances at it.

"It's by way of apology. For yesterday."

"*You've* got absolutely nothing to apologise for."

CHAPTER FOURTEEN

I t's wonderful to be out in the fresh Spring air. I've always
loved Roundhay, especially at this time of year when the
grass surrounding the vast lake is a carpet of crocuses. And
Natasha is always good company.

"You look knackered," she tells me as we walk around the
perimeter of the lake.

"Cheers." I try to laugh.

"She's right," Julie chimes in.

"What have you been doing to yourself?" The concern in
Natasha's face makes my eyes bulge with tears.

"It's just the tablets I've been on." I brush the tears away. I'm
sick of crying. "I'll be OK. Let's get a brew." Despite my lethargy,
it's great having some female company after weeks of literally
just spending time with Hugh.

The waiter brings our sandwiches and pots of tea as we sit in a
window seat looking over the lake. Happy voices, crockery and
cutlery tinkle all around. The ordinariness of it all is like balm
on sore skin. I have missed so much life lately.

"OK..." Natasha's voice slices into my thoughts. "I take it you know about everything that's going on with Nicola, Julie?" She gestures towards me.

"What do you mean?" Oh God. Here we go.

"Bits and pieces," Julie replies.

"Right - I'm just going to come out and say this to you... I can't believe you've gone and got married to that awful man Nicola. What are you going to do?" Natasha glances at her watch, then back at me, her eyes heavy with concern. I wish I was going back to work with her. Having said that, I'd probably fall asleep whilst standing at the lectern.

"About what?"

She hesitates as though wondering how blunt to be with me. "This depression you're signed off with? The marriage you've got yourself into? Nicola, I hardly recognise you anymore. What's happening to you?"

Julie adds nothing to the conversation, but appears to be listening intently. I know they've both got my best interests at heart here, but I honestly feel like a rabbit in front of an oncoming car's headlights, not knowing which way to run.

"Look," Natasha continues. "I saw your husband first-hand yesterday, didn't I?

"She's said she's sorry," Julie says. "I heard her when I got in the car."

"It's not up to Nicola to apologise for her husband's behaviour is it?" Natasha doesn't look at her, but keeps her eyes fixed on me.

I don't know how I've not noticed before that Natasha's eyes are green. Though right now, I'm so tired that they're blurring together. Surely it can't be normal to feel this drowsy in the middle of the day.

"And I'm sure," Natasha goes on, "that he was trying to keep a lid on himself towards you with me being there, and if that's not him at his worst, then I dread to imagine what he's like when you're alone with him."

I let a long breath out. "He can be really lovely, you know. You don't know him like I do." At least, he used to be.

Natasha's face says it all. Evidently she doesn't believe a word of it.

"Honestly, there really is another side to him." I hold her gaze.- I don't want her going back to work and worrying anyone. That would be so humiliating. "When things are going well between us, I couldn't ask for a nicer husband."

"That's what most battered wives say. Look I'm sorry Nicola, it's true."

"I'm not a battered wife," I retort, but then recall being walled up by him. However, that's not being *battered*. I've seen abused wives and wondered how they can live like that - with their black eyes, swollen lips and bruised limbs. Hugh would never do that sort of thing to me. Deep down, although my neediness and unresolved grief have driven him to the brink of distraction, he only wants the best for me. I know he does.

No man can keep up the appearances he did for over two months in the lead up to our wedding. No, who he was before that fateful day is who he is, and it's *me* that's altered in recent weeks. I've got the tablets and the sick note to prove it.

"There's different sorts of domestic abuse," Natasha goes on. "Being hit is only one of them." She takes a deep breath. "Look, I only want to help you." She glances at Julie as if silently asking for back up, but Julie still stays quiet. I expect she's letting Natasha, who's known me for much longer, do the talking.

"So you've met me today because you feel sorry for me." Great. I thought she was my friend.

"Not at all. But men like him have to be challenged. And stopped."

"Look I know you mean well, but he does love me. Really. If I had my phone with me, I could show you all the text messages I've had from him. Honestly, he's really nice once you get to know him."

Natasha frowns as she bites into her sandwich, clearly not convinced. She's obviously unaware of the extent to which he's looked after me since I became ill. And I haven't been easy.

"I'm going to organise some counselling," I tell her after a few moments of uncomfortable silence. "I need to come to terms with what my dad did last year, once and for all."

"She seems very affected by what happened..." Julie begins.

At least she's sticking up for me.

"As soon as I stop being so depressed and start being a better wife, and..."

"Have you heard yourself Nicola? *Be a better wife!* What would you say if roles were reversed? Come on, what would you say? If it was me going through what you're going through. Or one of your other friends?"

"I don't know. I wouldn't want to take sides."

"Rubbish Nicola. If I was living with what you're having to put up with, you'd probably have kidnapped me by now."

It's irritating that Natasha thinks I'm living with domestic abuse of some description. I know things haven't been brilliant. But it's not domestic abuse. "I know you mean well Natasha, but honestly, everything's going to be OK. Can we change the subject now? Please?"

"OK. I'm only saying all this because I'm worried about you.- Everyone keeps asking after you. At work, I mean."

"It's just wonderful to do something normal." I stare across the lake. "To you, it's just lunch by the lake – to me, it's called living again. I've been stuck in that house for what feels like forever. Let's not spoil it by discussing things that don't need to be discussed."

116

"I'm really glad you're feeling better today." Julie brushes crumbs from the side of her mouth. "The tablets must be kicking in at last."

As we pass the end of the street to Julie's side of the terrace, my heart falls into my stomach at the sight of the red Porsche parked alongside my gate. Julie and Natasha spot it too but hopefully my face doesn't give away how I'm really feeling. I badly wanted to get my head down for an hour when I came in, but I won't be able to if Hugh starts on at me for going out. He wanted me to work on my novel. Plus, I rang, having a go at him about my phone earlier. I'm probably in for it. Which is an expression I'd have used as a kid having to face my dad over something. *I'm probably in for it.*

"Will you be OK going in on your own?" Then Natasha's eyes widen at the car. "Rich, is he? Is that the attraction?"

I shake my head.

"What does that mean? No, you're not going to be OK, or no, he's not rich?" She pulls the handbrake on.

"Neither. I'll be fine. You get yourself back to work." I can't help feeling annoyed at her. I know she means well, but she's made me feel more stupid than I already feel.

Natasha reaches into her glove box. "There are a couple of cards here for you." She thrusts them at me. "Everyone is thinking of you, you know. Just hurry up and get yourself better."

"Mental illness isn't like a cold you know." Julie leans forward between our two seats. "Nicola's on tablets. It takes time for them to work properly."

"I'm just a bit down, that's all." Though to deflect their negativity, I fold my arms across my chest. "I'm not mentally ill, as you put it."

"Look I'm sorry Nicola." Julie sits back in her seat again. "I didn't mean... Do you want to come into mine for a cuppa?"

"No. I'd better go inside and face Hugh." I stare at the house.- It's not exactly inviting. The light reflects from the windows so I can't see into any of them, but I bet he's watching us.

"I thought he worked during the day?"

"So did I."

He'll have probably turned up because of how I spoke to him earlier on the phone. I can't blame anyone but myself for this one. There I was accusing him of tampering with my phone, when in all honesty I've been so preoccupied lately and operating from within a massive brain fog that it's probably something I've caused myself. It's not as if I'm getting any proper sleep. I either lie wide awake, tying myself in knots as the night ticks by, or I fall into some sort of coma. There's no in-between.

"You know where I am Nicola." Natasha rests her hand on my arm as I reach for the button to release my seat belt. "I know you're saying everything's OK, but it won't stop me from watching out for you."

"Or in my case, listening." Julie laughs. "There's not much I don't hear. Anyway, thanks for letting me tag along."

I slowly depress the handle on the garden gate and creep towards my front door. Hugh is standing in the kitchen, his back to me as I walk in. I linger in the doorway, wary of going any further. This seems to be his default position and stance when he's about to let rip at me.

"I've been trying to call you." His voice gives nothing away, and he doesn't move. "Several times, in fact."

"The screen on my phone is cracked. I dropped it."

"Sure you did. I heard the mood you were in earlier." His voice lifts slightly. "You're going to have to get that temper of yours under control Nicola. You could do a lot of damage with it."

"I don't have a temper." I try to keep my voice from shaking. "It was frustration more than anything." It's true. Even as a kid,

I was really easy-going. Kieren was the fiery one out of the two of us, and he often felt Dad's slipper on his backside because of it.

That Hugh keeps his back to me is really unnerving. I need to see the expression on his face. If only we could return to the days when I could barely get in the door without him enveloping me in one of his hugs. Back to evenings when I could hardly wait to get home to him. Whoever said that marriage puts the death knell on a relationship got it right. We've become like strangers since the wedding. Even the mundanity I got into with Jason would be preferable to this.

"Where exactly have you been Nicola?"

Here we go. "I just went for a walk... and a bit of lunch. I needed to get out of here."

"Who with?" He turns now and looks straight at me. His skin looks tighter on his face as he grips his bony fingers onto the edges of the worktop.

"No one." I try to keep my face straight, but I've always been rubbish at lying. Maybe I could be honest about Julie. He seems to have accepted her to some degree, but I imagine he'll be livid about Natasha. I slip the two get-well cards into my bag. He doesn't seem to have noticed them.

"You're lying to me."

Maybe he knows anyway. Maybe he followed me to the lake. I have a strange feeling that he's been nowhere near any of his showrooms this morning. It was deathly silent in the background when we were on the phone earlier.

"What is it with you and that woman?"

"Who? Natasha? Or Julie? What do you mean? *What is it with us?* I'm friends with them both." I feel like he's insinuating something here and I don't like it. All I wanted to do was have a sleep. Not face more drama.

"Since when?"

"I need my friends whilst I'm having a difficult time." I stare at the beautiful bouquet in the centre of the kitchen table which Natasha brought yesterday, trying to draw strength from it. Hugh hasn't binned it, which is amazing. Although I might have to bin the lilies. When they open, they give me migraines. Pretty though they are, I can't take any more pain.

"Oh, here we go. Poor little Nicola." Hugh tugs on his lips as he mocks me. "It's no wonder your father topped himself. I would if I had a daughter like you."

I stare at him, paralysed with shock. Could the man who's supposed to be my husband really have just said that to me? The man who's gazed into my eyes and promised that we'll look after each other forever? The man who told me a few months ago that he's waited his whole life to find me?

He looks thoughtful for a moment. "I think it's time you made a choice. Then we can decide where we go from here."

CHAPTER FIFTEEN

The way he's talking, anyone would think I'd been cheating or something. "What are you talking about? Make a choice about *what?*"

"It's me or her."

"Who?"

"That woman from the university." He jerks his head towards the window. "If you think I'm going to stand by whilst you ridicule me in front of your work mates, you've no chance." His voice echoes around the quiet kitchen.

"I'm not ridiculing you in the slightest Hugh."

"It starts with her, but then there'll be another woman, then another, then another. Before I know it, the entire world will know our business."

"You can't force me not to have friends."

"We're bloody married, for God's sake." His eyes narrow.

"That doesn't mean you own me." Good grief. How did things get this bad?

"Nor would I want to. You're lucky I'm even here. In fact..." his lip curls as he stares down at me. There's at least six inches difference in our height but right now I feel smaller than ever.

"I think it's time I wasn't here. A spell apart might make you appreciate me more."

"A spell apart?" I gasp without meaning to, imagining a night similar to the night after our wedding. I had pictured everything, from him being with another woman to him lying dead in a ditch. All reason suddenly leaves me as he strides from the kitchen and ascends the stairs. "What are you doing?" I dart after him, adrenaline dissolving my previously felt exhaustion.

"Getting some things together." His voice has lost its earlier passion, if that's the right word. It's now flat - devoid of any emotion. It's as though he doesn't give a toss.

"I would do anything, *anything*, to have things back as they were before the wedding, Hugh. If that's what it takes to change things, I'll stop seeing my friends." I don't mean it though. I'll pretend to stop seeing them and only plan things when he's working. "Please don't go. Don't leave me."

"You've changed Nicola. You're not the person I thought I was marrying. It was all an act, wasn't it? It must have been."

"What was all an act?"

"The minute we were married, you changed like the weather. I should have seen it coming. You were good fun, sexy, and confident before. Now you've turned into a miserable, shrivelled, boring..."

"Stop it!" I clasp my hands over my ears. It's no wonder I'm so depressed. He used to constantly compliment me. Now, all I get are taunts and insults. What the hell has happened to us?

"Don't worry. I'll be out of your hair in a few minutes."

I stand in the en-suite doorway, watching him throw his toothbrush and shaving gear into his toiletry bag. An image of him packing it on the morning we were setting off to Alnwick to get married enters my mind and my eyes flood with tears. How has it all gone so horribly wrong? He was quiet even before we set off that day, but I'd put it down to pre-wedding anxiety. Little did I know how spectacularly the day was going to fall apart beyond that.

"It's not me who's changed." I'm trying not to cry, but I can't help it. "It's you. It's like you're a different person. I just want the old Hugh back."

It seems to irritate him more when I'm in tears. I keep trying to swallow my misery when I'm around him. Cry when he's not here or when he's asleep. It's no wonder I constantly carry a lemon-sized lump in my throat. Recently, I've had to learn to cry silently but sometimes it's not possible. Like now.

"Please Hugh. Surely you don't need to go?"

"Leave me alone." He doesn't look at me as he marches past me, towards his side of the wardrobe. I watch as he tugs out jeans, jumpers and shirts – definitely enough clothes for several days.

It's strange now to recall Jason's things filling that wardrobe.- I've so much regret for rushing headlong into another relationship now. I should never have let my friends talk me into that dating site. And even if I had, I should have insisted that things moved along more slowly. Much more slowly.

"Why are you doing this to me?" I can't stop crying now and my sobs are erupting in huge angry bursts. I feel as though I'm drowning in misery. "What the hell have I done to you to deserve it?"

"I'm not enough for you Nicola. We both know that."

"Of course you are! Why are you saying this?"

"And if the truth be known, I need a break from..." He waves his arms around. "All this. Gary was right. You're definitely dragging me down to your level."

Whatever Gary has said about me, I don't want to know. It's not as if his opinion particularly matters to me anyway. I sink to the bed and decide to let Hugh leave. It crosses my mind to go round to Julie's, but I quickly decide against it. My spending time with friends has caused enough trouble. And I don't want to put my problems on other people. Then I think about turning up at Kieren's, but he'll be furious if he sees me in this state. I dread to think what he would do to Hugh. Besides, he normally goes to his in-laws for dinner on a Tuesday night.

After I've watched Hugh drive from the street, I wonder what on earth to do with myself. If I stay in these four walls, I'll go mad. It's time to put at least one of today's former plans into action – I'm off for a swim. It will kill two hours and hopefully wake me up too. This bone-dragging exhaustion has become my way of life and I've got to fight it. If I let myself sink much lower, I worry I won't be able to get back.

"Hello stranger." The receptionist smiles warmly at me as I swipe my card at the gym barrier. "Where've you been hiding?"

I try to force a smile back. I can't really be bothered with small talk. Earlier I felt like I needed company, but right now I need to retreat. Just not to within the four walls at home. "I've not been too well."

"I'm sorry to hear that. Are you feeling better now?"

"So so."

"Well, take it easy, won't you?"

"I'm just going to have a swim and a steam." I feel brighter now I've made it a reality. When I'm out of Hugh's company, I can root out a strength within myself. But when I'm with him, I go to mush. I can't explain the effect he's having on me. At times, it's as though someone could have drugged me. I feel like a very distant version of myself.

"And what have you been up to?" She points at my left hand with a manicured finger, her smile widening.

For a moment, I feel like hiding my hand behind my back. But it's too late – she's already seen them – the rings that really do feel like two nooses. More so with each day that passes. I know I should get out and get away, but I don't seem to have the volition.

"Let's see them."

I edge up to the desk and hold out my hand, fighting back the all-too-familiar tears as she inspects the sparkly new diamond nestling alongside my shiny wedding ring. My finger is the only part of me that says radiant newlywed.

"How gorgeous." Luckily, she keeps her gaze on the rings and not on my face. "Who's the lucky man then?"

I snatch my hand away. "I'm sorry. I've got to go." Now I'm torn between dashing back towards the exit or carrying on towards the pool.

"Nicola," she calls after me. "Are you alright?"

I've already swiped through the barrier, so it's easier to run to the pool, as planned, rather than back out into the dusk. Besides, I really don't want to go home just yet. I'm feeling so horrendous that there's a part of me that's feeling empathy with what Dad did to himself. I burst into the changing room, realising it's time for me to get some proper help.

As I jump into the water, I gasp. It's cooler than usual, but the chill gets some much-needed energy circling within me. It's so good to be here, in surroundings that are familiar but also different. I wanted to be around other people, not having to talk to them, but just be in their presence. However, there are only a couple of other swimmers here. I guess it's that time of day when everyone is picking their kids up from school and thinking about what to make for dinner. These thoughts make me feel even more on my own. If that's possible.

However, as I plod up and down the pool, I'm glad it's quiet, and begin to feel like Nicola again. I've left my rings in the locker and with each length I swim, my breath evens out a little more, and my mind clears. I might love Hugh, but we're not happy anymore. The happiness only lasted a matter of weeks. I'm going to have to summon every bit of fight I have and give him an ultimatum. Either things go back to how they were before the wedding, or I want him to leave. I cannot go on like this.

And I need to get back to work. It suddenly dawns on me I have had nothing formal from work about my absence. Natasha has visited, but that's hardly official. I would have expected an email from Human Resources at least. And I've not even heard anything from Tom. It's very odd.

I head towards the steam room. Coming somewhere that I've never been with Hugh before is liberating. Doing something I did pre-Hugh makes me feel as though I can reclaim myself. This is what I need to do more of.

After I'm dressed again, I decide to have my evening meal in the gym bar area. I'm not the only person dining alone, which makes me feel better. Nor am I the only woman. Suddenly I recall the last time I ordered from a menu – when I was out to lunch with Hugh. I'm not looking forward to returning to my dark and empty house. I remember I've got some wine in the fridge, so that will help me sleep tonight. But no more tablets for me. No way. I know I keep saying it, but it's fightback time. It has to be. *He reckons I'm dragging him down?*

As I turn the final corner into my street, I half expect to see the Porsche returned to its usual place. I've stopped trying to recoup the money for it. It doesn't matter anymore. It's only money. What matters is how we go on from here.

I let myself into the dark house, sighing as I reach forward for the hallway light switch. I kick my shoes onto the hallway mat, not knowing whether to feel miserable or relieved because Hugh isn't here.

Having taken the time to blow dry my hair at the gym, and eating a proper meal for a change, I *was* feeling better until I got back here. Suddenly, the loneliness hits me like a bus. I flick the light on in the kitchen and pad across the floor to the cupboard. The click of the wine glass against the marble counter is loud in the house's silence. The wine glugs into it and I gratefully take a sip, calming me some more as it slides down my throat. I'll be fine. Before Hugh came along, I survived, and I'll do it again.

I lean against the counter and stare out into the darkness. This time of year doesn't do me any favours. Exactly a year ago, Dad was alive, and Jason was still with me. Well, in body, anyway. My life had already been rocked by Mum's death, but at least I'd been prepared for that.

Next week marks the first anniversary of Dad's suicide and then the following week marks Jason walking out. I don't know which hurt me most. When Dad died, I was bereft and after Jason left, I felt like an abandoned dog. For nights on end, I had lain awake, imagining him lying in bed with the woman he'd left me for. Then, when I discovered she was pregnant, and that they were getting married, it was like being crucified.

When I met Hugh, I thought I was finally getting to leave all that pain behind, but now look at me. What is so wrong with me that men think they can treat me like this? Even my father thought I wasn't worth sticking around for.

The front of the house is suddenly lit up. I'm startled to notice that it's the Porsche. Hugh evidently has had second thoughts and come home to apologise. Surely he won't mind that I've been out for a swim and had my tea at the gym. I can still cook him something and sit with him whilst he eats. I wouldn't want to do anything else today that might put him back in a bad mood with me.

He'll sense as soon as he looks at me that I'm more myself than I was earlier. My make-up had slid off the last time he saw me, and my eyes were raw with all the crying I've been doing lately. I look better now, and I'm relieved he's come back. Perhaps I'll be up to giving him that ultimatum I was considering whilst swimming. When he sees the strength I've recaptured, this could be the first night of the rest of our lives together.

I jump as the doorbell echoes through the house. Why is he ringing the bell? He's got a key. And in any case, I didn't lock the door behind me. This is a decent neighbourhood, one where I'm not inclined to keep myself behind lock and key. I feel safe here. That is, until I hold the door open to Gary. Without invitation, he strides in, that awful smirk emblazoned across his face.

"Where's Hugh? Isn't he with you?" I look beyond him, expecting to see Hugh's tall frame appear at the gate.

"It's you I came to see, actually." Gary brushes past me into the kitchen, leaving a cloud of cheap-smelling aftershave hanging in the air. He tugs a chair from under the table, then turns it around, sitting astride it, back to front.

I fight the urge to laugh. Who the hell does he think he is? "You haven't answered my question. Where's my husband?"

He laughs now. "Your husband?" His voice rises, possibly to the top of its range. "He's your *husband* now is he? When it suits you to call him that?"

"Why are you driving my car?" I glance out of the window to where it gleams under the streetlight.

"Your car?" He arches his eyebrows. Or should I say eyebrow?- They join in the middle, but because he's blonde, it's not so obvious. "Since when is it your car? It was a gift to Hugh, remember?"

"You're not even insured for it." I wonder then if we could get into trouble for allowing him to drive it. Then I remember the drink drive allegation that Hugh reckoned I'd somehow dreamt up after the wedding. I never got to the bottom of that.

"The arrangements I make with my brother are nothing to do with you." He looks at me like no one ever has before. Like I'm some sort of insect. It's been an awful year for me, the worst I've ever lived through, but with the job I have, I'm used to a certain level of respect from people. I can't believe this man is even in my house. *Come on Nicola, find your kick-ass. You're going to need it.*

"Your arrangements are everything to do with me when you're both driving a car that he's not even paid me for."

"I don't give a shit about all that." Gary's such a charming man. "I just want to know what's going on here." He extends an arm and sweeps it right to left.

"Look Gary. You'd be the last person I'd confide in. I didn't invite you into my home, and I don't want you here." I try to load power into my voice, but I can hear the tremble in it as it leaves me.

"You need help. Do you know that?" His voice drips with sarcasm. "Serious help. Even Hugh's said it. You come across as relatively normal one minute – then you're losing it the next. No wonder my brother feels like he needs to get out of here." He rests his arms on the back of the chair like an actor in an eighties film might. His midriff spills over his waistband as he leans forwards. "Have you ever had a diagnosis?"

Suddenly, I don't feel safe around him. Backing away, I lean against the kitchen sink. I'm in the house, on my own with this man. I don't really know him and from what I do know of him, well... at least if I yell out, Julie will probably hear me.

Then her earlier words about mental illness tie in with Gary's question about a diagnosis, and I feel about as shitty as I can ever remember.

"I'd like you to leave. Now."

"You're on tablets, aren't you Nicola?"

"Mind your own business. Did you hear me? I said I'd like you to leave." I try to keep my voice steady. Maybe I should just let him say his piece. But I'd be lying if I said I wasn't scared.

He's had it in for me from the moment he clapped eyes on me in November when Hugh introduced us over a meal. I'd been looking forward to meeting his twin, but Gary had soon put me in my place.

"You're not his usual type," he had said when Hugh went to the loo. And smiled as he raised his pint of beer to his lips.

"Oh. Right." What was I supposed to have said to that?

"You're older than we are, aren't you?" He had then put his glass down and seemed to appraise me with a sneer.

"Yeah. Thanks for reminding me." I forced a laugh but knew my gut reaction to this man was spot on. Nothing but a greasy, sarcastic neanderthal.

"University lecturer, is that right?"

I'd nodded.

"Good money?"

"It pays the bills."

"It sounds like your parents left you well provided for too." Not only was his line of conversation wholly inappropriate, especially for a first meeting, it made me wonder what Hugh had told him about me.

I was relieved to watch as Hugh headed back towards our table, but perturbed to spend the rest of the meal fending off questions about what had happened to my dad. Questions such as *why did I think he'd done what he did? What was it like finding him?* And even more inappropriately, *did I visit him in the Chapel of Rest after he was dead?*

"I knew you weren't wired right as soon as I saw you." Gary's voice slices into my gloomy memories. "Just make sure you stay on those tablets. I wouldn't want my brother coming to grief because of you."

"Get out of my house." I point at the door.

He doesn't move. "You're a schitzo Nicola. You're going the same way as your father."

I step towards Gary. "Don't you dare talk about him."

He smirks and rises from the chair. "Or else? What will you do? Is this the treatment you give my brother? Threats of violence? Totally unhinged, aren't you?"

"It's the two of you that are unhinged." I clench my fists at my sides. But I won't go for him. My losing it is exactly what Gary seems to be inviting. I'm totally unsure of his agenda, but I'm not playing any further into his hands. "If you don't get out of my house, I'm calling the police. I mean it."

Gary holds his hands in the air as he passes me, this time on his way to the door. Thank God. "I just wanted to let you know that I'm watching you, Nicola. And I'll be right at the front to watch you fall."

"Get out!" I scream the words at him, then jump as he slams the door. "Get out! Get out!"

Taking my wine to the table, I spend several minutes trying to regulate my breath. I'm shaking like a leaf. In the last eighteen months, I've had several panic attacks, but none since I met Hugh. We were so happy that I assumed I'd put all the heartache behind me. I take a swig of the wine but struggle to swallow it and start coughing. Calm, Nicola, calm. I can't take much more of this. From where I'm sitting, I can see the shine of the car roof still under the streetlight. Why isn't it moving? I dart to the door and lock it – something I should have done as soon as Gary slammed out. My brain is so woolly all the time.

Watching the car and locking the door takes the focus away from my breathing. By the time I've drained my glass, it's nearly gone back to normal. In fact, it's probably slower than normal. The wine mixed with what's left in my system of the tablets is probably having a sedative effect.

The car's still out there. I stride to the window and close the blinds. Then I go upstairs to find what's left of my phone. I'll still be able to make an emergency call with it if he comes back. As I reach the landing, I hear voices from next door. They're too low to be discernible, but one is obviously Julie, and the other is... I listen for a moment. Yes, it's Gary.

Oh God! Hugh must have told him that me and Julie are friends. I can't believe I've put her in this position. Who the hell does he think he is to go around, having a go at her? And in the mood he's in. I grab my phone and race back down the stairs towards the door. I unlock it, then dash around to the other side of the building, before repeatedly ringing Julie's doorbell.

"What the..." She yanks the door open. "Oh, it's you."

I'm taken aback by her hostility, but it's no wonder, really. Not with what she's now having to deal with. All because of me.

Gary forces his way past her and strides towards the gate.

"What happened?" I gasp as he turns the corner. "I'm so sorry. What did he say to you?"

"Nothing much." She leans into her doorframe, and I wait for her to invite me in. She doesn't. I can't blame her. All the same, I'm gutted – I could have done with offloading about all this.

"Are you alright?"

Her cheeks are flushed and it's clear she's been caught off guard. "Look Nicola. I'm busy right now. I'll speak to you another time." Then, as though it's an afterthought, just before the door closes, she opens it again, "you just make sure you keep taking those tablets – right?"

I turn away, tears blinding me once again. I thought I'd found a friend in Julie, but it seems that in between my so-called husband and my arsehole of a brother-in-law, that she's been frightened off. She probably wishes that she'd never got talking to me.

Chapter Sixteen

I see every second of every minute, and every minute of every hour as the night dawdles by. My spinning mind won't allow me to drop off, but I haven't got the energy to get up, either. I must thump my pillow into a hundred different positions as my dark thoughts conspire against me sleeping. But no way am I giving in and taking a sleeping tablet. I've been so out of it each night for the last two or three weeks that I've wondered if the doctor has started me off on the wrong dose, or if the pharmacist has given me stronger tablets than they should. But perhaps it's me, getting muddled and taking more than I've been prescribed. I don't trust myself at all these days.

Then there's the anti-depressants. Because I'm already woozy from the sleepers, the anti-depressants make me feel deathly sick and completely unable to function – which all has the knock-on effect of making me even more depressed. After all, how is it possible not to feel low when so ill and completely useless? And I can't get Gary's words or Julie's hostility towards me out of my mind. The more I try to get to sleep, the more it all whirrs around.

However, I must eventually drop off for an hour or two. And I've become so tuned into the sound of the throaty engine noise of the Porsche that I'd recognise it half a mile away. Now, at six thirteen am, it's pulling up outside the house. Instantly, my heart beats faster and my breath comes more rapidly. I've gone from zero to two hundred in the space of ten seconds. Well, from fitful sleep to a state of heightened alertness. I just pray it's Hugh and not the return of Gary. And, if it *is* Hugh, I hope to goodness he'll be OK with me. I've got all the fight left in me of an October wasp.

I listen to the rattle of the gate, followed by an almost silent opening and closing of the front door. But no matter how quiet he's trying to be, nothing can stop that door from squeaking. It *must* be Hugh. Unless he's given Gary his key. But Gary wouldn't be in the kitchen, filling a glass with water and opening and closing the fridge and cupboard doors.

I swing my legs over the side of the bed and tug on my dressing gown. OK, so I'm dreading what I might be about to walk into, but at the same time, I'm also feeling gratitude because I'm not as nauseous this morning as I have been on recent mornings – even if I have tossed and turned for half of the night. There's nothing as awful as feeling sick. I would rather die.

Innately knowing which stairs creak, I tiptoe down them without making a sound. I don't know what I'm going to find when I reach the kitchen, but I want to catch whoever it is unaware. When I get to the bottom of the stairs, I can peer through the crack in the door. Hugh is sitting at the kitchen table, and is scrolling through a screen on my work's laptop. I've no idea how he's got into it, or what he's looking for.

"What are you doing?" My voice is shrill in the stillness. Hugh gasps as he twists around to face me. I've evidently made him jump out of his skin. Good.

"What are *you* doing sneaking around like that?" He slams the laptop lid down and glares at me.

I stride across the room and snatch it from the table. "What is it you were looking for Hugh?" Placing the laptop on the counter, I pull the lid back up. After a moment for it to wake up, I can see that Hugh has been looking at my emails. I scan them in a panic, in case there's anything from Tom that Hugh could misconstrue. But with a heavy heart, I realise nothing has hit my in-box for over two weeks. Even my students must have been redirected to another lecturer.

"I wanted to Google something," he says. "I thought I'd wake you if I went up to the office for the main computer."

"Yeah right. I wonder why I don't believe you." With not having taken my antidepressant, my mind is clearer and I'm feeling stronger. I fill a glass with water. "I was already awake."

"Didn't you take your sleeping pill?"

"I don't need bloody sleeping pills." I sip my water, then set the glass down.

"We've discussed this already Nicola. Clearly, this is what's happening when I'm not around to keep an eye on you. You can't even be trusted to take prescribed medication."

"I'm a grown woman, for God's sake. I'll take what I want, when I want. Not when you tell me."

His face darkens. "Don't take that tone with me."

For a moment it's as though Dad's in the room, though he might have added young lady to the end of the sentence when I was in my teens.

"What I'm trying to tell you Hugh." I attempt to soften my tone, "is that I'm feeling much better without them. Can't you tell?"

"You're a depressive Nicola. And depressives need to be on medication." The lines around his eyes are more prominent this morning. Once they'd have crinkled with his smile – now, it's because of his frown. I used to make him happy. I really would give anything for us to be like we were. For the first couple of months that we were together, he couldn't do enough for me and excitement would pool in my belly every time I thought about him. Now is a feeling of dread which pools there. Which version of Hugh is the real one? I know which one I'd rather have.

"Who says I do? *You?*"

"Not just me." His voice has mellowed. "There's your doctor too. And look at your family history." He glances towards the photograph of my parents. I wish I'd never told him anything about any of it. "Remember what your dad did. Aren't you the least bit worried about following in his footsteps?"

"Only if I stay married to you." I mumble the words, but he's on them straightaway. He's not used to me standing up to him. I'm feeling brave this morning. The time I had out of this house yesterday has strengthened me.

"What did you say?" His nostrils expand as he stares at me. I'm taken aback by the venom in his voice, the voice that used to be velvet-warm towards me.

"You heard."

A silence hangs between us for a moment. I'm back. *I'm really back.* And I'm going to lay it all out on the line for him. Give him that ultimatum I decided on. I can do this. If we can't have the relationship we had in the beginning, I can't stay with him. I can't believe how much my life has disintegrated. Mum, Dad, Jason and now all... *this.*

"So where were you last night Hugh?" The million-dollar question. His shirt is crumpled, and his hair is on end. More to the point, who has he been with?

"What's it to you?" His voice takes on the snarl of his lovely twin brother. They might not look alike. In appearance they're as different as a cat and a chicken, but they're more alike as people than I could ever have imagined. If I'd only seen this side of Hugh before I went and married him.

137

"I'm supposed to be your wife. You haven't been home all night. Where were you?" It's hardly an unreasonable question. I can't even go out for lunch and have a walk with friends without upsetting him.

"I'm here now, aren't I?"

"That's not good enough." I realise that I'm standing with my hand on one hip. This is a Nicola he's never seen before. I'm certainly better this morning than I have been.

"I'll tell you what's not good enough, shall I?" He slams his fist onto the table and cranes his neck to look at me. Oh God, here we go again. "You're not good enough, that's what." He rises from his chair and starts towards me. "That's why I stayed out last night. Do you think I want to come anywhere near *you?*" He's so close that I can smell the stale breath from his unbrushed teeth. "You depress the shit out of me."

"Who have you been near then?" I stand firm. Normally, I would have backed away. But he needs to believe that I'm not scared of him. Perhaps I need to hear the answer to this. If he's slept with another woman, it will give me complete volition to throw him out. I can start again. Accept that things have not worked the way I thought they would and pick myself back up. Admittedly, from the floor. I should never, ever have embarked on *any* relationship last year. I wasn't in the right place after everything that had happened. But somehow, I'll get myself sorted. I'll come back from this.

He smiles now. "Wouldn't you like to know?" He looks rough. Looking at his chin, there's about two days' growth there.

"Yes, I would like to know. That's why I'm asking." He's such a bastard. Why has it taken all these weeks for me to realise?

"Her name's Debbie."

"What?" Despite my former bravado, it's like being slapped across the face. *Debbie.*

"That's where I've been all night." His gaze doesn't waver.

I turn away, stung from his words, and try to distract myself by rolling the blind up. The peachy sunrise outside is beautiful. No matter what he's doing to me, at least I can still appreciate a beautiful sunrise. He hasn't taken everything from me. Not yet. "Have you...? Did you...?"

"Well, we haven't been playing Monopoly all night, have we?"

A tidal wave of gloom washes over me as I get a sudden memory of being close to him in the weeks before we got married. "How could you do this to me Hugh? Who is she? Why?"

He grins, clearly getting off on my misery. "We've been at it like newlyweds, Debbie and me. Sorry, bad word to use – I don't mean to touch a raw nerve."

"You bastard."

"A raw nerve is the only thing I'd want to touch of yours, though. Anyway, I'd better go for a shower. Wash the night away, if you know what I mean." He winks at me as he turns to leave the room.

"You absolute bastard." I launch at him and find myself on his back, thumping at him wherever my fists will connect. If anyone was observing us, we would probably look like something out of a sitcom. Only this life I've found myself living is far from funny.

Almost instantly, Hugh throws me off. "Get a fucking grip on yourself, you crazy bitch."

I'm sprawled on the floor, wheezing like a forty a day smoker. I can't believe I'm behaving like this. What's happened to me?

"Don't you ever come at me again." Hugh's fists are clenched at his sides as he yells at me.

There's a thumping at the back wall. It's so loud it could be coming from the next room. "Keep it down, do you hear me?" It's the muffled voice of Julie. "I've bloody had enough of you."

I don't blame her for having had enough. Off and on since she moved in early last year, she's had to endure listening to my endless dramatics. Being visited and probably warned off by Gary last night may well have been the final nail in the coffin of our friendship. Before it's even begun. I can't imagine he'll have been very pleasant to her. He hasn't got a nice bone in his body.

"I'm sorry," I shout back before slinking towards the lounge.- All the previous fight has seeped from me. Well, nearly all. As I press the door handle, I turn back to face Hugh. "I want you out of my house. Today." The lounge door clicks behind me. This is it. Enough is finally enough.

All goes quiet for several minutes. Then I hear the shower. Sighing, I head back to the kitchen and neck the rest of my water. My throat is raw after yelling at him. But at least I'm not crying for a change. I'm too shocked to cry. After how Hugh behaved on our wedding day, nothing should come as a shock. However, the confession he's made about spending the night with Debbie has winded me.

I wake, dry-mouthed and squint in the bright sunlight. This room always gets the sun in the early afternoon. Early afternoon. I glance at my watch. It's just after one pm and I feel as sick as a pig. Not just nauseous. Really sick. My body lurches from the sofa at the same time as my stomach and I make it to the sink in the kitchen just in time.

I pick up the empty glass next to it, noticing traces of something in the bottom. Hugh's probably taken an Alka-Selzer or something. It was obviously a good night for him. I rinse and refill it, needing to wash the awful taste away.

I slide down the kitchen cupboard to the floor, clutching the glass as I try to assemble my muddled thinking. Why do I feel so rough? What happened? Why have I woken up on the sofa? Why is it one o'clock in the afternoon? I don't know what day it is or whether I should be at work today. I can't think straight. Where's Hugh?

I don't know how long I'm on the floor, but after a while I grapple for the edge of the work surface and haul myself back up. I've never felt as dizzy in my life, and just like I did after the tablets two or three days ago, only worse this time. But I've stopped taking them so it can't be that. And I only had one glass of wine last night, so it can't be that either. It's either the stress I'm under, or something I ate. Whatever it is, I need to lie down again. But first, I need to know if Hugh's around. I hope not. I glance out of the window. There's no sign of the car.

Feeling my way upstairs, my heart sinks at the sight of the bed, which has only been slept in on one side. My side. Then I remember. He spent the night with someone else. Debbie. My stomach heaves again and I dash into the en-suite.

I was ill like this after Dad died, then again after Jason left. Only for some reason, because of Hugh, who I only met at the beginning of November, I now feel ten times worse.

When I wake again, it's nearly dark. What a total waste of a day, one which I'd actually intended to spend on my novel. I fumble around in the dusk for a drink of water then lean back against my pillows again when I can't find one. Tears trickle from my eyes. I've never felt so lonely or abandoned. What a mess I've made of my life. But at least I don't feel as sick as I did earlier.

I don't know how long I lie here but am startled by the bang of the front door then the footsteps which quicken up the stairs. Oh no – here we go. I hold my breath as Hugh curls his head around the bedroom door.

"You OK?" He says, looking genuinely concerned. He's wearing his work badge and a tie I bought him for Christmas. It's like a lottery every time I see him. I don't know whether I'm going to get nice Hugh, indifferent Hugh, or nasty Hugh.

"What the hell would you care?"

I feel his weight as he sinks into a space beside me. "Actually, I care very much. It's awful to see you like this."

"I'm like this because of you."

"There's no way I'm prepared to bear the weight of that sort of responsibility." He shakes his head. "I'm sorry Nicola. You're like this because you're not well." He looks at me so earnestly that for a moment, I wonder if he genuinely does love me after all. But then he can't. Men who love their wives don't have sex with other women. I wonder then about him getting her pregnant. How would I cope? Then I think about sexually transmitted disease. But he comes nowhere near me, so that side of things isn't really a concern.

"The tablets are making me feel dreadful. And I've had some sort of bug today, so I definitely don't want to take them anymore." I realise that we're holding a civilised conversation, which is incredible after what he's admitted to earlier. This shows how desperate I've become for human attention and company.

"So how are you feeling now love?" He reaches out and smooths some hair from my face.

"What are you doing?" I jerk my head away from his hand. He rarely ever calls me love. And just hours ago, he had me in tears with his two hundred decibel voice. "Isn't it Debbie's hair you should be stroking?"

"Oh, that." He laughs. "I was only messing about. Nothing happened. Nothing at all." He pats my hand. "It could have done, but I told her I was happily married."

Despite the absurdity of it all, something lifts inside me. But then it falls again just as quickly. *Happily married.* He's taking the mickey. "I don't believe a word that comes from your mouth Hugh. Not any more."

I'm no longer angry, just sad. Sad for the loss of the wonderful life I thought we'd have together. Sad for everything that went before that, and sad for me. For what I've been reduced to.

"I promise you Nicola. Debbie crashed on Gary's sofa, and I fell asleep on the floor after having a few. That's why I didn't drive last night. I felt bad about what had happened between us the minute I left here."

"You said you were leaving me for a few days. You said you needed a break." I'm utterly bewildered with the whole thing.- Why would he tell me he's been having sex with someone if he hasn't? It's like the drink drive thing.

"I didn't mean it. We all say daft things sometimes. You know, in the heat of the moment." His face looks softer than it did before. Not just because he's had a shave – there seems to be a trace of remorse in there.

"So, who is this Debbie then?" An imaginary woman swims into my mind. Blonde, buxom and full of cheer. The complete opposite of me.

"She's someone who Gary knows, really. He'd buggered off out somewhere. We just had a few drinks and talked."

"How cosy." Hugh never talks to me. Not for the last few weeks, anyway. "Why did you say you'd slept with her then? At it like newlyweds," I draw air quotes as I speak.

"I said it to hurt you, I guess." At least he has the grace to stare at the floor.

"To hurt me?" I stare at the outline of his face, unable to read his expression in the semi darkness. "Well, you succeeded there." I clap my hands. "Well done."

"Really, I didn't sleep with anyone, I promise."

"Why should I believe you?" I say. "Despite what you're telling me, I think you *have* slept with that woman. I meant what I said earlier. I want you to leave." *Do I?* Do I really mean what I'm saying here? Once he's gone, he'll probably *never* come back.

"Please Nicola. Don't be like this. I don't know what I was thinking of earlier. I know it's not a defence, but I was just fed up." He reaches for my hand, but I tug it away. My thinking has cleared to what it was this afternoon and I need to protect myself against how he's treating me.

"How do you expect me to be?"

"I crashed on Gary's floor all night. It's the truth. I didn't feel like coming home."

"One minute you're saying you had too much to drink, and the next, it's that you didn't feel like coming home. Which one is it?"

"It's not as if we've been getting on, have we?"

"Whose fault is that?" He doesn't reply, so I continue, feeling braver than I have for a while. "Do you know your brother turned up here last night? First having a blast at me, and then at Julie."

"Julie? How come?"

I can't believe Hugh's jumped on Gary having had a go at Julie. Rather than at me. But then, it's probably more about appearances. He's already mentioned not wanting the neighbours to know our business. "I don't know. He was round here. Then at her house. What the hell have you said to him?"

Hugh looks uncomfortable for a change. "I might have mentioned that you've been talking to her. But that's it."

"It's more than that. He's deranged, your brother. I don't know why he's so interested in me. Why doesn't he just get on with his own sad little life?"

"Look I know you and Gary don't see eye to eye. But please don't pull me into the middle of it. Sad life or not."

We sit in silence for a moment, then he reaches for my hand again. "Do you want a cup of tea?"

I resist the urge to tug it away. Maybe I should try to believe him. "Yes please. And a piece of toast. My stomach feels better now."

I lean against my pillows, listening as he bustles around the kitchen. It does feel good to have another body in the house, especially after the months of loneliness I had prior to him coming along. I stare at the walls which I painted last year to keep busy after Jason left. Then, after I'd met Hugh, I bought new curtains and cushions to create a home he'd come to want to share with me. However, I'd had to clear the way to fit Hugh's belongings in here sooner than I could ever have imagined.

Why don't I listen to others? I don't know. *Fools rush in where angels fear to tread* had been the words of wisdom Natasha had imparted when I'd disclosed we were getting married. No one seemed to understand how much we were in love. At least I thought we were.

I take the tea and toast from Hugh.

"Thank you." I smile, despite my misgivings. At least he's being nice to me.

"So you believe me, about Debbie, I mean?" He sits back on the bed beside me.

"I don't know what to think at the moment." I sip my tea. One thing that can be said for Hugh is that he can make a good cuppa. I'm dehydrated from being ill earlier, so it's going down nicely.

He's watching me intently. I can tell he wants me to believe him. But we need to talk more. However, I'm just too tired right now. I know it's important to sort things out with him, but I can barely keep my eyes open. What's wrong with me? I've slept nearly all day as it is. Maybe it's this bug. Maybe...

CHAPTER SEVENTEEN

I wonder where I am and even who I am for a few seconds. Sunlight is seeping around the edge of the blind. I try to lift my head from the pillow, but it's as though it's stuck there. It must be morning again. It feels early. If the sun's coming up, it will be around seven. I've slept like a corpse all night. Really, I should feel refreshed and full of energy, not like a dead slug. In fact, a dead slug would have more get up and go than me at the moment.

But I need the loo. No way can I just lie here where I've been for the last who knows how many hours. I haul myself to a seated position and pad unsteadily across the floor to the en-suite. Thankfully, I don't feel sick anymore, but I'm still absolutely shattered. It's a tiredness I've never felt before – right through to my bones. I'm really going to have to go back to the doctor.

Splashing my face with water, I then head back to the bedroom, and fumble for my watch in the drawer. It's after eight. I've been in this bed for fourteen hours. Prior to that I slept all day on the sofa. I roll the blind up and throw the window open, gulping in the fresh air as I do.

Where is Hugh? His side of the bed is untouched, but he must have placed a fresh glass of water at my side of the bed at some point. I'm so parched that I want the water to be as cold as possible. So I empty what he's left me down the sink and refill the glass, downing it and then refilling it twice. It makes me feel instantly better. And even more so, after a shower and a change of clothes. Then I head down the stairs to see what's going on. What fresh drama is today going to bring?

I linger at the bottom and regulate my breathing. He's on the phone. At this time of day, he should probably be heading off to work not pacing up and down the lounge. I catch bits of what he's saying above the breakfast news.

"I've got it all under control. Stop worrying."

"We've just got to hold it steady." Yet his voice is anything but steady.

"Good things come to those who wait."

Then, "I've just got to get her trust back."

He's talking about me. He must be. But who's he talking to? I push the door open.

"Got to go." He says quickly, colouring up as he sees me. I notice that he avoids eye contact as he drops his phone into his pocket.

"Who was that?" I stride to retrieve the remote control from the top of the mantlepiece and point it at the TV. I've got the headache from hell and can't listen to that racket. The news drains me at the best of times.

"Erm no one. I didn't hear you getting up." He eyes me with what appears to be wariness. "What were you doing... sneaking around?"

"I want to know who you were talking to. Was it Debbie?" My stomach churns as I say her name.

"No, it wasn't Debbie." He rolls his eyes.

"What if I don't believe you? Especially after what you told me about her." I study his face, really wanting to trust him.

"Look Nicola. I've been honest with you. What I said – I said it to hurt you."

"Well, you succeeded. Like I've said." I want to ask him what on earth he'd want to hurt me for, but haven't got the energy to get any deeper into this conversation. I don't think I've ever felt so knackered in my life, even when I went through all the grief with my parents.

"No really. There wasn't any truth in it – as I'll prove to you." He drags his fingers through his hair.

"How are you going to do that?"

"I don't know, but I'll find a way. Are you thirsty?" He starts towards the door.

"No, I woke up feeling like I was in the Sahara, but I've just downed three glasses of water."

"Did you get the glass of water I left beside you?" He looks at me for the first time this morning.

"Erm yes. Thanks."

I watch as he strides past me, wondering what he's going to do to provide proof that he hasn't slept with a woman called Debbie. I pause for a moment, thinking, and then follow him through to the kitchen. He jumps as I notice him looking inside a box of tablets.

"What are you doing?"

He colours up again. Guilty conscience or what. "Just checking that you've been taking what you're supposed to. Look love." He takes a step in my direction and for a moment, I think he's going to hug me. "I do care about you. I just want you to get better and for us to get back to how we were."

His words warm me. It's the first time he's referred to getting back to how we were. "I feel fine today," I lie.

"*Do you?* Good."

But he adds the word *good* almost as an afterthought.

I take a deep breath before my next sentence. He isn't going to like it. "I'm going to get out of this house today. Over thirty-six hours is long enough to be cooped up."

The creases in his forehead deepen. "What's that supposed to mean? Where are you going?"

I pull a loaf of bread from the bread bin and some cheese from the fridge. "A long walk is in order. Then I can churn some ideas around about this novel. Fresh air is just what I need."

I can't believe I've lost another entire day through sleeping. What a waste of life. I glance out of the window at the sunny day outside. If it wasn't for Dad's anniversary looming, this would normally be my favourite time of year. Still, I'm looking forward to finding a picnic table amongst the crocuses with my laptop and getting my head into something else for a change.

"Where are all the knives?" I tip the knife block towards myself and then open the cutlery drawer.

Hugh shuffles from one foot to the other. "I've moved them."

"Moved them. Where? Why?"

"I'll put them back when I'm satisfied."

"Satisfied? With what?" I shut the drawer. Now I am baffled.

"That you're getting better." He strokes at his chin as he speaks.

"I still don't understand."

"Look. I'm doing this because I care about you. You don't want to go the same way as your dad, do you?"

"But I won't." I stare at the cheese.

"Look Nicola. You're obviously suffering mentally. Your dad committed suicide last year. I don't want you to be next."

I stare at him now. "It's never crossed my mind." That's not completely true, but I'm not going to let Hugh know that. He'd probably have me sectioned or something.

"You can't deny that you've been going downhill lately. Seriously downhill."

"Never mind making a sandwich. I'll find a café." I shove the cheese back in the fridge and look at the kitchen table where my laptop last was. "OK, so what have you done with my laptop?"

"I've returned it to the university."

"You've... what?" I lean against the kitchen counter. My life really isn't my own anymore. He's taken it over. And I've let him. Up until recently, I was a successful woman giving lectures to a packed auditorium, now I've been reduced to a gibbering wreck incapable of making a straight decision. *What the hell has happened to me?*

"Well, you don't need it anymore, do you?"

"I haven't made a final decision about my job yet, if you must know." There it is – I've said it. He's confessed to sleeping with someone called Debbie, so I'll say what the hell I want.

"I thought you were leaving your job?"

"You'll be the first to know when I make my mind up."

"It's too late."

"What do you mean, it's too late? What's too late?" *Oh God, what has he done?*

"Look Nicola. You need to remember that I'm your next of kin now. I'm your husband."

Yeah, but you don't act like one, do you? I want to say, but obviously I keep my mouth shut.

"And," he continues, "you haven't exactly been coping have you?" He cocks his head to one side as he surveys me.- "Especially over these last few weeks. So, I called in yesterday with your laptop and had a word with your line manager."

"Tom?" I stare at him in horror. The thought of what Hugh might have said to Tom fills me with dread. I don't want everyone at work knowing about my business. Natasha promised she won't repeat anything from a few days ago. They all supported me last year, but this, all this, well I've only got myself to blame. They warned me to take things slower than I have.

"Yeah. To be honest, it surprised me when he agreed to see me without an appointment. But he's fine about you leaving, if that's what you're worried about. In fact," his face eases into a smile, "an advert's already gone out for your post."

"You're kidding me. But I'd discussed taking a sabbatical with Tom. In case the novel doesn't work out."

"A sabbatical? It's the first I've heard of it. As usual, you never mentioned it to me."

"Well, it's just..."

"It doesn't matter now. You can relax and just get on with your writing, can't you?"

"But..."

"No buts. I know what's best for you and taking this time for yourself is long overdue."

There's a tiny part of me that is heartened by his concern, but, even so... "Look, you might mean well Hugh, but I need the company of other people, you know. My work colleagues, my brother, my friends."

"Aren't I enough for you? Isn't what we've got, enough?" He actually looks hurt. I've never known anyone whose moods are as changeable as Hugh's. Perhaps *he's* the mental one.

"Maybe if things had stayed as they were over the first couple of months, but, look Hugh, I don't know if I can even trust you anymore..."

"We've been through all that. I've told you I made it all up. What I said before."

"Look, I'm going. Since you've got rid of my laptop, I'll just take my notepad and pen."

"I'd rather you..." The rest of his sentence is swallowed into the air as I leave the room. I'm going out today and nothing

151

Hugh says will stop me. Unless he locks me in. And even then, I'd climb out of the window.

My first port of call is a new phone. I'm told it will take a day or two for my number to be transferred to it, but I feel better knowing that I'll soon be back in the land of the living. It's been a rough few weeks, but if I keep away from those tablets and start looking after myself better, I should be OK.

I still haven't got Kieren's number, but I've decided that I'll turn up at his house tomorrow. It's the first anniversary of Dad's death, so Kieren and I should be together for it. I can still ring the university though – find out what's been said between Tom and Hugh. I sink to a bench outside the phone shop.

"Nicola." Tom's voice has a cautious edge. "This is a surprise. I was only talking to your, er, husband yesterday."

It still doesn't sit comfortably, having Hugh referred to as my husband. Even less so in the last twenty-four hours. "So I gather."

"Are you feeling any better? I've been wondering when you might get in touch. Obviously, we've had your sick notes, but..."

"It's been a bit rough. But yes, thanks. I'm much better now." I watch as a woman drags a toddler past me. If I'd been lucky enough to become a mother, I'd never have dragged my child around.

"Well," he clears his throat, "that's not what Hugh told me yesterday. He seemed really worried about you."

"Really? What did he say?"

"Look, it's not really my place to go into it all, I don't want to inter..."

"I need to know what he's told you Tom." I stand and pace up and down the pavement, feeling my previous strength slide from me.

"You should talk to him yourself, really. Look Nicola." Tom lets out a long breath. "You don't sound like yourself at all. If there's ever anything I can do to help."

His use of the word *ever* feels as though he's just saying what he thinks he's supposed to say. I thought Tom was my friend, yet it sounds as though Hugh's hoodwinked him. If he really wanted to 'help' me, he'd suggest something specific.

"Not advertising my job would be a great start." I stare into the sky. My life has changed beyond recognition. I should never have listened to Hugh. It's not the money that's important, but without the sense of purpose my career offers me, who knows where I'll end up.

"But you said you were leaving Nicola. I've got your email." Tom sounds really uncomfortable speaking to me. Totally different than when I was last in his office.

"We talked about that though. In your office, do you remember? We agreed you'd consider a sabbatical. Did you ask the management team about it?"

"I'm talking about the email you sent in late last week." He's clicking around on his computer as he speaks to me.

"What email?"

"The one offering your final resignation on medical grounds. I'm just pulling it up now."

"I don't remember sending anything of the sort." This has got me really mixed up now. It's happening too often that I'm forgetting things I've done or said. Either that, or I'm remembering things which haven't even happened. Maybe I need to start writing everything down. *What's happening to me?*

"It came from your university email address. It's right in front of me."

"I don't know..."

"Hugh said you might not remember sending it. That you've been confused and having a few issues with your memory."

"Yes. But I'm getting better."

"I'll read it to you... *Hi Tom. As you'll know, I haven't been too good lately and I've been signed off with anxiety and depression. The medication is making me feel worse, and the prospect of returning to work is unthinkable. I need to take some time for myself and work through everything.*

Therefore, I have decided not to return to my job at the university and wanted to give you as much notice as possible so you can advertise for my replacement.

Please don't try to contact me about this as I'm not up to dealing with anything at the moment.

Regards, Nicola."

I try to swallow the golf ball that's forming in my throat. My job's gone. My bloody job has gone. "I really don't remember sending that. Really Tom, I don't."

"I want you to know, Nicola," there's a weariness to his voice, "that no matter what, I'm always here for you."

"But you don't want me to come back to work? Is that what you're saying?" I watch as two women dressed in suits cross the shopping park in front of me. They're heading into the coffee shop. Probably going to have some sort of hotshot business meeting. Their lives have got meaning. I've... got nothing.

"We don't think, given the circumstances, that it's in your interest, or the best interests of the university right now for you to continue. Hugh told us..."

I press the end call button, shaking with emotion. I don't want to know what *Hugh told us*. Whether I'm shaking with fear, anger or misery, I don't know. Probably a combination of the three.

Who the hell does Hugh think he is, going into my workplace and discussing my personal circumstances? It's like he wants to make all my decisions for me. Yes, I do want to write a book, but

I didn't want to forgo every other aspect of my life to achieve that. I wish I'd never said anything to him about it.

I return to my bench, open my notebook, and stare at the page where I've written the word novel at the top.

Then I scrawl the word bastard over the top of it, pressing so hard that the nip of my pen stabs through the page. Then I slam the book shut.

CHAPTER EIGHTEEN

Within a couple of hours, I'm walking back towards home. The repetitive motion of walking has somewhat calmed me, but as the house comes into sight, it doesn't feel like home anymore. It's become like a prison.

Whilst walking, I've been trying to come up with a way forward from all this. But no matter how hard I try, I can't think straight. I certainly can't get my brain into writing, and no doubt, Hugh will press me for a progress report. The more I procrastinate, the worse this state of complete brain fog is getting. I'm starting to wonder whether I'm ever going to get anything done. Thank goodness I've got plenty of money in the bank, especially since I seem to have lost the option of returning to my lecturing post.

"What have you told Tom about me?" I haven't even closed the door behind me as I fire the question at Hugh.

"Oh, first-name terms, is it?" Hugh slams his cup into the washing-up bowl. "When have you been speaking to him?"

"Earlier today."

"I thought your phone was broken."

I don't know how Hugh can look at me so accusingly, especially after his recent confession about Debbie.

"I bought a new one. I need a phone."

Hugh appears to flinch. "Right. OK. Look Nicola. I just told your manager the truth. That I thought you were suffering from delayed grief and that you need to be looked after for a while. Nice bloke, isn't he? Very understanding."

I watch as he gesticulates wildly whilst he speaks. I've noticed that he does that when he's uncomfortable about something. It's funny – I've learned more about Hugh's moods and mannerisms in a few months than I learned about Jason in twelve years. I guess reading Hugh has become part of surviving.

He grabs his phone from the kitchen counter the second it rings. "Debbie – hi. Thanks for ringing back."

An icy hand clutches at my chest. Debbie. With all this job drama, I'd almost pushed her to the back of my mind. Almost. He was lying about her after all – he didn't really sleep with her, did he? He was joking - testing to see how I'd react. So why is he on the phone to her?

Hugh glances at me and it's clear from his expression that he's enjoying my reaction.

"Yeah. I'll pass you over." He thrusts his phone at me.

"I'm not speaking to her." I back away. "Why would I want to speak to a woman you spent the night with?"

"That's precisely why you should speak to her." He presses the phone into my hand. "So, she can tell you the truth about what happened. Or more to the point, what didn't happen."

There's a knock at the door which Hugh heads towards. I slowly raise the phone to my ear. It's probably for the best if I speak to her without him listening anyway.

"Hello." I attempt to load confidence into my voice.

"Nicola. My name's Debbie. Hugh's asked me to speak to you."

"Yeah, I know." I can't help but feel jealous as she uses his name.

"Is he there with you now?"

She actually sounds nice. Perhaps someone I'd be friends with in different circumstances.

"No, he's gone to answer the door." I glance towards it. "In fact, I think he's gone out into the garden." I crane my neck to find out who he's talking to, but I can't see.

"OK, that's good. Listen to me carefully."

I want to ask why should I listen to anything she has to tell me, but instead I stay quiet, and wait. I will learn nothing by ranting into the phone.

"What's Hugh told you about me?" Her voice is gentle, to the point of sympathetic.

"He told me initially that he'd slept with you. But now he's saying that he made it all up to hurt me."

"Nicola." Her voice softens even more, and she seems to take a deep breath. "He told you the truth. I'm sorry."

"What?" I glance at a bottle of red wine, corked on the counter. A glass might slow my heart rate down.

"To be truthful, I had no idea he had a partner until the other night," Debbie continues. "He's always made out like he's single."

I glance out of the window. There's still no sign of Hugh. Is Debbie really telling me the truth? I've no idea anymore. All I know is that my heart feels like it's going to jump out of my chest.

"Look," she says, as though knowing what's in my head. "Hugh begged me to tell you that nothing happened between us, but really, I think us women need to stick together, which is why I've told you the truth."

"I'm not his *partner*. I'm his wife." It's a struggle to get the words out. My breathing feels shallow, just like it did when the intensive care nurse came out and told us that Dad had passed away.

"Gosh." Debbie pauses. "Hugh never mentioned you were married. I'm really sorry. I'd never have gone anywhere near him if I'd known that. Blimey – you think you know someone."

I close my eyes. I believe her. They *have* slept together. We've been married a matter of weeks and he's sleeping with other women already. What's so bloody wrong with me? That's what I want to know. Tears blur my vision. I so wanted to believe what he's told me. That he'd made it up.

"Plus, I was drunk the other night." Debbie's still talking. I should get her off the phone but feel a compulsion to hear whatever else she has to tell me. The truth should make me stronger, instead of like this wreck I've become just lately. "I only seem to end up with Hugh when I'm drunk. I'd never go near him sober."

"This has been going on for a while then?"

"Yes. But it's just been sex. I wouldn't have let it go any further than that. I'm only too aware of his darker side."

"What do you mean?" I walk the width of the kitchen, side to side, and then back again. Hugh's gone to the other side of the garden wall and I can now see who he's talking to. Julie. Today is getting better and better. It looks like a heated discussion. I hope he's not having a go at her, especially as she had Gary to contend with recently. I can't imagine her wanting to be friends with me for much longer.

And I can't take much more today. I'm thinking it's a good job that Hugh's moved the knives out of my way. The way I feel right now, I could cheerfully stick one in his back. But then it's strange how he's moved knives but left all my tablets around. Surely, I'd be more likely to damage myself with those? Having done lots of research into suicide after Dad did what he did, I found out that overdose is the most common way.

"I'm single. I thought Hugh was single." Debbie's voice jolts me back into the present. "But I've heard since about how Hugh treated his ex, so I'd have never got more involved than I have."

"So how did he treat his ex?"

"I don't know too much about it. Only that he fleeced her out of some money and became violent on occasion. I heard he smashed her house up."

"Really?"

"Yes. She ended up having to get an injunction to keep him away."

"Were they married?"

"No."

At least she could walk away, I think, bitterly. How am I going to walk away? He's going to take me for everything I've got. I'll have to get Debbie to admit to adultery. Then maybe I can divorce him.

"Listen Nicola, I'm really sorry to be part of all this. I'm sorry that it's because of me, you've got so hurt."

"Sorry doesn't really cut it at the moment."

She must hear the sorrow in my voice. I wipe my eyes on my sleeve. Hugh and Julie are still going at each other. The last thing I want is for him to come back in here and see me in this state. I need to work out what to do.

"You should leave him, you know. No woman deserves a man who cheats on them. Look I never expected to be saying this to you, but you sound like a decent person."

"Why are you saying all this? So you can have him to yourself?" I glance back at the window. Hugh's wagging his finger as he speaks. I can't see Julie's face. She's too far back.

"I wouldn't want him. We've had an arrangement for nearly a year. No strings."

"Nearly a year? How often?" Do I really want to know? It's as though I'm pouring even more salt into my wounds.

"Often enough. But now I know he's married, I'm not going to have anything to do with him again. Besides," she lowers her voice, making me wonder who's listening to her. "He was really nasty the other night – I haven't seen that side of him for a while. You need to watch yourself."

"Why do you say that? What do you know?"

"I know he's interested in your money. For a used car salesman, finding a woman of your means must be like winning the lottery."

"A used car salesman? But he said..."

I jump as Hugh comes up behind me and plucks the phone from my hand. He takes one look at my face and snarls "you bitch" into the phone. Then he chucks the phone onto the kitchen counter. "So now you know the whole story." He turns to me. His eyes bear no trace of remorse and I'd go so far to suggest a hint of a smile is playing on his mouth.

"How could you?" My voice sounds alien as it echoes around the kitchen. "You're a liar and a cheat. What I don't understand is why you ever wanted to marry me. You've treated me like shit."

"I've done nothing but ask myself the same question if the truth be known." He leans an elbow onto the kitchen counter as though he owns the place. "Why on earth did I marry you?" He drums his fingers on the edge of the sink. "I wonder."

I have to get him out of my life. No way can I go on like this. The lump in my throat is the size of a grapefruit now. And I feel as bitter as one too.

"And as for me sleeping with Debbie, you weren't exactly putting out, were you? What was I supposed to do?"

"I've tried to instigate some kind of sex life over and over again with you, but since we got married, you've done nothing other than reject me." My words are spilling over with emotion. In all the time I was with Jason, I don't think I ever felt as gutted as I do now.

"And who could blame me? Have you looked in a mirror lately?" Nasty Hugh is well and truly back. Not that he ever really left.

I wish I could leave here, but I don't really feel as though I've got anywhere to go. Plus, I don't really want to drive – I'm too wound up and I'm not sure how much medication might be left in my system. But that will not stop me from having some wine to calm me down. I grab the bottle and a glass and stride past Hugh towards the door.

"You stay away from me, do you hear me?" I turn back towards him. "What I said before about wanting you out of my house still stands."

"Half my house Nicola. Half my everything, in fact." He has the gall to grin at me. "Actually, you might need a good solicitor. Not that anyone's going to pay much attention to what you've got to say."

"We'll see about that."

"It's all documented, you know." He folds his arms. "Your mental state, I mean. How you've been behaving. The risk you pose to yourself... and to others."

"The only thing that's been wrong with me is not seeing who you really are earlier."

"Don't forget I've got witnesses," he calls after me.

Slamming the door, I pour myself some wine, thinking that I might need more than half a bottle. I've been trying to stay sane and awake, but oblivion might be the best way forward now. There's more wine in the kitchen should I feel the need.

What have I ever done to deserve this treatment? At least Hugh hasn't followed me into the lounge, but I want to know what he and Julie were discussing outside. I need to know more about what his intentions are and what it will take to get him out of my life. Quickly, I drain the glass, feeling calmer. But I'm so tired. Really exhausted. I need more sleep.

Chapter Nineteen

I t's dark when I wake, freezing cold in a foetal position on the sofa. I reach for one of the throws and drape it over me. I lie here for a few minutes, trying to process the events of the previous day whilst attempting to ignore my raging thirst. But it's no good. I'm going to have to move.

As I haul myself into a sitting position, the room swims around me. I feel my way along the wall and flick the light on. Its glare makes my eyes ache. I stagger to the kitchen and fill a pint glass with water. As I gulp it down, I realise I barely ate yesterday. It's no wonder half a bottle of wine has had such an effect. I peer around the edge of the blinds. The Porsche is there, so Hugh must be upstairs, warm and comfortable in my bed. Rage prickles at me. I cannot believe I'm in this predicament. And in a few hours, when it's daylight, I'll be marking Dad's anniversary.- But right now, I need the loo, then I need more sleep. Morning will come soon enough.

To say how rough I felt in the night, I'm not too bad this morning. I throw off my makeshift blanket and stretch out in the clothes I've been wearing for twenty-four hours. I badly need a shower, but I'll have to make sure Hugh's out of the way first.

163

The car has gone. Thank goodness for that. I can't face any more angst right now. I make a coffee and sit at the table, gazing at the picture of my parents for a few minutes.

"This would never have happened if you were still around." My voice sounds strange in the silence of the house. Heat rushes to my eyes as I'm transported to this time a year ago, sitting with Kieren in the family room of the intensive care unit, willing Dad to pull through. And Hugh thinks I'm capable of doing to myself what Dad did. "I really miss you both, you know." If Hugh was here, he'd think I'm even more deranged than he does already, sitting here alone, talking to a picture of my dead parents. "Anyway," I continue, "today is going to mark the first day of the rest of my life. I promise I'll get it sorted. Just please keep watching over me – both of you."

My eyes flit from my mother's face to my dad's. I look more like her, with the same dark, wavy hair and olive skin.- Kieren takes after Dad, with his sandy hair, height, and thick set everything. Tears are streaming down my face again. We had our moments, of course we did, but fundamentally, we were once a happy family. Mum and Dad had their moments too, but Kieren and I never really wanted for anything.

No matter what, I will get over to Kieren's today. I'm a bit baffled why he hasn't just turned up here, especially after how aggrieved he was when he learned of the wedding. Perhaps it's best to hang on a while longer, to make sure I'm definitely able to drive, given how shocking I felt when I woke in the middle of the night.

But today belongs to remembering Dad. Suddenly, I feel compelled to dig some of the photo albums out. Emptying their house had been like a punishment at the time and still makes me shudder to recall how tough it was. To condense sixty years of life into bags and boxes, then sell the house we grew up in was heart-breaking. Kieren and I talked about one of us living there, but when it came to it, neither of us could bear to.

Since my huge inheritance, I could afford somewhere far more affluent than the terrace I'm in, but until I get myself properly sorted out, I haven't got the energy to even contemplate moving.

Whilst thoughts of bags and boxes are in my mind, I recall the mountain of them in one of the cellar rooms. Since lugging them here last May, I haven't been able to bring myself to look at any of them. I know, however, that I've got the box which is full of our photo albums. I need to remember the happy times and see the faces of people who loved me. Really loved me.

I check the front door is locked, rinse my cup, and tug a fleece from the coat rack in the hallway. I slide the bolt back on the cellar door and shiver as my bare feet connect with the stone steps. To make sure all the heat from the house doesn't escape into the cellar, I close the door behind me and flick the light on.

There's so much space down here - I should really have used it for more than just storage - a gym or something. Not that I'll be here for much longer, I don't think. I drag boxes from the top of the stack and place them at my feet. Eventually, probably when I move, I'll get around to looking through everything properly. But for now, it's just the photos I want to see. Naturally, the box containing them is at the bottom, and right at the back of the pile.

I'm huffing and blowing by the time I sink onto the old pouffe which Dad used to use as a footstool when he was watching TV. He had joked about adding it to the campervan, but Mum had forbidden him. She was always threatening to take it to the tip.

I flick through their wedding album, trying to ignore the nagging voices which compare their happy day with the one I recently put myself through. The edges of each page in the album are delicate and yellowing, so I turn them carefully. Mum and Dad totally belonged together and, in the end, they proved that. Death didn't separate them for long. I just wish Dad had talked to me or Kieren. Between us, we could have pulled him through.

I flick through album after album. Nicola, Filey, 1978... Kieren, Cornwall, 1982, Nicola, first school photo, Kieren, cub camp 1984. I don't know how much time passes as I perch here, on Dad's dusty footstool, become lost in who I was, a shy but happy child. Then I became an awkward teenager, peering out at the world from behind the fringe I always hid behind.

But my parents were my constant – apart from once, that is. I can only recall a few rows between them, around the mid-eighties. Kieren and I used to perch at the top of the stairs, listening. We were worried they might get divorced, or that Dad might leave, as Mum kept screaming about *she, her* and *that woman.* But thankfully, whoever or whatever was causing them problems, they came through it.

And now I'm on my own in life. Work has gone. Over the course of the last eighteen months, I've been gradually losing touch with the few friends I had, and Kieren seems to be too busy with his own life to be overly bothered about me.

As I wallow in self pity, I suddenly become aware of voices above me. One is Hugh's, and the other is a woman's. I creep to the foot of the stone steps and turn out the light, so that neither of them will notice it shining beneath the bottom of the cellar door. The female voice sounds familiar, but takes me a moment to identify. Julie. This must be a continuation of whatever discussion they were having outside yesterday whilst I was on the phone to Debbie.

"No, she doesn't suspect a thing." What's Hugh on about now? Don't say he's having it away with someone else as well as Debbie. Not Julie, surely. He's already accused her of looking *like a man*, as he so nicely put it.

"Well, the more we're seen talking together, the more likely she'll be to find out sooner than we want her to," Julie replies.

There's a scrape as one of them pulls a dining chair from beneath the table. I tiptoe higher up the steps. I'm thankful I rinsed my cup. If it had still been warm, they might have looked around for me. *Find out what?*

"The money's pretty much under control. She doesn't appear to have noticed what I've transferred so far. It's the tablets I need to keep on with. Make sure she stays completely out of it. And her mental state is the biggest thing that will prove what I'm saying."

"Well, I've been on at her to take them." Julie again.

Does she want me to keep taking the tablets because she cares about me, or is there some sinister motive here? I thought Julie wanted to be friends with me, but since Gary went to her house, she seems to have cut me dead.

"Well, *keep* on at her. You've seen how she's been over the last few weeks. I've convinced her boss at the university about her state of mind, so it shouldn't be too hard to convince the powers that be as well."

The powers that be? What on earth is he talking about? The power to what?

"That's if she doesn't do something to herself first, of course.- The more cut off from others she's becoming, the more depressed she's getting."

"I know." Julie lowers her voice to the point where she sounds almost pensive.

167

"And," Hugh continues. "I take every chance I get to remind her *like father, like daughter.*" He laughs.

How dare he laugh? I sink to a step, five from the top, hardly daring to breathe. From what Hugh's saying, he seems to be admitting to Julie that he's purposefully trying to drive me to hurt myself, or at the very least, to completely discredit my state of mind. But why? Is this all about my money?

There's silence for several moments before Hugh speaks again. "What's up with you?"

"It's all going too far if you ask me," Julie says. "I would never have agreed to this if I'd have known things would get dragged out for this long. It's been weeks since your wedding."

I close my eyes. Has Julie got something to do with the ruining of my relationship with Hugh?

"I need you to hang in here with me," Hugh says. There's another chair scrape and a creak of the chair. He must have joined her to sit at the table. "All we need to do is continue to keep Nicola out of the land of the living, and make sure that her confidence levels stay exactly where they are."

"You never said it would be like this Hugh. You never said..."

"She's improved over the last couple of days, if you ask me." Hugh's talking over the top of Julie. "And if she fights back anymore, we've had it. All this will have been for nothing."

"The problem is," Julie says slowly. "I'm really not feeling good about this anymore. Any of it. When we planned it – to start with, I mean, I hated Nicola's guts."

I continue to listen, bewildered. Why did Julie hate me? She didn't know me. I don't understand.

"After all, she has everything that should have been rightfully mine..."

"All the more reason to keep slipping as many of those tablets in her drinks and her food as we possibly can. In fact, you should invite her around for a glass of wine tonight."

"I actually quite like her now, if I'm honest," Julie continues.- "The more I get to know her, that is."

"Gary warned me you were going bloody soft." Hugh's tone changes. "Come on Julie, get a grip of yourself, for God's sake. Look, Terry Donnelly was your father as much as he was Nicola's. You should have got a third of what was left behind — we both know that. And we're going to get it. And more."

It's all I can do not to gasp out loud. Did he really just say *Terry Donnelly was your father?* My thoughts are tumbling over one another. That makes her my... How? When? It's all I can do to stop myself from bursting in there and demanding some answers.

"Look, I'll carry on with all this, but on one condition," Julie says.

"What's that?"

"That Nicola doesn't get hurt. I'm fine with you driving her into some hospital for treatment, but driving her to do what *he* did to himself? No, I'm sorry — I can't live with that."

"Even after what he did to you and your mother? She'd still be alive if it wasn't for how he treated you both."

"But that was completely down to Donnelly. It's hardly Nicola's fault, is it? I couldn't see it a few weeks ago, but I can now."

"Oh, for God's sake."

"All I'm saying, is that there's been enough tragedy in my life. And she is my sister."

"Cut the bloody dramatics, Julie. You were too young to remember your mum topping herself. Tragedy! And Nicola's hardly acted like your sister all these years, has she?"

169

"I might have been too young to remember what my mother did, but I wasn't too young to remember being shunted between foster homes and children's homes. All because Terry Donnelly wouldn't accept any responsibility. He wouldn't get away with it in this day and age."

"Right, that's enough memory lane." I hear a clap of hands. "We need to be talking about the future, not the past."

"Maybe when all this is over, I'll come clean about who I really am to her."

I'm in utter shock. She must have got it wrong. How can she be my sister?

"Come clean! Don't be so ridiculous." He laughs. "Do you think Gary will let you do that?"

"Gary doesn't control me." Julie's voice hardens. "And neither do you. In fact, once I've got my share of the money, I've decided that I don't want to see either of you again."

"Gary won't let you go that easily." Hugh laughs again, and it's a laugh I recognise well. It's the one I hear when he's thinking, *just how stupid can you be?*

"He won't have any choice."

"That's what you think. He's all set for moving in with you. You've got your place nice for someone on such a low budget."

"Things have changed. I've changed. I've had a lot of time to think, especially since I saw Gary the other night."

"Don't you even think of letting us down Julie. Besides, even if you wanted to, you're in it up to your neck."

"I know I am." Her voice fades to the point where I only just catch what she says, and there's silence again. "Look, when Nicola gets back, tell her I've invited her for a drink then, will you?"

"That won't work," Hugh replies. "I've spent weeks trying to keep her apart from any friends. An invitation from you can't come via me – she'll be suspicious."

"I understand why you've tried to isolate her from some people, but not from me."

"If she'd have suspected any link between you, me and Gary, she'd have been on to us. To act like I discourage any sort of friendship between you both gives us more cover."

"Which will be blown if she catches us talking like this. We've already sailed close to the wind a couple of times."

"She didn't see you yesterday. She was too busy on the phone to Debbie."

"Well, I'd better get back around to my house, just in case she comes back."

"You've only been here a few minutes. It'll be fine."

"So where is she, anyway?"

"I've no idea. Which is exactly what I'm getting at." His voice rises. "We need to get more of that medication into her. For a while, we had it nailed. We've allowed her to become alert enough to be able to go out. She could be with her bloody brother for all we know."

I listen as their conversation pings backwards and forwards some more. Well, it's more Hugh. He's talking timings, referrals and being next of kin. Where I go from here, I don't know.

"Well, I'll get myself back home then." I hear Julie get to her feet. "I'll come back later and invite her for that drink myself if you think that's the best way of going about it. Which pills shall I put in this time?"

"The sleepers at night. But triple the dose. I'm still thinking that the accumulative effect is the best way."

"I'll double it. Tripling it could push her over the edge. Plus, she'd be more likely to taste it in her wine."

"Nah, you're talking bollocks. She hasn't tasted anything so far, has she? Look Julie, do as I tell you. I've got this all planned out."

I'm rooted to the spot. Julie is claiming to be my sister, yet between her and Hugh, they're trying to overdose me. My teeth are chattering. The front door bangs, then after a couple of minutes, I hear a lesser bang from the other side of the building. Julie must have returned to her own home.

Cupboard doors are opened and slammed in the kitchen above me, then the slams are followed by a rattle of keys, then another bang of the front door. I let a long breath out. Thank God they didn't find me down here. And thank God that I've now got an idea of what I'm up against. I can finally accept that this sham relationship was just that all along. A sham.

CHAPTER TWENTY

I wait for a few moments, feeling my breath return to normal. I'm in real danger here. No wonder I've been feeling so drowsy. That wine I drank last night was laced with additional sleeping tablets, probably far higher than the prescribed levels.- Possibly triple, according to what Hugh's just said to Julie. He's putting me at risk of a heart attack, and who knows what else?

When he's brought me tea or water in the morning, it's heartened me that maybe he's trying to look after me. Now I've found out he's been adding tablets to my drinks too. He'd left the house whilst I was still sleeping this morning, so thankfully, I didn't drink the water that had been left next to the sink. At least I know what was wrong with me all day yesterday. Why I could barely lift my head from the pillow. Not to mention why I've been feeling so sick all the time.

I need to see Kieren. Find out if he knows anything about this 'sister' thing with Julie. If it turns out to be true, then Dad must have had some sort of affair. Maybe I should go round straightaway, and ask Julie outright, but now I know she's in it with Hugh and Gary, there's a chance I could put myself in more danger. Maybe I should go to the police? No, I'll go to

Kieren first. He'll know how to handle this. My thinking is still so muddled that I don't trust myself to make the right decisions. The best thing I can do is get Kieren on board with this.

I peep through the crack of the cellar door into the kitchen, in case he hasn't really gone. After all, he's done that before – pretended to leave the house in the hope he'll 'catch me out.' With what, I've no idea. My eyes ache with the glare of the morning light after the gloom of the cellar. I'm scared. Really scared.

It was my intention to drive, but as I pace up and down the kitchen, trying to decide on the best way forward, I veer between wired and woozy. Venturing out feels daunting, yet I'm safer out there than I am in here.

Resentment gnaws at me as I walk past my Audi towards the bus stop. Hugh is trying to take everything from me – even my freedom to drive. Why? I'll never know.

It will take two buses for me to get to Kieren's. But as it happens, the time surrounded by mundane ordinariness lifts my spirits. From waiting at the bus stop, watching life go on as normal, to observing people as they get on and off the bus. Mums with prams and babies, elderly ladies, a pair of love-struck teenagers. I listen as their conversations float around me. I enjoy watching the world go by; fields and trees and buildings I haven't seen for a while. They look new to me. And it's good to be near other people, OK, so they might be complete strangers, but they are a reminder that there is a world beyond the miserable life sentence I've found myself serving at the hands of Hugh, Gary and Julie.

By the time I reach Kieren's street, I've almost decided on the way forward from my predicament. As I walk up the garden path, I remember that I've not seen my brother and sister-in-law since

October. We've never gone as long as this without meeting up. We would have normally got together over Christmas, especially for the first Christmas without both our parents. However, Hugh had insisted on me and him spending the entire time together on our own. We had to make our first Christmas special. He had insisted on it. One we would never forget.

The door knocker squeaks as I tap it twice against the door, then I hear the squawky bark of Nellie, their Border Collie. Claire throws the door open and her familiarity is such a welcome sight that I have to stop myself from launching at her.

"Nicola." She catches hold of Nellie's collar as she lunges towards me. "This is a surprise." But her smile doesn't make her eyes crinkle in the corners as it normally would, making me wonder if she's offended by me turning up out of the blue. Or because of me cancelling with Kieren just after the wedding. Normally, she'd give me a hug and I could really do with one. Especially with what I've just found out. And particularly on a day like today. Unfortunately, Dad's anniversary has been swallowed up by all this going on.

"Is Kieren around?" I try to look beyond where she's standing.

"Erm no, he's away on a course for three days. He's not home until tomorrow." She folds her arms and continues to stare at me.

"He's away over Dad's anniversary? I'd have thought he'd have wanted to get together with me. Especially with it being the first one." Maybe she'll be more welcoming now that I've mentioned it being Dad's anniversary. She might have forgotten, although she's normally good at remembering important dates. I only started getting birthday cards from my brother after he'd met Claire.

"I think you made your feelings quite plain to Kieren on the *getting together* front Nicola."

"What do you mean?" A wave of tiredness sweeps over me, and I realise I need to sit down before I fall down. I must get these tablets completely out of my system. I can hardly even think straight. "Look, can I come in?"

There was a time when I barely needed to knock on their door. Now I'm having to ask to be let in. *What's wrong with her?*

"I suppose so."

Claire steps back, and I follow her into their lounge. The familiar smell of their house is like balm on a sore. It feels more like home than home does. She's not normally so unfriendly though. In her presence, I feel shabby as she beckons for me to sit down. I'm still in yesterday's crumpled clothes whilst she's wearing her yoga ensemble, has her fingernails immaculately manicured and her blonde hair is swept into a bun at the top of her head. No way would she have fallen for, and put up with, what I have over the last months. She's got too much respect for herself. And I've still got to prove everything that's gone on. All that my parents and I have worked for could be lost because of my gullibility.

"You look dreadful Nicola. Really dreadful. Are you OK?" Finally, there's a look of something other than contempt from her. Thank goodness.

I lean back into the cushions, and tears spring to my eyes at her crumbs of kindness. "I've been better, to be honest."

"Can I get you a drink?"

"As long as you don't lace it with sleeping pills." I laugh through my misery, then kick the ball away that Nellie noses at my feet. Normally I'd play with her, and she knows this.

"What?" Claire's eyes widen.

"Long story. I'd love a coffee though. It might wake me up."- Because Hugh has not managed to get any of the antidepressants down me today, I should be able to stomach a coffee. For weeks now, I've been feeling too sick to go anywhere near it. Usually, I have to curtail how many cups I get through.

As I listen to Claire clanking cups around in the kitchen, I sweep my gaze over my brother's lounge. Their wedding photo presides in pole position, forcing me to draw the usual comparisons with my own wedding.

I was their bridesmaid and was treated to the same top to toe pampering as Claire. It was one of the happiest days of my life. Jason and I had only been together for a couple of years then. I'd hoped that the whole loved-up atmosphere would awaken marriage stirrings within him. But alas, not.

Then I notice the framed picture he's got of our parents in the bay window. They're much younger than they are in the photo on my wall – I think it was taken not long after their rough patch in the mid-eighties. Which might coincide with what Julie appears to be claiming. I'd say she's around ten years younger than me, so the pieces of all this seem to be fitting together. I need some answers from her directly though, and no matter what it takes, I'm going to get them. But first, I need to protect myself.

"Here we go." Claire breezes back into the lounge and slides a coffee onto the table in front of me. She sits in the armchair opposite and crosses one shapely leg over the other. Nellie trots back into the room after her and drops a ball into my lap. Claire and her home blend well together, soft, girly and everything in place. Everything I'm not.

"So what did you mean when you said I've made my feelings plain to Kieren?" I take a large sip of coffee, hoping it will wake me up. One minute I feel as though I'm coming around, and the next, I could sleep for a hundred years. I wonder how many sleeping tablets were in that wine I drank last night. "Is it because of the wedding? Because I couldn't invite you both?"

"Well, that was a big part of it." Claire wraps her fingers around her cup. "And that's aside from the fact that we've barely heard from you since last October. Kieren's been gutted about it. Christmas would have been difficult anyway, but without you..." Her voice trails off.

"Has he? Been gutted? *Really?*"

I'm surprised if the truth be known. Kieren and I have often gone months without being in touch. He always knows I'm there for him though. I refrain from pointing out that he could have got hold of me too – no relationship is a one-way street. It's nearly always been me who does all the running.

"I'm three months pregnant Nicola." Claire looks me in the eye now and rests one hand on her belly. "Kieren was so excited about telling you. But you've done nothing but ignore his calls and texts, and that message you sent..." She shakes her head.

"What message? What calls? Hang on." I glance towards her flat belly. There's certainly no sign of anything yet. "Wait. What? You're pregnant?"

She nods and her initial irritation with me appears to fade.- She can probably sense from my voice, my joy for her. They've tried for a baby for years. Almost since they got married. I'm never going to be a mother, but I can be the next best thing. I can be an amazing auntie instead. For the first time in weeks, a flutter of excitement dances in my belly. I'm still me. Hugh has tried everything to flatten me as a person, but I'm back despite his best efforts. I've still got things to go on for, and to look forward to.

"Three months? So how are you? How are you feeling?"

"Grim, to be honest. Hence, I'm drinking this rubbish." She holds her cup towards me to reveal bits of ginger and a slice of lemon floating around in hot water.

Through my smile, I grimace at the sight of her drink. "I'm so happy for you Claire. But I can't believe you've only just told me." Really, I want to hug her, but we haven't quite broken the barriers down yet.

"You don't know how many times Kieren has tried to ring or message you. From his phone and mine too. Nothing has even shown as delivered, so he assumed you'd blocked us both. Same with social media. We can't even find your profile on Facebook anymore.

"Why on earth would I block you? Either of you? Don't be daft."

"That's exactly what we thought. Which is why Kieren came to see you."

"Did he? When?" There's a shriek in my voice. All this time I've thought he didn't give a toss, not knowing that he's ever been around to the house. I must have been sleeping, or something. I've certainly been doing enough of that lately.

"The first time was about three weeks ago. But that's not the only time he's been to the door. He's tried three or four times as far as I know."

"It must have been when I've been out... or sleeping."

"At least he got to meet your husband." Her lips purse in distaste. "Pleasant man by the sounds of it."

"He never said a word to me about it. Honestly."

"You really don't know Kieren's been to your house?" I can see in Claire's eyes that she suspects I'm lying. I can't blame her really.

"Of course not."

"Well, the lovely Hugh sent Kieren packing. Every time. After giving him a mouthful about his attitude towards you."

"What attitude?"

"I think it was because Kieren had been upset about not seeing you at Christmas, and then not being invited to your wedding. He made his feelings quite plain both times, didn't he?"

I nod as Claire continues.

"I kind of understood, or at least tried to, but Kieren didn't." Claire sips from her cup, not taking her eyes from me as though she's watching for my reaction. No doubt she'll be reporting back to Kieren. "But to be honest, nothing could have prepared us for that message you sent."

"What message? When?"

"The email from your work email address."

It's all falling into place today. First Julie, now Kieren. At least I'm getting some clarity. If only the same could be said for my mind. "I really haven't sent any messages Claire. I swear to you. What did it say?"

I can tell from her face that she's sceptical. "I saw it with my own eyes."

"He must have hacked into my email account. Probably my phone and social media too." I think back to the moment I realised that some of my numbers had been deleted and my passwords changed. It's the only explanation I can come up with. "He's even lost me my job."

"How's he managed that?" Her voice goes up an octave or three now and her eyebrows raise with it.

"He's been sending emails, pretending to be me. That's a whole different story. Tell me about this message I supposedly sent first. I need to know what's going on."

"Oh Nicola. It was awful." Claire's face drops. "I couldn't believe it. You told Kieren never to contact you again, and..." Her voice fades away.

"What?"

"Here's the worst bit. You said that you blamed him completely for your dad's suicide. If he wasn't so self-centred...," you said, "and..."

She keeps saying you said. "I *said* nothing of the sort Claire. It wasn't me. I promise you." Tears fill my eyes again. I need

Kieren and Claire beside me. I can't fight all this on my own. "Why on earth would I ever blame Kieren for what Dad did?"

"There was lots of other stuff besides that. Look, I'll get Kieren to show you the message. That's if he hasn't got rid of it. Like I said, he was really upset with you."

"Bloody hell." I put my cup down on the coffee table and drop my head into my hands. "It really wasn't me who sent it. Kieren should have kept trying. He should have forced his way past Hugh. He should know me better than this."

"What the hell's been going on with you?" Claire moves from her chair to sit beside me and drapes her arm around my shoulder. The rare human contact is comforting. And despite everything, I can't wait to see my brother. I should have known he wouldn't just abandon me without what he thought was good reason. Despite Hugh trying to convince me he had.

Claire listens as I spill the whole sorry tale. How Hugh was Mr Wonderful before we got married, but how I can now see that he wanted me all to himself. To manipulate and subsequently bring me down.

"It sounds as though he's been trying to isolate you from everyone." Claire tucks her hair behind an ear. "And it's clearly worked. I wish now that we'd tried harder to get through to you. But in my defence, I've spent the last couple of months feeling as sick as a pig. I haven't been able to think about much else." She rests her hands on her belly. I certainly know how that feels after the tablets they've been poisoning me with lately.

I tell her about the wedding day, and about Gary, the Porsche, the joint accounts, and the bank transfers.

"Why the hell didn't you get in touch with us?" She pulls her arm away and twists to face me. "We're your bloody family, for God's sake Nicola." Her eyes are puzzled. "In fact, you're the only family Kieren's got now."

"Only for the moment," I smile through the tears that are welling and place my hand on Claire's belly. "I'm so, so happy for you. Really, I am. And I'm happy for me too. I can't wait to be an auntie." My voice wobbles. "I'm sorry to have only just found out. I'll make all this up to you, I promise."

"Nicola. You've got to sort yourself first. You need to get this appalling man out of your house and out of your life. Do you think you should involve the police?"

"I've been completely drugged up for the past month, near enough," I tell her. "Totally out of it, in fact. But I've not had anything since yesterday, so I'm feeling better today." I really am, thank God. Still not well enough to drive, but well enough to take some control back.

"You haven't had any what?"

"Sleeping tablets and antidepressants. Hugh's been spiking my drinks and food with extra doses. As well as forcing me to take what I was prescribed whilst he watched. I didn't really want to be on them at all." As I say the words, the realisation hits me at just how serious all this is.

"He told Kieren that you were on tablets. Whilst blaming him for it, of course."

"I don't even need to be on them – maybe counselling, but not tablets. I just need to find my strength again. My self-esteem is on the floor. And you haven't heard the best part of it yet."

"There's more?" She raises an eyebrow before sitting back against the cushions. She looks exhausted, and I feel guilty for laying all this on her when she's pregnant. "Nicola. Tell me."

"It turns out all this wedding stuff is some sort of set up and has been since the start." I feel so stupid now. So blind. How could I have been taken in by this man? "I haven't got to the bottom of it yet, but it seems I've been targeted all along."

"By who? And for what?"

"Hugh obviously, but his twin brother Gary – he's a right slimeball – he's been in on it all too. Then also my neighbour, Julie, who I thought was my friend, but it turns out that she could be mine and Kieren's half-sister."

"What! How?" Claire looks like she wants to spit her tea, or whatever it is, out. She swallows and sits up straight again. *"Half-sister!"*

"I haven't had it out with her yet. Julie, I mean. I only overheard their conversation when I was in the cellar this morning. That's when I found out they've been drugging me. Which is when I came straight round here."

"You've done the right thing. Blimey, this is like some sort of bloody TV drama." She smiles at me, though it's a weak smile.

I shiver as I recall sitting on the cold cellar step in the darkness a few hours ago. It's a right curveball that's been thrown my way, but I'm glad it has. At least I'm piecing everything together now. "It seems Dad might have had an affair."

"No. No way." Claire shakes her head vehemently. "Not your dad. He adored your mum."

"That's what I'd have thought. But now I'm not so sure." An image of Julie's face swims into my mind. "Julie does have a look of Kieren and from what I heard of their conversation; it didn't sound as though it was being invented. What they were saying really sounded genuine. I know it was years ago, but still..."

"Bloody hell." Claire closes her eyes and then opens them again. "Kieren will have a fit when he hears about this."

"Do you think he'll come home early? I could really do with talking to him."

"I'll message him in a minute. But whether he comes back today or tomorrow, you're not going back to that house." She shakes her head again. "You're staying here with us."

"I don't want to drag you and Kieren into all this. Especially now." I point at her belly.

"You're not safe at home, you know that. Besides, I won't rest if you go back there. And I need my rest." She smiles at me. This time it's more genuine. Hopefully, I'm forgiven.

"I can't let Hugh drive me out of my home. And if I leave, I might not be able to get him out then."

"Of course you will. It's your house, for goodness sake. You've got the law on your side."

"But we're married now, aren't we? That gives him rights. Not to mention that I've let him put his name on things."

Claire sighs. "Look, somehow, we'll figure a way through this."

"He's got access to my money Claire. And you'll never guess – it turns out he's a used car salesman. He told me when we met that he owned a string of car dealerships."

"You've been well and truly had, haven't you? But listen." Claire rests her hand on my arm. "You won't be the first and you certainly won't be the last woman to be duped like this."

"It's not just about the money though. I'm not sure what he's been hoping to achieve with the tablets. The more I think about it, the more I believe he's capable of really hurting me. Or worse."

"We need to get in touch with the police. Then a solicitor." Claire shoos the dog away with her foot.

"You're right, I know you are." I pause, "but before I go any further, there's one thing I need to do." I can't let anyone talk me out of this.

"What's that?"

"I've got to speak to Julie. Just me and her. Once I've got my answers, I can give the police a straighter story. Right now, I'm totally unsure of what's been going on, or how I came to be on Hugh's radar."

"What do you mean?"

"I'm going to ask her some questions." I press my hands together. They're clammy at the thought of what's in front of me.

"What sort of questions?"

"About things over the last few months and then, obviously, about my dad."

"I'm really not sure it's a good idea." Claire frowns as she tucks a stray hair behind her ear. "I really think we should let the police handle things from now on."

"If I go to them straight away, I might never get the chance to get the answers I need from Julie. And at the moment, I can only tell them half a story anyway."

"Yeah, I get that, but Kieren will go barmy with me if I let you go back there. It's not safe Nicola." Claire shakes her head, her bun wobbling from side to side with the movement. "You're putting yourself in danger and I can't let you."

"No more danger than I've been in for the last few months." Thank God it's behind me now. My fight is back and the only way is onward and upward.

"Do you think Julie will even talk to you? If she's in on everything, I mean. For all you know, they might be threatening her too."

I nod. "Though, from what I heard this morning, I don't think it'll be too difficult to persuade her where her loyalties should lie."

CHAPTER TWENTY ONE

I can't face any more public transport today, so take a taxi home. Although it doesn't feel like home anymore. Home should be a place of sanctuary. Somewhere you want to be. If the Porsche is parked outside the house, I'll go straight around to Julie's. I've no idea what sort of reception I'll get, but I'm not going to risk bumping into Hugh.

Claire wanted to drive me back, but I'd never forgive myself if anything happened to my unborn niece or nephew. She offered to wait outside in the car, but I refused. If Hugh were to come back and realise Claire was supporting me, who knows what he might be capable of? Maybe not straight away, but further down the line he might try to find her. It's not worth the risk.

There's no Porsche. I breathe a sigh of relief and decide to nip into my house for the loo before I talk to Julie. I suddenly recall Hugh telling her to invite me round, which reassures me I probably won't get the door slammed in my face.

But first, I could do with knowing where Hugh is. I need to keep him in the dark about what I know for as long as possible. Act normal.

He answers his mobile on the second ring. It's quick for someone who's supposed to be at work.

"It's me." I try to make my voice as nonchalant as I can. Inside, I'm quaking.

"Where the hell have you been all day?" Wherever he's speaking from is in absolute silence and his words are dripping with anger and suspicion. I can picture him on the other end of the phone, the man whose hard face and stony eyes have replaced the face of the handsome husband I thought I'd found for myself. I really hoped he was my happy ever after. What an absolute idiot I've been. So desperate for love and companionship that I jumped at the first man who showed an interest. All this has taught me a valuable lesson.

"I went to sort some more tablets out." This should appease him.

"You've been to the doctor? On your own?" His voice rises some more. "You should have asked me to go with you. How did you get there?"

"On the bus. It was good to get out of the house for a while. Be around people." It's not a complete lie.

"It's better if you don't handle things like that without me."

"Thanks, but I was actually OK." I want to ask him how he thinks I ever made it to the age of forty-five without him, but obviously I don't. I'm beyond relieved that some of my former 'kick-ass' seems to have returned, but he doesn't need to be aware of that. He'll find out soon enough.

"Going to the doctors doesn't take until this time though, does it?" His tone returns to suspicious.

I imagine him glancing at his expensive wristwatch, the one he bought with *my* money, and can visualise his jaw clenched with frustration at the thought of losing control of me for a couple of hours. From what I heard this morning, that's one of his main goals – to know exactly where I am at all times.

"I had to go to the chemist, then I needed to go for a drink to be able to swallow my tablets." I've never had to explain my whereabouts in this much depth to anyone before. Not even to my parents when I went AWOL as a teenager.

"You went for a drink?"

"Just to a café. And I've been having a mooch around the shops. You know I enjoy doing that."

He stays silent. Actually, he doesn't know I like doing that.- We've only been together for a short time. He hardly knows me at all. Nor do I want him to. He's only interested in my bank balances. Finally, I've come to my senses, and I'll never go near any man again after this is over.

"I made a few notes on my novel too." That might shut him up.

"It sounds like you've had a productive day." I sense he's trying to create a lift in his voice. "Though I thought we'd agreed you'd only work on your novel at home. That's why I sorted the office out for you and got you the computer."

Yeah, with my money. But I don't say this, of course. He sounds more subdued than usual, making me hope he hasn't sensed too much of a shift in me. He mustn't realise I'm fighting back until it's too late.

"Yes, I suppose I have. Anyway, I'm back home now. I just wanted to let you know."

"Have you taken your tablet today?"

I wondered when he'd ask this. I'm surprised it wasn't his first question. He's obsessed with my tablets. "Yes. Like I've just told you. That's why I went to a café." I need him to believe I'm still on them.

"The antidepressant?"

"I'm not going to take my sleeping tablet at this time of day, am I? I wouldn't get anything done." I force a laugh. What a performance. I should be on stage.

"I'm sorry." His tone softens. "I'm only asking because I worry about you. Someone's got to."

Not so long ago, a sentence like that would have melted my resolve. "I know. And thanks. It's good to be worried about. Are you at work?"

"Yeah. Where else would I be?"

Just as I decide it's time to wrap the conversation up, he continues.

"Anyway, are you OK Nicola?"

"Yeah, why shouldn't I be?"

"No more silly thoughts then? I couldn't believe what you said to me yesterday. I haven't been able to stop thinking about it."

"About what? What did I say?"

"About doing something stupid."

"Like what?"

As far as I can remember, I was out of it most of the day yesterday. However, now my head is a little clearer, I wonder what the truth is about lots of things I've supposedly said. Perhaps I've been talking in my sleep, or maybe Hugh has misconstrued something.

"You were on about hurting yourself. Honestly Nicola – you really worry me sometimes. Especially after what your dad..."

"I haven't had any silly thoughts. I've no idea what you're talking about."

Despite my new-found strength, a cold knot of fear twists in my stomach. I've been low, and not well, but surely, not that low and unwell to verbalise my fleeting thoughts out loud.

"Oh Nicola. You and your memory." Hugh laughs. "Honestly. Never mind, it's not your fault, is it? At least you've got me to take care of you. It's a good job I came along when I did."

I've got to be honest, he sounds so plausible. It's no wonder he's constantly made me doubt myself.

189

"It's me and you now," he continues. "Just like I keep telling you. Me and you against the world."

I really haven't got an answer to that. Act normal. Act normal. "What time will you be home?" I ask. "I'll cook us something nice for dinner."

"Around six, I should imagine. Usual time."

We could almost be an ordinary married couple. *What time will you be home? I'll cook us some dinner.* "I'll be waiting," I tell him. And I certainly will.

Good. I seem to have thrown him well and truly off guard. And I've got over two hours before he'll turn up here. Plenty of time to persuade Julie into my way of thinking.

As I fill a glass of water, I shudder to recall the recent efforts that have been made to add medication to my drinks. Hugh and Julie. I won't be drinking anything whilst I'm around her. It's important to really be on my guard. I now have a better idea of what's been going on, so I must protect myself and what I've got. Somehow, I can get through this. In my teens, I was repeatedly dumped by friends and boys and Mum would always trot out one of her stock phrases, *it will pass*, or, *you won't feel like this forever*, or her favourite, *what doesn't kill you makes you stronger*, words that should empower, yet this last statement sends a chill right through me. No matter how hard I try, I can't quell this sense of foreboding that's expanding inside me.

As I rinse my glass, my gaze is drawn to the window as the gate squeaks open. It's Julie. I wonder if Hugh's let her know I'm back home. It would probably have been safer for me to go to her house, but she's here now. And Hugh's not due back for a while yet. Right. Here we go. Act normal. Act normal.

I fling the door open before she rings the bell. "Hello stranger." I force a smile.

"Yeah." Her gaze is down at her feet. "I'm sorry I've been a bit off with you. It's just, you know..."

"Of course I know. Hugh hasn't made you feel too welcome here when you've been around. He's the same with everyone, not just you." I'm gabbling like I always do when I'm nervous. "I don't know what it's all about, but I don't want it to spoil us being friends. It's his problem, not ours."

Her shoulders seem to relax as she stands in front of me. She does look like Kieren. Same nose, same eyes... and Dad. I always used to want a sister, but not like this. And if she is my sister, then she hasn't exactly made it straightforward, or even desirable to move on from here.

"Are you OK?" She frowns at me. "You seem to have zoned out. And you're looking at me strangely."

I'd welcome her concern if I didn't know the truth. "Sorry. It's just the tablets I guess. They're zonking me."

"Are you taking them properly now? You said they were making you feel ill before." She passes her keys from one hand to the other as she stands in front of me.

"Yeah. I've got to. I want to get better, don't I?"

"Anyway." She smiles. "I came to ask if you'd like to come round to mine for a glass of wine later? Or two?" She laughs. How can she laugh, knowing what she knows?

"I'm sorry. Tonight's no good." I shake my head. "I've promised to cook for Hugh."

"Really?" She looks puzzled. As well she should.

It's my turn to laugh. "I'm not completely incapable, you know. I can still cook. Why don't you come in for a drink *now*, instead?" This conversation needs to be done with well before Hugh returns.

"Where is Hugh?" She glances behind her and along the street.

"At work, of course. He won't be back until after six. And I've got a couple of bottles of wine in the fridge." I step aside to allow her in. "There's no time like the present, is there?"

Her voice sounds uncertain. "It's a bit early for wine, isn't it?" However, she walks past me and into the kitchen. So far, so good.

"It's never too early for wine!" I laugh as I tug the fridge door open. "I'll just have a small one with me being on these tablets."

"You'll be fine. I drank whilst I was on tablets."

You would say that, I think to myself as I stride across the kitchen.

"You sit if you want. I can get the drinks," she offers.

I bet you can. "Thanks, but I can manage."

"You seem a lot better than you have done lately." She pulls a chair from under the table. I turn and notice her glance at the photo of my parents as she sits. It's still unbelievable to think that my dad could be hers as well. And try as I might, I wouldn't have had him down for someone who would turn his back on a responsibility like another daughter. Unless Mum forced him. It's the only explanation I can come up with.

"Yeah, for now." I tug two glasses from the cupboard. No way will I be letting this drink, or Julie out of my sight for a moment. I still haven't decided which way to play this. Ask her straight out about everything or test the water first. Though it's not as if I've got time on my side. I just have to go with my gut. Somehow, I'll find the right words. Or they'll find me. I need to move with this. Fast. I glance at the photo as I head to the table, mentally saying a silent prayer to my mother to watch over me throughout all I'm about to face.

"So... how are things with you?" Julie smiles as she takes the wine glass by the stalk and brings it towards herself.

I can't imagine how she and Hugh have found it acceptable to lace my drinks with extra tablets. What sort of person does that to someone else? Hopefully, soon I'm going to find out.

"I'm seeing things a hell of a lot more clearly to be honest." As I speak, I'm nodding in time to my words. Should I just tell her what I know? No. Instead, I'm going to try something that could go one way or the other.

"Like what?" She looks puzzled.

"I've had some good news today." Another alien sensation of joy floods me. No one knows where Kieren lives, so I should be safe taking this course of action. *Everything happens for a reason*, Mum also used to say. Hugh never wanting to go to Kieren's house has provided me with a place to escape to where the location is unknown to Hugh.

"Oh?" Julie raises an eyebrow, clearly unaccustomed to seeing me smile.

"Yes. I met my sister-in-law earlier. It turns out I'm going to be an auntie." I screw my face up with excitement.

"Kieren?" Her face darkens and I realise that I've probably never actually mentioned his name to her, so that's more evidence.

"Yes, it's Kieren's baby. I've only got the one brother." I study her as she narrows her eyes. "I've always wanted to be an auntie." I keep my fingers wrapped around my glass after I've lowered it to the table. "Have you got any nieces or nephews Julie?"

"No." She puts her glass down with an abrupt clink against the polished table. "I've told you about my background."

"About your parents, but I don't think you've ever really told me about any other family." I'm watching her closely as I speak. "Do you have any brothers or sisters?"

She drops her gaze and appears to stutter over her reply. "Actually, I do." Hopefully, this is the moment where my plan goes the way I want it to. Julie raises her gaze from the table to look at me square on. "A half-brother and a half-sister. But they don't even know I exist." Her voice drops as her sentence ends. It's a combination of bitterness and regret, and I'm unsure which emotion will win out. But I'm sensing there's something I can work with.

"Oh? Why's that then?" I've got her on the back foot, I can tell. There's an unmet need in her, a yearning I'll be able to tap into. Thank God I've finally found out the truth about everything.

"I was the result of an affair." She continues without further prompting. "And my father didn't want to know me or my mother." She spits the word *father* out as though it's a piece of rancid meat.

"That's rough," I reply. "Not at all?"

"He had his wife and two children already." She takes a large glug of her wine. "My mother was his best-kept grubby secret. Until she wanted more from him, that is."

"What did she want from him?" I'll have to keep this line of questioning going for as long as I can. It's the only way I'll get my answers.

"I never got the chance to ask her. But I imagine she wanted support, acknowledgement, help... She was very young." Her voice fades to almost a whisper.

"How young?"

Shit. What was Dad playing at?

"Legal. Only just though."

Only just legal. Suddenly, I realise her age might be part of the explanation of why he wouldn't acknowledge them or fully accept responsibility. I really thought I knew my father. Not only was he spineless enough to take his own life last year, he also... I can't even think about it.

"Have you ever met him?"

194

She shakes her head. "Yes. Long enough to be told where to go. And my mother, well, as I've told you before, I wasn't enough for her to stick around for either."

Julie's telling the truth. I knew it. *She's my bloody sister.* What a bloody cruel twist of fate that both her biological parents have taken their own lives.

"What happened to you? When your mother died?"

"Her parents, my grandparents, took me in, but I got too much for them." She drops her head into her hands but quickly, as though she suddenly remembers what she is dealing with here, lifts it again. At least she's confiding in me. It's all going to plan so far, and will hopefully make it easier for me to take this conversation to the next level.

"Did anyone try contacting your dad to help you after your mum died?" It's beyond weird is this calling my dad *her dad.*

"He didn't give a shit. Even less so after his wife found out."

It sounds just as weird to hear my mother referred to as *his wife.*

"She was perfectly happy," Julie continues, "to let me rot in children's homes and foster homes. So long as I didn't wreck her cushy little life." She stares into her glass. "And bring their reputation into question. That's what I've been told anyway."

I wait for a few minutes. This can't be put off any longer. "I know who you are, Julie." My voice is so gentle it surprises me.

She raises her gaze from the table to the picture of our dad, then to me. Her face is hard to read. "You've lived the life that should have belonged to me," she says. "It's not fair."

CHAPTER TWENTY TWO

We sit in silence for a few minutes. This is where things could really take a turn for the even worse. But I've come this far, and I've got to keep going.

"I'm sorry," I say eventually. "I'm sorry for everything you've been through, Julie. Really, I am."

"I came to detest you over the years," she replies. "I tried getting in touch with him so many times in my teens."

"Did you?" I stare at her, feeling sure I'd have been able to remember if I'd ever answered the door to her. With her height and her build, she's quite distinctive. Of course, she's probably altered since her teenage years. I still can't imagine my dad just ignoring her though. That's not the sort of man he was. Although, I've found out today about a side of him which I never knew existed.

"I used to watch you together." Julie tilts her head towards me, then immediately up at the picture. "I couldn't work out why you were so special to him and why he wouldn't even acknowledge me."

"Did you?" I say again, feeling somewhat creeped out by the whole thing, thinking of her watching me. I had absolutely no idea. But now I need to push this discussion onto how she's linked with Hugh, and also Gary. I'm aware of time ticking on.

"I'd see him dropping you off in his big, posh car, or picking you up from somewhere and taking you home to your big, posh house, being *your* dad," she points at me, "when he should have been *mine*." She gestures towards herself.

"I can see why you'd feel like that, but..."

"You were born with a silver spoon in your gob. It's really not fair." She's pointing at me again. I hate being pointed at usually, but in the circumstances, I'll let it slide.

"None of this is my fault, Julie." My voice is surprisingly even as it echoes around my quiet kitchen, and I intend to keep it that way. No way will I rise to the emotional level Julie's at right now. I need to keep the situation as calm as possible.

Glancing at the clock, I see there's less than an hour until Hugh is due back. I consider the idea of moving our conversation onto more neutral ground, like a café or a pub. I quickly dismiss it though, deciding against breaking the mood and momentum of our conversation. She's opening up to me and I want to keep it that way.

"If it's really true Julie," I clasp my hands together on the table in front of me. "If you really are mine and Kieren's sister, we can make up for lost time. We can find a way through this. We can-"

"It's too late." I jump as she thumps the table with her fist and rises from her chair. "Can't you see that? I'm in too deep now. It's all too late."

"What do you mean?" She strides towards the window and peers up and down the street. What if she knows something I don't about Hugh's impending return? I glance around for something to defend myself with if I need to. The wine bottle is probably the best weapon I can come up with. After all, Hugh's moved the knives.

"It's all gone too far." She turns back to me. The sunset outside casts warmth over the kitchen and an orange glow across her face. This could be a pleasant moment. Two sisters sharing a drink in an early spring kitchen. Instead, my job is to get to the bottom of *it's too late* and *it's gone too far.* I rub my head, thankful that I seem to be thinking straighter for the first time in weeks. What those bloody tablets have done to me...

"Sit down Julie. We can talk about this."

Surprisingly, she does as I suggest. "I'll have a drop more of this, if you don't mind."

Taking my glass with me, I rise from the chair and head to the wine bottle in front of the window. I can't risk her slipping anything in to it. It could stop me from ever being able to leave the house again. At least Claire knows what's going on now – she and Kieren would help me. I pour some wine for Julie, but not for myself. My thinking needs to remain as clear as possible.

"There you go." I place the glass in front of her and sink back onto my seat. "OK, so my dad had an affair with your mum. It's tragic what happened with your mum, and then, my dad..."

"Our dad."

"Our dad. Sorry. He's behaved in a really shitty way. I get all that. I get why you'd be so pissed off with him. But why take it out on me? I was in the dark the whole time. And why didn't you tell me who you were earlier?"

"I hated you, Nicola. You've no idea how much. You and your brother."

"*Your* brother too." I echo the connection she's just attached to Dad. Who knows what Kieren will make of all this? The hatred she's been harbouring is written all over her face. It's no wonder Gary is the only man she's been capable of attracting into her life. With the amount of venom and jealousy she seems to have swirling around inside.

"I was certain you must have known about me all along. That they must have mentioned me to you." She takes a big swig of her wine. "I told myself that you must be as poisoned towards me as your parents were."

"Well, I wasn't. You should have talked to me," I say gently. "I wish I'd have known. It could have been so different."

She shakes her head. "Over the years, I've built you up into something. Not so much Kieren, but definitely you. It was you I hated the most. You, who I felt had taken everything from me."

"That's understandable, to a point. After all, we're both girls, but..."

"It's only in recent months I've realised you're actually alright." There's a ghost of a smile on her lips. "I've even grown to like you, if I'm honest."

"Erm, thanks." Perhaps I'm getting somewhere. I place my hand over hers, but she tugs it away as though she's been burned. Evidently, there's still a long way to go. I glance at the clock.

"Honestly. It was such a shock. To find I liked you, I mean. I'd spent my whole life hating you to the point where I wouldn't have cared if you'd died alongside your parents."

Charming, I think to myself, but keep quiet. She obviously needs to let this out.

"You don't know how hard my life's been Nicola. I know I wasn't an easy kid but who would be, shunted from pillar to post. My father didn't want me. My mother was barely more than a kid herself and didn't want to stick around and bring me up. Then, my grandparents couldn't cope." She stabs at the table with her finger as she reels off her list.

"What about whilst you were in care?" I try to keep my voice soft, so as not to aggravate her further. "Surely you were fostered by people who chose to foster you? Who wanted to look after you?"

"What planet are you on?" Her voice is a shriek as she tugs at the cuff of her jumper and flicks her hair behind her shoulder.- Because of her height and broad build, her hair is one of the more feminine things about her.

I find myself wondering what her mother looked like. And I still can't believe that my own mother was involved in all of this and behaved like she did. But I suppose she was also betrayed.

"I'm sorry. I just can't..."

"There was one set of foster parents who used me as a glorified babysitter for their own younger kids, another who put me on a diet to save themselves some money, oh and one where the dad..." She draws air quotes in the air as she says the word *dad*, "had an interest in me that was anything but fatherly. Then there were the children's homes."

"I can't imagine what it must have been like for you." It's true. I can't. And I do believe she's my half-sister, although Kieren will probably insist on a DNA test. Particularly before we part with any of our parent's money. Which I really think will be the right thing to do. But first, I've got to survive all this.

"Yeah. I got bullied to high heaven in the children's homes." There are tears in her eyes as she continues, and I wonder if she's ever talked to anyone about it all. She probably should. "And at school. Just because I was different. Bigger, taller, and in care. Kids are shits, aren't they? I stopped going to school in the end. I was the only kid at my school who was in care. And I kept running off from the homes, but the police always took me back. It was shit. Shit. Shit!"

She pauses. Still, I keep quiet.

"I couldn't have anything there, you know. Not a thing. Any stuff I had, any money I got. It was always pinched. It was alright for you in your big house with your parents, and your brother, and your holidays, and your education. I bet you had your own room, didn't you? I had to share with three others in the last place I was in." She pauses to glug more wine.

"Have you ever spoken to anyone about all this?"

"I'm speaking to you, aren't I?"

"You know what I mean. You've obviously been through a lot."

"Only Gary."

I sit up straight in my chair. It's time for me to get to the root of Gary and Hugh's involvement in my life. Especially *now* she's the one who's mentioned him.

"I've been seeing Gary on and off for a few years." Julie avoids my gaze as she continues. I would in her shoes, admitting to having any sort of relationship with that weasel.

"You could do so much better than him Julie. I can't imagine what anyone could possibly see in him. He's been a right pillock to me."

"He was alright to start with," she continues. "But he often used my past as a stick to beat me with. I thought he was all I deserved, if I'm honest. But at least I've been able to hang onto some of the better elements of myself." She looks at me with what looks like scorn. *Unlike you,* her eyes seem to say. "And at least I was sensible enough not to ever move in with him. Or get married." She smiles now, and it's definitely with scorn.

"You knew Gary, well before I knew Hugh then?"

"Yeah. But obviously, I was keeping tabs on you all along.- So, when the house behind..." She gestures towards the back kitchen wall, "went up for sale early last year, I pulled out all the stops to raise the money to buy it. I had to beg, borrow and steal the deposit. And the mortgage is crippling me. I've been getting repossession letters. Being on my own and being self-employed. I bet you paid cash for this place, didn't you?" She sweeps her gaze around my darkening kitchen. I'll probably leave the house after this.

I did pay cash, but I'm not getting into the money side of things with Julie. "So, where were you living at that time? Before moving here?"

"In a shitty council flat near Gary's. It's a world you wouldn't know."

"Did Gary not want to move into the house here with you when you got it?" I tilt my head towards the back wall. I've seen where Gary lives on the occasions I picked Hugh up or dropped him off when we were first seeing each other. The area is the pits. I can't imagine Gary choosing to be there, rather than here. But then, they'd have blown their cover with me.

"He had Hugh living with him by then. They're up each other's arses, them two – as you'll have found out for yourself."

I nod in reply and the memory of Gary having a go at me outside the registry office swims back into my mind.

"Hugh had treated his ex like crap, by all accounts. He controlled her money, what she did, where she went... Anyway, he was on bail after smashing her house up."

"I've heard something about that." The conversation with Debbie flashes back into my head. I forgot to tell Claire about her. Even Debbie tried to warn me, and it doesn't seem to be just so she can have Hugh for herself. "I've only just found that out, though. So they bailed him to stay at Gary's then?"

"Yeah. And between us, no one had much money."

"You've got your own business, haven't you?"

Julie laughs. "What – as a self-employed seamstress? I'm hardly Richard Branson. And Gary can't hold a job down for more than five minutes. Anyway, whilst I was waiting for the house sale to complete, I told them about you, and who you were, and the fact we were becoming neighbours, it was then when a plan started to come together."

I bet it did. Hugh was never remotely interested in me. But he's a good actor, I'll give him that. "Whose idea was it to fleece me?

Hugh's? Gary's?" Not that it's important, but it's all information I can give the police.

"Gary's, to start with."

"Well, there's a surprise."

"Hugh took very little convincing though. And to be honest, neither did I. I really had it in for you."

"You said."

We sit for a moment, listening to the ticking of the kitchen clock, which she then cuts into as she continues.

"I've heard everything through these walls over the last year.- Everything." She cocks her head toward her house again. "You crying over your dad – our dad. Arguing with Jason. Him leaving. You crying some more. Then I've heard everything between you and Hugh."

"I must have done your head in." Hopefully, I'm getting her on side here. To the point where she won't want to continue in league with Hugh and Gary. Where she'll see the sense of trying to establish an allegiance with me and Kieren instead. Though how any sort of relationship between us can pan out after all this, I don't know. I'm not sure I'd ever be able to trust her. How can I? She was part of a conspiracy to have me sectioned. Or worse. Much worse, by the sounds of it.

"Yes and no," she replies. "I was biding my time. Watching. Listening. Waiting."

"What for?"

"The chance to get back at you, I guess. And to get hold of what's rightfully mine. Especially after he killed himself."

To hear what dad did put so bluntly sounds awful. It's something I rarely talk about. Hugh has repeatedly brought it up, particularly over the last few weeks. I just want to put that awful memory into a little box and send it as far away as possible.

"What I will say," Julie says, "is that I've felt better knowing you were going through some of what I've had to deal with for a change. The misery, the confusion, the lack of..."

"I still don't understand why you didn't just talk to me Julie. It didn't have to be like this."

"Like I've told you, by the time I'd decided you weren't the spoilt, selfish bitch I'd built you up to be, it was too late. I was already in it up to my neck."

"Already in what?"

She lets a long breath out. Here we go. This is when I get the full story. Then I can go to the police. Get a solicitor. Go back to Claire and Kieren.

"Do you remember when you joined that dating site?" Julie glances at the clock now and I find myself worrying whether she's really on Hugh and Gary's side and telling them everything that's being discussed between us. Surely not. If she has, we'll be finished as sisters before we ever get started.

"What?" How on earth does Julie know about me joining online dating?

"You were out with a group of women. In some fancy wine bar." Her face contorts into a sneer. "There were some right posh cows there."

"You must mean my workmates. Or at least they were my workmates. They're not posh, really. They're great once you get to know them."

"Anyway, I was sitting at the table beside you."

She really was stalking me. How on earth I didn't recognise her, I don't know. Julie is very distinctive. And I've never had any kind of sense that I was being watched. I remember that night well – even though I'd had a few drinks. Surely I'd have spotted Julie. The more I look at her, the more I see Kieren.

"I was worried at the time you might recognise me as your new neighbour."

I shake my head. "That night's a bit of a blur to be honest." I point at my wine glass.

"You'd obviously been so far up your own arse all those months that you hadn't taken a blind bit of notice of me having moved into the house behind. I might as well have not existed."

"I'm sorry. Really, I am. I used to say hello to you though." It's my turn to look at the clock again. Three quarters of an hour to go.

"Yeah, but I obviously wasn't someone worth taking much notice of, was I?"

"Julie. I'm sorry. Like I said, we can make up for all that now."

"I heard every word from your table that night. Right down to the dating site they set you up on. You were all having a right laugh, weren't you?" Her sneer has returned, as though it's a crime to have a right laugh.

"So that was why I matched up with Hugh so quickly from that site. In fact, it was the same night." Why didn't I ever suspect? Or maybe I did. I spent several weeks thinking it was all too good to be true.

"I got him to register and find you on there," she explains. "I never could have imagined things would be so simple from then on."

I let a long breath out. Yes, I was simple alright. At least Julie is talking. I'm confident that I'll draw the whole story from her now.

"I wasn't sure what we were going to do at that point, just that a dating app would make it easy for us to get to you. Well, via Hugh, that is."

"I really thought he was interested in me." It still makes me feel sad when I think back to those heady November days, when for a time, Hugh made me forget all I'd been through with Dad and Jason. He certainly put on a convincing act. "Then what happened?"

205

"Look. I've probably said too much as it is." She closes her eyes, then opens them again. "I hated you then."

"But you don't now?"

She shakes her head. "Look, I really do regret the part I've played in all this, but unfortunately it's too late to do anything about it."

"Of course it's not. We could join forces here Julie. Against Gary and Hugh, I mean." I can tell by her face it's a fruitless request.

"They've got more on me, not just with the situation with you, but with other stuff, more than you could ever imagine." She lowers her gaze. "That night Gary was at mine. It was to warn me."

"Warn you about what?"

"He sensed mine and your friendliness might go beyond what had been agreed."

"I don't understand. What had you agreed?"

"I was supposed to be Gary and Hugh's eyes and ears. Report back anything you said to me. And ensure we kept piling the medication into you."

"But why would you do that?" This is the part I'm going to find the hardest to forgive.

"The money side of things I was fine with, after all, you owed me – you still do, but the other thing..." Her voice trails off and she doesn't seem able to meet my eyes.

"What?"

She takes another swig from her glass and pauses, as though summoning courage. "Driving you into an early grave through an overdose, or sending you out of your mind, I really didn't agree with. More and more so as the weeks have gone on."

So that's what they were doing. Trying to overdose me – they'd have probably told the authorities that I'd done it to myself. And if I'm honest, Hugh hasn't been far away from sending me out of my mind. All the lies, all the things he's told me. Conversations we've supposedly had, things I've agreed to. Not to mention the isolation. And the cruelty.

"You stupid bitch."

Julie slams her glass on the table as we both turn to the voice at the door. We've been so engrossed in the conversation that we haven't noticed Hugh pull up outside.

My gaze lowers from his face to the glint of metal in his hands. He's clutching the spade Tom got for me from the maintenance cupboard at work when it was snowing before Christmas. Hugh must have taken it from the boot of my car.

"What are you doing? What have you got that for?" I rise from my chair, my eyes darting around the kitchen again for a weapon that could match his. Something better than a wine bottle. Only he knows where the knives are, which in itself is worrying. There is nothing for us to defend ourselves with. Or more to the point, there's nothing for me to defend myself with.

He's early. Perhaps Julie has tipped him off. Maybe the spade is for me.

CHAPTER TWENTY THREE

Hugh's narrowed eyes flit from me to Julie, then back again. "What's going on here?" His face is white and pinched. It's an expression I've come to know well. One that I've learned to fear.

"Julie's popped round for a glass of wine." My voice is bright. Too bright. But that's what Hugh wanted – me and Julie to get together so she could spike me some more. Isn't it?

"It's all over." Hugh steps closer to the table, his fist tightening around the handle of the spade, which he brings to rest beside his foot.

I catch the glint of metal as he twists it this way and that, making grooves in the linoleum. I've definitely nothing in this kitchen to match that if it comes my way. I look around again. A pan perhaps, or the pipe from the hoover. Hopefully it won't come to me having to defend myself against Tom's spade.

"What's all over?" I don't take my eyes off him.

But he's not looking at me. He lunges towards Julie with more venom in his face than I've ever seen.

"How much have you fucking told her?" Spittle flies from his mouth as he shouts, towering over her, lifting the spade and ramming it back to the floor.

"Nothing." She leaps from her chair and steps around the back of it, evidently as threatened by the spade as I am. "She'd found out we're sisters. We were talking, that's all."

"Half-sisters." His sneering words increase my conviction that Julie is my half-sister. "But you were doing more than just talking, weren't you?" He reaches under the table and plucks a black plastic device which must have been stuck beneath it. Bloody hell. He's bugged us. If only I'd gone around to Julie's instead of inviting her in here. But for all I know, he, or Gary, have installed something there as well. They probably have. Panic crawls over me. I need to check my coat, my bag. He could have heard every word I said to Claire today. He can't know that I've told her anything. My unborn niece or nephew could be at risk.

His next words begin mockingly before rising to a crescendo.- "Do you know how much you've fucked everything up Julie?" I jump as he shouts the word *Julie.* It's horrendous being so scared of a man. I've never known anything like it.

"I haven't fucked anything up Hugh." Julie's tone has a pathetic edge and I wonder to what extent she's keeping up appearances here. "We can still go on with what we planned to do. We've got the money behind us now, haven't we?"

Does she mean what she's saying to him? One thing's for sure. I can't trust her. Not yet. But maybe she's just trying to placate him.

"I heard every word you said." He points the spade towards me. "Every. Bloody. Word. Where are your tablets?"

I nod at the cupboard.

"Show me."

I thread myself past him and grapple for the box on the bottom shelf, sending boxes of paracetamol, plasters and indigestion tablets showering to the counter below.

209

He snatches the box from me. "They're the old ones. Where are the tablets you picked up today?"

"They're upstairs." I try not to sound too eager. "I'll get them."- This is my opportunity to get away and call for help. I think of my bag in the hallway.

"You'll stay exactly where you are. You can take these for now."

I stop in my tracks as I get to the door.

"You can swallow them right here, where I can see you." He thrusts the packet back at me.

"But I've already taken my tablet today." What is it with him and these bloody tablets? Surely there would have been quicker ways for him to bump me off if that's what he wants to do. I expect he's ensuring that he'll get away with it by overdosing me slowly. He can then blame it on my confused state. He knows what he's doing.

"I didn't see you take it. So you can swallow another in front of me, just to make sure."

"What difference does it make to you what I take or don't take?" I'm two steps from the front door. As I lurch towards it, I feel cruel for leaving Julie behind, but hopefully, I can get some help for both of us.

Shit. He's locked it.

Hugh dives towards me. "Did you really think I'd have left it open?" He grabs the edges of my jaw in one hand and presses my head against the door frame, his face contorted into a grimace, and his whiskey breath in my face. "I said, take the fucking tablet." As I stare back at him, I can hardly believe this is a man I thought I was in love with.

"In fact, you can take two of them." He grips my face tighter.

I bruise easily so I'm going to look a right sight after this. It's more evidence for the police though. That's if he doesn't kill me first. Perhaps Claire was right - I should have gone straight to them for some help.

"You're that bloody deranged, you should take as many tablets as you can get down your gullet. Then you can fuck off to bed and get out of my sight." He squeezes my face one last time before releasing it.

There's no way I'm swallowing anything. I'd rather fight off that spade first. Julie's still gripping the back of the chair. I follow her gaze to the bunch of keys by the microwave. Hugh's standing between us, and judging by the look on his face, he seems poised to strike whichever of us crosses him first. And even if Julie manages to grab the keys, she needs to isolate which of them will open the front door. Whether Julie wanted to swap allegiances, it seems that Hugh bugging our conversation has made that decision for her.

"I'm waiting. You either get them tablets down you or I'll shove them down your throat myself."

If he goes for me first, Julie will get the chance to run for it. But will she call for help for me, given what's gone before with Dad? I silently plead for someone to walk past the window and notice what's going on in here. But we're in semi darkness now, and the only light source is from beneath the cooker hood.

Hugh swipes at Julie's half full wine glass, then snatches the strip of tablets from my hand. Balancing the spade between his legs, he presses three tablets out of the foil with trembling hands onto the counter, then slides the wine glass alongside them. "Get them down your throat," he growls. "Now."

"No chance." The old me is back. It's someone Hugh has barely known before, and he certainly won't like it.

The spade drops to the floor with a clatter and before I can think about what I'm doing, he's thrown me to the floor after it. I've barely time to put an arm out to break my fall before he's sat astride my chest, his fourteen-and-a-half stone weight bearing down on me. I can smell the leather from his jacket and his cheap aftershave.

He twists himself around to face Julie. "Pass me the tablets and the glass. NOW."

She reaches towards them and for a moment, it looks as though she's going to obey him. Instead, she grabs the keys then sprints towards the door. Hugh's off me and after her in the blink of an eye.

"Give them to me." His voice is a growl as he grips her by the throat and rams her against the door. He's trying to wrestle the keys from her with his free hand. She's putting up a valiant fight against him getting them, so whilst this is going on, I see my chance to grab the spade. However, Hugh's back at me before I have a chance to get to my feet.

"You mental bitch." He throws me back to the ground. "You're going the same way as your lunatic father. You do know that, don't you?"

Julie's spluttering in the doorway. I jerk my head to the right, hoping she'll somehow take the hint that my handbag is in the hallway. If only she can get to my keys, or my phone...

"Whatever made you believe you were worth me killing myself Hugh?" I'll keep him talking whilst I continue trying to draw Julie's attention to the bag. I haul myself from the floor onto my elbows, again tilting my head in the direction of my bag, but to no avail. Julie's too busy rubbing at her neck. I know how she feels. My face is stinging from Hugh's grip, but I won't give him the satisfaction of showing him he's hurt me. Not anymore.

"And nor am I mental, as you keep putting it," I continue. "If I've appeared to be, it's only because of what a bastard you've been." I smile through my fear. "I'm so over you Hugh. There's nothing more you can do to me."

"You reckon? That's what your pathetic excuse for an old man thought as well." It's Hugh's turn to smile. "As I locked him inside his garage."

"What the hell are you on about?" I haul myself into a seated position. Julie is leaning against the door. I glance at her, hoping my expression conveys what I'm thinking. *We're going to have to join forces to overpower him. The door's locked. Our only way out of this is to immobilise him. Properly. And I can't do it on my own.*

Hugh retrieves his spade from the ground and digs it again repeatedly into the linoleum, this time beside my foot. I find myself feeling angry that it's going to need replacement after this. Although, perhaps I need to get out of here unscathed before I consider what's needed on the kitchen floor. I shrink into the corner of the room, finding my back up against the washing machine.

"I could tell you what I know." He grins. "But then I'd have to kill you."

"You never even knew my dad."

Hugh's expression says otherwise. I look from him to Julie.

"He didn't know him," she confirms. "I told him and Gary about him being my biological father and how he abandoned me, but that's all."

"Perhaps I took matters into my own hands." His grin widens. "After all, his death ensured the inheritance was immediately available, didn't it?"

The door of the washer is digging into my back. I'm sure the spade is just bravado. He's not going to do anything with it. He's violent, yes, but covertly. Over the last few weeks, he's proven that. Things either get thrown around or he holds me against walls rather than lashing out at me. But, if I'm honest, what he says and how he makes me feel is more punishing than a fist in the face or a boot in the back.

I really need to find out what he means by saying he locked my dad in his garage. And I want to know whether Julie knows about any of this. Surely though, it's just another of Hugh's mind bending stories. Over the last months, he could have told me the sky was green, and I'd probably have believed him. I've fallen for so much other crap from him.

"His campervan was up for sale, wasn't it?" Hugh leans on the handle of the shovel, rocking front to back from the balls to the heels of his feet as he switches his gaze between me and Julie. His anger appears to have been replaced by some sort of amusement. Gritting my teeth, I long to wipe the sadistic grin clean off his face. I'll get my chance, if it's the last thing I do.

Unable to look at him, I nod. How does he know about Dad's campervan? What's he going to tell me?

"Well, I thought it was time that daddy-kins got exactly what he deserved."

"Deserved? What do you mean?"

"After how he'd treated Julie." He points at her. "And then, my thinking centred around the fact that if he was dead, Julie would have a claim on all that estate of his. Only she didn't, did she? Your dickhead brother put a stop to that."

"My brother? What's he got to do with anything?"

Shit. What the hell did Kieren know about all this? And for how long? If he knew anything about Julie, he's never uttered a word to me. Is there anyone I can trust? Anyone?

"I'll come back to brother dearest in a moment. Anyway, pleasant man, your father, wasn't he? Very trusting?"

"What did you do to him?" I glance at Julie. "Did you know about this?" I try to get to my feet, but as Hugh raises the spade from the floor, I cower back down.

"No. I didn't. Not a thing." She lowers her eyes, then raises them again. They're clear and I can see truth in them. "As far as

I knew, he'd committed suicide. But I thought it was apt, given it was what he'd driven my mother to do all those years ago."

"Only it wasn't suicide, was it?" Hugh smirks. "Not for dear-daddy, anyway. Lethal, them exhaust fumes, especially from an older vehicle locked inside a garage."

I stare at him as I recall the police telling us that the key had been snapped inside the ignition. This, they'd said, would have been Dad's way of ensuring he couldn't have second thoughts.- The campervan doors and the garage doors were locked, but I'd assumed dad had done that himself. I should have known that he wouldn't have knowingly left us.

"It was you. You killed my dad."

"Well, not entirely. I had a little help from someone else with a vested interest."

"Gary?" Julie's voice sounds strangled. "Gary helped you murder our dad?"

"How touching. Calling him our dad. He didn't want to know you, you stupid bitch. Anyway, I don't like the word murder. Let's call it assisted suicide, shall we? A far more pleasant term. All we did was put him out of his misery. We did him a favour, and you."

I'm silent for a moment, trying to take it in. "Which is what you've been trying to do to me." My voice is strangled. "Assisted suicide." And he has. Just over a more prolonged period. And using a different method.

"You can't prove anything Nicola. It's my word against yours. And who's going to believe you, given your current medical condition? It's all on record." His face breaks into a smile. "They might even investigate *you*. After all, you had plenty to gain from his death."

"I'll make sure she can prove it," Julie says. Thank God. She's definitely joined forces with me.

"Do you reckon?" He twists his torso to face her. "You'll be too busy serving a stretch for murder to be proving anything."

"What are you on about?"

"Nicola's murder. I'll make sure your prints are all over this spade after I've finished with it. And then obviously I'll be making a detailed statement, describing how you battered your half-sister to death in a fit of jealousy. I'll tell them how I did everything I could to stop you from hurting my wife."

I open my mouth to speak as I notice how dead his eyes are. He raises the spade again, above his head this time.

"Please... no." The words reverberate around my skull as the spade comes crashing onto it. And again. Then again. I don't know how many times he hits me, but eventually I don't feel the pain. Instead, I feel... nothing.

CHAPTER TWENTY FOUR

A faint glow from the streetlight casts shadows around where I'm laid. I'm bone cold. I try to raise my head from the floor. It's killing me. It feels like a youthful morning after a night on jagabombs and sambuca.

As my hand brushes the floor towards my head, it passes through a pool of liquid. I dip a finger into it and bring it to my nose, then my lips. It has a salty, irony taste – blood. Bile burns the back of my throat and I swallow it down. I raise my hand to the side of my head. There's an egg-size lump and my hair is matted with what must be blood. My blood. I squint in the darkness, trying to make sense of the shapes around me. I can hear what sounds like laboured breathing to the right of the table.

"Nicola?" A voice eventually whispers. "Are you awake? Are you alright?"

I struggle to place the voice at first. I seem to be enveloped in a peculiar sensation, like I'm not really here. Maybe I'm dead.

"Nicola?"

The events of before I was unconscious spool into my spinning thoughts. Hugh's crazed expression as he brought the spade crashing down on me. And again. And again. Thank God

217

it's Julie's voice rather than Hugh's. But where is Hugh? Maybe he thought he'd killed me, so he's made a run for it. God, I pray he's gone. I've got no fight left in me now. I can no longer defend myself against him. If he's still here, I might as well write my own death certificate.

"Yeah. I'm OK, I think. It's just my head." I get to my elbows and haul myself up against the fridge, rubbing again at my eyes. "How long have I been out?"

"I don't know." There's a rustle of clothing and the slide of Julie's weight against the floor as she drags herself from the wall towards where I'm slumped.

"Are you OK?" I ask her. "Where is he?"

As she reaches me, I see the whites of her eyes in the weak light. I hope I can trust her. "Tell me where he is." I feel the same as I have recently when my drinks have been poisoned with medication. Since I've got myself up to seated, I've come around some more. Head wounds always bleed a lot. With a bit of luck, he won't have done me as much damage as the blood suggests. "Switch the light on."

"I will in a minute." Julie's eyes don't leave mine. "But before that, I need to close the blinds." However, she doesn't move and instead, she reaches for my hand. "I did what I did for you Nicola. You're my sister." She tightens her grip around it. "Promise me we're in this together."

"In what together?" I close my eyes against the crushing pain. I can't tell whether it's affecting the inside or the outside of my head. All I know is that I'd better find some painkillers. Strong ones.

"You've got to promise me before I tell you."

Whatever she's done, it seems to have got Hugh out of here.- And I think I can trust her. I squeeze her hand in return. "I promise."

She rises unsteadily to her feet and staggers towards the window. She tugs the cord for the blind, plunging the kitchen into complete darkness apart from the cooker hood. Then she snaps the overhead light on, causing me to scrunch my eyes against its sudden glare. When I open my eyes, the first thing I see is severe bruising to Julie's arm and two spade-shaped gashes which are oozing with blood.

"Oh my God. Julie! What's he done to you?"

She glances at her wounds, and then towards the door which leads down to the cellar. There behind the table, lies Hugh, his head surrounded by a pool of blood, probably five times the size of the pool which I've generated. She slides down the wall, facing me.

"Oh my God! Is he...?"

Wide-eyed, she nods. She's trembling like a frightened child.

"How? What the hell happened?"

"He'd knocked you to the floor with that spade. You weren't moving. I honestly thought you were dead. Then he was going to do the same to me. He killed our dad Nicola. Who I know didn't want me, but he might have done in time, especially since your mum had gone. I'm sorry to say that. I'm sorry. I'm really sorry. I didn't know what to do. He was going to kill me. I thought he'd killed you. I only did what I had to do."

She goes on and on. She's delirious. Whilst I'm numb. I'm struggling to find any words. I can't seem to piece my thoughts together.

"Julie. Stop. Please. I need to think."

I need her to be quiet before my head explodes.

She stops talking and all falls silent for several moments. I take some deep breaths, trying to quell the pain.

"We need to call the police." For once in my life, I'm the voice of reason. Plus, I don't see that we've got a lot of choice.

"No. No. No. We can't. We really can't. Gary will tell them everything. *Everything*. He knows all about what Hugh was trying to do to you. And I was in on the plan with the tablets, and in on the plans about the money."

"Why Julie? Why didn't you just come to me? None of this would have happened if you hadn't been so..." I search for the right word but can't think straight as I gesture towards Hugh's lifeless body, unable to take my eyes away from the man who I thought I'd be with for the rest of my life. He's dead, and we can't handle this on our own.

"You owed me. But..." she says quickly re-composing herself. "But honestly, I didn't know what they'd done last year, in the garage, in the..."

Hugh's confession comes back to me with the force of a lightning bolt. He and Gary killed my father. How could Hugh lie in bed with me, knowing what he'd done?

And now he's dead on the floor. That's if he is dead. I should check but I can't move. Julie looks panic stricken and as though she can't get her breath in.

"What have I done?"

"Look, we've got mitigating circumstances Julie. All this will be OK. We'll have some questions to answer, there's bound to be a ton of them, but we'll get bail, maybe a suspended sentence at worst..."

"What makes you such an expert?" Her voice is the most normal since I've re-gained consciousness.

"Nothing. But it was all self-defence, wasn't it? He's the one who brought the spade into the house and threatened and attacked us with it."

"Maybe it will be OK for you, but how can it be for me? Gary will make sure I go down. You don't understand. Plus, it's me who's killed Hugh, isn't it? Not you. You can carry on living your privileged life, whilst I rot." She's throwing her hands around as she rants away, in the same way our dad used to. "You've always had everything, haven't you?" The bitter edge has returned to her voice. "Whilst I've had to scrap my way through life. I can't do it anymore. I can't go to prison. I just can't. Please Nicola. There must be another way out of this. I did it for you. To stop him. To save you." Her voice softens. "We're only just getting to know each other, aren't we?"

She's playing the sister card now. I'm not sure how I feel about that. In the weeks I've known her, I've never heard her talk so much. "OK. Julie. Just calm down for a minute. I need to think. And my head hurts."

Her silence barely lasts a moment. "I can't believe I've actually killed him. I've never killed anyone – I've never even seen a dead body. Oh God." She drops her head into her hands. "What am I going to do?"

"What are *we* going to do?" I crawl across the floor towards her and reach for her hand. "We're in this together." My head's suddenly not hurting quite so much. The shock of seeing Hugh's body must have somehow anaesthetised the pain.

"OK. So what are we going to do then?" Some of the panic appears to have drained from her, which is a relief for me too. We need to stay calm.

"Tell me exactly what happened Julie. We need to get this straight before we can plan what to do next. I remember the spade over my head." My hand instinctively reaches for it and I wince in pain. "Then - well nothing."

"He tried to do the same to me. I couldn't get away from him. He had me boxed in, there." She gestures to the corner of the kitchen, next to the cellar door. "He had the spade above his head, ready to knock me out, or whatever. Same as with you. I put my arm out to stop him. To protect my head. " She holds her arm out as she inspects it. "I might need stitches. I think you will too."

"You did well to get the spade off him. He could have easily killed both of us."

"I'm not sure how I did, to be honest. Somehow I managed to grab it as he swung for me. Then I rammed the handle back at him. Into his chest. It was enough to knock him off balance and he tripped backwards over the chair."

"Then what?"

"He dropped the spade as he fell." She steps towards the chair and turns it back onto its feet. "That was my moment to get hold of it. Properly hold of it before he got back up again." She's gasping for breath as she relays what happened. "I didn't know I could hit someone as hard as I have. I used to be a scrapper in the children's homes, but thought I'd got beyond all that.- However, once I started hitting him, I couldn't stop."

"I can tell." I glance across the room to where he's lying.- Perhaps I should feel something – grief, regret, or guilt, but I don't. Not a thing. I can't. Not after how he's treated me and what he's taken from me. "How many times did you hit him?"

"I don't know. All my pent up God knows what came tumbling out. That's the problem. If I'd hit him once, I could argue it was self-defence but, I carried on even after he was on the floor. He was probably dead, and I was still hitting him. What sort of person does that make me?"

"I don't know what to do." My teeth are chattering. "But what I do know is that we need to sort our injuries out before we do anything. And get ourselves cleaned up."

"Does that mean you're not going to ring the police?" Julie looks hopeful.

"I don't see how we can avoid ringing them, but we can stall until we decide how to handle this. I can't face being locked in a cell. Not in the state I'm in right now. We both need to get some painkillers down us." I crouch beside her. "If we ring the police, they'll definitely lock us up. Besides, I need to see my brother first."

"Can I see him too?"

I nod. "He'll know what to do, and he already knows about you according to what Hugh said. Us turning up there shouldn't come as too much of a shock."

"How will he know what to do?" Her expression suggests she doesn't believe me.

"I don't know. He just will." My brother's face makes its way through the pain and emerges in my mind. "He'll probably sort us a solicitor to speak to before we go to the police. Get some advice on what to say. Especially about how many times you've hit him."

"Any solicitor would tell us to turn ourselves in. They'll probably do it for us."

I'm surprised at how calm I've become now I know Hugh can't hurt me anymore. "Let's just give ourselves some breathing space whilst we work out what we're doing. Hugh's not exactly going anywhere, is he?"

Julie looks at his body, then back at me. "I can't believe what I've done to him. When Gary finds out, he'll..."

"He might not have to find out. Not the full truth, anyway. Like you said, we've only just found each other – as sisters, I mean."

That statement seems to jolt Julie out of her misery. She gives me what could be nearly described as a smile, and says, "I don't suppose you've got any brandy?"

I pour generous measures into two glasses, then we sit facing each other on the kitchen floor for ten minutes, lapsing between panic and silence as we bathe and soothe our respective cuts and bruises with wet tea towels and bags of frozen vegetables. To say I was unconscious not so long ago, I don't feel too bad.

"I can't look at him Nicola," she suddenly cries out.

MARIA FRANKLAND

"Then don't." I press two painkillers from the blister pack I found in the cupboard and pass them to Julie.

She takes them from me. "We need to move him."

I slop more brandy into our glasses, then follow her gaze, inclined to agree. But where? And how? And won't that just get us into more trouble? Other than my parents, I've never seen a dead body before. And knowing he was alive and swinging a spade just a short time ago...

"We'll get him into the cellar," I say after a few moments. "He'll be OK in there - just until we've seen Kieren and perhaps a solicitor too." As I say the words, part of me wonders if we could just leave him there. I mean, no one ever goes into the cellar.

That's it. We've got a plan. Of sorts, anyway. At least we're not going to get thrown into a cell. Not yet.

I drag the rug from the lounge into the kitchen and between us, we manage to roll Hugh onto it.

"I can't do it," Julie cries at one point.

"Yes you can. Remember, we're in this together."

We're already panting profusely. I look from the top of the steps into the dark void at the bottom. I think of my parent's things stacked down there. This bastard killed my father.

We begin dragging the fourteen-and-a-half stone of dead weight down into the cellar. Both of us are streaked with a mixture of sweat, fibres from the rug and blood – probably a mixture of my own, mingled with Hugh's.

Our puffing and grunting echoes around the concrete walls, as between us, we gradually inch him, a step at a time, three quarters of the way down. By now, my hands are slicked with his blood, as are Julie's. I glance at her and she looks back at me, and we lose our grip on him. He tumbles the rest of the way, landing with a sickening thud as his head slams against the

224

concrete floor. Bile rises in my throat again as I fight to regain my breath.

I should retreat up the steps and resist the urge to have a final look at him. Instead, I observe his face in the weak light, already knowing that this image will haunt me for the rest of my days. I married this man. I thought he loved me. Now he's dead.

Then, looking back up the steps, I observe the terror in the face of the woman who has abruptly become my sister. What an absolute mess.

CHAPTER TWENTY FIVE

"It's Gary." Julie hisses as we face each other across the kitchen. The look of terror returns to her face. Mine probably mirrors it.

"Well, we can't exactly answer the door, can we?" I hiss back.- "Just keep quiet for a minute. He'll go away."

"Hugh?" I hear his muffled voice from the porch. "Are you in there?"

"He's going to know someone's here," she whispers. "The lights are on. The cars are outside."

"Shh. He'll have to give up eventually."

"I wonder if he's been to my house. Shit. Nicola. What are we going to do?" She slides into a crouch against the wall.

I put my finger to my lips like a schoolteacher, and frown at her as I shake my head. If Gary gets even an inkling that we're in here, he'll force his way in, I'm certain of it. The image of the spade in the cellar alongside Hugh's body fills my mind. If Gary gets in, I'll have no hesitation in retrieving it. I'm reeling from the knowledge that they murdered my father. And all this time, I thought he'd rigged that hosepipe up himself.

"Come on." I jump as he shouts again. "Open up. I know you're in there."

I can hardly breathe as Gary repeatedly bangs on the door and both the kitchen and lounge windows. Several more minutes pass. His footsteps shuffle around outside and I wonder if he's ever going to give up.

"I'll be round at Julie's when you decide to talk to me." Gary bangs again on the door, then his footsteps die away around the side of the house.

"Shit. Does he have a key to your house?"

She nods.

What a daft question. Of course he has a key – they're in a relationship. I gave Hugh a key to this place within the first couple of weeks. Suddenly a wave of melancholy sweeps over me so powerfully it almost winds me. I can't bear to think back to last November. If only I could turn the clock back to before I responded to his message on that stupid dating app. I can't believe I'm thinking such trivial thoughts. Hugh's body is lying just feet beneath us. Both mine and Julie's lives could be in tatters here. She's been through enough in her life. God, what an absolute nightmare.

"Do you think he'll wait there long? At your house, I mean?"

She shrugs. "I don't know. What the hell do we do now?" She looks at me as though I have all the answers.

"We finish cleaning this place up. We clean ourselves up. Then we get out of here."

"Where to? And what if Gary gets to us on the way out?"

"Look, I don't know about you, but I can't face spending the night in a house where a dead body is lying in the cellar." The image of Hugh will not leave me. I doubt it ever will.

We both jump as there's another thumping at the front door.-

"Where's Julie?" Gary's yelling at the top of his voice from outside. "Open this door. I know you're in there."

"I wish he'd piss off," I whisper. "He's drawing attention to the house. If the police end up doing house to house the neighbours will remember him being here..."

It feels like an eternity before a car door bangs. Then I hear Hugh's phone ringing. Damn. It must still be in his pocket. What if his whereabouts can be traced through it? I wonder for a moment if we should retrieve it. Then I shake the thought away. I can't face going back down there and really, we just need to get out of here.

After a few minutes, the sound of a car engine roars and moments later, fades into the evening. I let a long breath out and Julie takes a sharp one in as though she's been holding it. "Thank God for that."

"Shall we stay at my house tonight?" Julie wipes at a bead of sweat that's rolling down the side of her face.

I shake my head. "It's too close to it all. Plus, Gary might come back."

"You're right. What about Kieren's?"

I think for a moment. Really, I'm not sure if I've got it together enough to see him straight away. "We should get some sleep first, get some of our strength back, and then go tomorrow."

"Perhaps we should go to a hotel." She cranes her neck towards the clock. It's after nine.

"Surely it's too late now?" I get to my feet to inspect my head in the mirrored door of the glasses cupboard. "Besides, how can we go anywhere, looking like we do?"

"We'll be fine after a shower," Julie replies. "It's only my arm and shoulder that show any injuries and you, well, just put a hat over it."

"I suppose we've nearly got this place cleaned up." I glance around. We've got through the bleach from both bathrooms, as well as the spare bottles and about twenty buckets of water.- We've hopefully removed all traces of what's happened here in the kitchen, but that doesn't solve the problem that Hugh's still lying dead in the cellar. I can't shake the thought that we could leave him there. Perhaps in time, he'll just rot. It is underground, after all. I could have the cellar door bricked up and plastered over. I don't say anything to Julie. The idea is barmy, even to me. Plus, he'd be missed. Of course he would. I've met none of his friends. I'm not sure he even had any, but Gary will definitely report him missing. Or his work will.

"We need to get ourselves cleaned up now." Julie glances towards the washing machine. "I suggest we get everything in there on a hot wash, go up for a shower and then have a final mop round before we go."

"I'll put them on a quick wash so we can take them with us, just in case."

She shivers. "I won't be wearing those clothes again. The outfit I wore to kill someone. No thanks. Can I borrow something? It'll have to be big and baggy on you to fit me though."

"We'll get rid of all these clothes in a bin or a skip somewhere then. But we need to get the blood out of them as best we can."

"I hope you've got some good washing powder." She laughs and it sounds alien amidst all this.

"You get in the shower first whilst I get somewhere for us to go booked on line."

"Somewhere which will have a night porter to let us in." She begins peeling her bloodied clothes from her body, flinching as she's forced to pass what's left of her sleeve over her injured arm.

"A night porter." I laugh now, despite the awfulness of it all.-
"You sound as though you've done this before. I'll bandage that
up for you before we set off."

It occurs to me again that perhaps Julie was in on Dad's death
too, but I shake the thought away. I can't cope with any more
tonight. Besides, she looked as shocked as I did to learn of what
Hugh and Gary did to him last year. Poor Dad. Although, for
now, I need to push these thoughts away too. One thing at a
time.

It's been several hours since the brandy and nearly
twenty-four hours since they forced the last sleeping tablet
onto me, so I feel alright to drive. Although driving under the
influence of something is the least of my worries, given the
predicament of a beaten, dead body on the floor of my cellar.

I've booked us into a twin room at the Forest Lodge Hotel.-
We've both packed clothes for several days. I've no idea
how long we can leave Hugh lying where he is without doing
something, or whether anyone will come looking for us, but I'm
so exhausted that I'll leave it until I've had a few hours sleep
before I try to make any decisions.

"Nicola. Wake up."

It feels as though I've only been asleep for five minutes. I open
one eye to find Julie sitting on the edge of her bed, staring at
me. It looks to be nearly dawn, so I must have been asleep for
some time. My head throbs and for a moment, I wonder where
I am and what Julie is doing here. Then, steam roller style, the
memory of what we've done to Hugh flattens itself over me.

"What's up? What's happened?" I sit bolt upright, grimacing
with the pain of my head injury. Despite this, I'm the most
alert I've been for a couple of months. After all, I'm free of all
the tablets my drink and food have been laced with. Clearly,

I've got the constitution of an ox to have withstood the vastly increased doses they've been inflicting on me. Eventually, though, I'm sure the medication would have compounded in my system, causing who knows what sort of harm. There might even be damage done already. I stare at Julie, still uncertain about trusting her.

"Nothing's happened. Not since we left the house, anyway. I'm just scared about it all Nicola." She's rocking back and forth as she speaks, as though trying to comfort herself. "I can't sleep – not without knowing what's going to happen."

Swinging my legs over the edge of the bed, I pat the mattress beside me. In a dutiful way, Julie sits at my side, and I drape an arm around her shoulder. She leans into me, like a younger sister would, and in this moment, for the first time, fury boils in me towards my father for being at the root of this. Why couldn't he have just faced up to his responsibilities? Or at the very least, afforded Kieren and me the chance to make our own minds up about Julie. As a child, Dad was my absolute hero. As a teenager, I could see his flaws, but he remained my hero, nevertheless. Now, it seems I didn't have a clue who he really was. Then my fury switches to Hugh and Gary for dragging Julie into all this. I have to believe this was the case. And I have to trust her now. It's the only way I can cope.

"Today we'll drive over to Kieren's," I tell her. "I'll ring down for some breakfast and then we'll check out."

"I don't know if I can face food after yesterday. Or Kieren."

"We've got to keep going. Look after ourselves... and each other." I add the last words as an afterthought. Seeing how Julie appears to be struggling, it's what she needs to hear. Even if it feels forced.

"Do you want to eat in here?" She gestures across the twin room.

"I don't want to go into the restaurant. Everyone will take one look at us and know what we've done." I pluck the menu from the side of the phone on the bedside table.

"What I've done, you mean."

"Like I keep telling you, Julie, we're in this together. You were honest with me last night and I'll never forget that." I'm suddenly transported back to my kitchen, seeing the pool of blood around Hugh's head and the splatters up the back wall.

"I should have been honest before though." Tears fill her eyes. "I hate myself for being part of it. For being such a coward and getting sucked into what they wanted me to do. I was greedy, and I was blind."

"You did the right thing in the end. You could have really landed me in it if you hadn't." I shudder to imagine the two of them having joined forces and it being my body lying in the cellar right now.

"Like I said, I've come to like you." She squeezes her eyes together as though trying to stem the flow of tears. "I've got so much utterly wrong and made so many awful mistakes."

I reach for her hand. "Stop it Julie. We can't change anything. All we can do now is go forwards."

"Yeah." She raises her eyes, the same as Dad's and Kieren's, to mine. "Let's just pray that's not to prison. I have to say though, I don't know how we're going to get out of this."

"Do you think they'll let us share a cell?" I half laugh, despite the dreadfulness of it all and try to focus on the room service menu in front of me. Even though it's now thirty-six hours since I last had a tablet forced down me, my head still feels as though an army of hammers is at work inside it. I reach into my bag for more painkillers and remind myself that being welted God knows how many times with a spade won't have done it many favours. If I were a cat, I would probably have used several of my nine lives in the months of my life that I've wasted with Hugh. And now he's dead.

"Are we really just going to leave Hugh – where he is?" Julie strides to the window and drags back the heavy curtains.

The early sunlight streams through the window, offering hope that today can't be anywhere near as dark as yesterday. In the brighter light, I notice the streaks of blood on my pillow.

"I don't know what else to do." I lean back against the headboard of my bed. "But now that I've had some sleep, I'm thinking that we should have probably reported what had happened straight away to the police. We've definitely made things far, far worse for ourselves."

"We'd have been locked up though, without a doubt, like you said. In a stinking cell all night. And neither of us was in a fit state, were we?"

"We'd have been locked up to start with, yes. Until we could prove that we acted in self defence." I scrunch my eyes against the vision of Hugh's face, which suddenly floods my brain.- I knew as soon as I looked at it last night that it would be imprinted on my mind forever.

"We shouldn't have cleaned the place, should we?" Julie stares at the normality continuing beyond our hotel room through the window. "Or put him in the cellar."

She says *put him in the cellar* like it was an easy task. I look around the room as though to centre myself. My gaze rests on a painting of the nearby woods. In here I feel untouchable but once we get back out there... "It was to get rid of our blood more than his. If ours is found, it's curtains for us. As it stands, we might even be able to make it look like a break in."

"Do you think we bleached it well enough?"

I shrug. "I hope so. My DNA will be all over the place anyway – I live there. But blood is another matter."

"He was out after three hits." Julie's voice is full of anguish. "Why did I keep on smacking him with the spade? What the hell is wrong with me?"

"You've been suppressing it for many years," I tell her.

"I should have stopped. That I kept on smacking him will make it look like I attacked him, rather than the other way round."

"Come on, let's get some food, then we can get to Kieren's." I thrust the menu towards Julie. "Like I said he'll know what to do for the best."

⑦"Why? Has he dealt with the aftermath of murders before?" She looks like she might laugh at my faith in Kieren, which admittedly, is somewhat unfounded.

"Now that's what I call a car." Kieren's eyes widen as he looks past me at the Porsche. "How long have you had that?"

"Never mind the car. Are you going to ask us in, or what?" I glance behind me. For the entire journey, I've been expecting us to be pulled over and to have handcuffs snapped on us before being interrogated about the dead body in my cellar.

The situation keeps leaving my mind for a few seconds, but only for a few seconds. Then the image comes back to clobber me. I guess, in time, the seconds will turn into minutes and maybe even into hours.

Perhaps we should just make a run for it. Maybe we don't have to go back. Ever. It crosses my mind not even to tell Kieren. Not straightaway, anyway. Julie's clothing covers her injuries, and mine are largely hidden by the wide headband I'm wearing. I just want a day of normality. I don't want to talk about Hugh, about Gary, or about anything that's happened. Not really. I just want to spend time with my brother and sister-in-law. Be normal. God, I'd give anything for things to be normal.

"Are you going to introduce us to your friend?" Kieren asks. I glance at him. Clearly, he has no idea who she is. He knows of Julie but perhaps won't be expecting her on his doorstep straightaway. I can't believe he can't see the likeness of himself, or even Dad in her. Mind you, I didn't have a clue who she was until yesterday, either.

Claire appears behind him, smiling. I can always count on Claire. "Is this...?"

I nod. "Kieren. Meet your sister. Julie. Kieren. Kieren. Julie." I point from her to him and back again.

The smile fades from his face. "You've got to be joking." He's turned as pale as Claire and she's the one suffering from morning sickness. "What the hell have you brought her here for?"

Damn. I should have suspected we might get this reception. "Kieren - do you not think Julie's been rejected enough?" I cross my arms as I face my brother over the threshold of their doorway. "None of this has been her fault. And we also need to discuss why you didn't see fit to tell me about her the moment you found out."

"She's right Kieren." Claire lodges herself in front of him.- "Come in Julie. You're very welcome and it's lovely to meet you. I'm your sister-in-law, by the way. Take no notice of him. He'll be fine."

Thankfully, Kieren steps to the side to let us pass. "I didn't mean..." It's the first time I've seen Kieren grappling for words. "It's just that..."

"Leave it." I say, fighting Nellie off as she goes bananas at my feet, although I have to say, I appreciate her welcome more than ever.

Chapter Twenty Six

I t feels somehow wrong to be sitting in the kitchen watching Claire pour tea into mugs. We're doing something so ordinary, whilst Hugh is lying dead. His bloodied body fills my mind for what feels like the millionth time since last night. Julie must be going through the same hell – she was, after all, the one who finished him off. Big time.

"It's good to see you sis."

I frown at Kieren and turn my head towards Julie, who is sitting at my side. Hopefully, he'll get the drift from my expression that I want her to feel included, and it's best not to call me *sis* in front of her. Our entire dynamic has shifted. As far as I'm concerned, he and I need to make up for what Dad didn't do – emotionally, financially and otherwise. And it shocked me to learn last night that Kieren has known about Julie since Dad died. I'll get to the truth of that shortly.

"Are you both OK?" Claire lowers herself to the chair. "I've filled Kieren in on everything." Clearly Kieren didn't fill Claire in on everything before that though. She'd have told me yesterday if she had known anything. Namely Gary's visit to their house

236

last year. If Hugh hadn't let it slip last night, I would never have found out about Kieren keeping me in the dark.

"What I want to know is - why the hell you didn't come to me sooner?" His eyes blaze as he glares at me. Now he and Julie are together in the same room, they look even more like each other than I originally thought. As Claire looks from one to the other, I can tell she is probably thinking the same thing.

"To be fair, I was completely out of it."

"Claire said he's been doubling and tripling your tablets. Bastard." He interlaces his fingers and stretches his arms out in front of himself, cracking his knuckles at the same time. "He'll wish he'd never been born when I catch up with him."

Julie shifts in her seat and lowers her gaze. She's had little opportunity to be part of the overdosing campaign Hugh instigated against me, but I expect she's spiked me when she's made me coffees. Thinking back, she had every opportunity on at least three or four occasions. For now, I'd better keep quiet about the extent of her involvement in what they were doing to me. If I were to tell Kieren, he'd probably throw her out on her ear. And right now, I'm relieved that we're here. At my brother's house, I can almost pretend that nothing's happened. For a few seconds anyway.

"I shouldn't have been on those tablets in the first place," I tell Kieren. "But Hugh had literally frogmarched me to the doctors." I feel pathetic now, admitting to the control I've allowed some man to exert over me. "He really led me to believe I was going insane. Conversations I recalled, that he said we hadn't had. Decisions he said I'd made that I couldn't remember."

"You could have answered my calls, Nicola. You needn't have gone through any of this. I'd have got you out of that house in an instant if you'd told me what was happening."

I notice he's directing everything at me. He's avoided eye contact with Julie since we all sat down. And he's had lots more time than me to get used to the idea of her being our sister.

"I thought Claire had explained everything about why I didn't." I glance at her. She's prodding around at the slice of lemon floating around in her mug. I don't envy her sickness.- The side effects of the tablets were bad enough, so I know how she feels.

"She did. But maybe I want to hear it from you."

"Hugh had got hold of my phone and blocked your number.- Then locked me out of my social media accounts."

"Not that you ever go on them anyway." Kieren shakes his head. "I've tried everything Nicola. I've lost count of the number of times I've been to your house. At all times of the day as well. Doesn't Hugh go out to work through the day? He answers the door every bloody time."

It sounds strange now, hearing Hugh talked about in the present tense. "We'll come back to that Kieren. There are more important things to discuss."

Claire's hand flits to her belly and she gives me a knowing look.

"Firstly, congratulations." I reach across the table and squeeze Kieren's arm. Under normal circumstances, I'd have hugged him by now, but with Julie looking on, it doesn't seem appropriate. We're certainly not a conventional family anymore.

"Yeah, thanks. It would have been nice to have told you as soon as we found out."

"I'm sorry. I'd have liked to have known too. Really, I would."

"You're my only family Nicola. I had no one else to tell. No one who matters anyway."

"That's not true, is it?" I glance from Kieren to Julie, then back again. "How long have you known we had a sister, anyway?" There it is. Right at him.

"Not that long actually," Kieren replies.

"I only found out last night that Kieren already knew about Julie." Claire says. "If I'd known, I'd have told you Nicola."

"I know. I was just thinking that." And I do believe her.

Now it's Kieren's turn to look uncomfortable. However, he still shoots Claire a look which seems to say, *your loyalties are supposed to be with me.* I know my brother almost as well as I know myself. Even though I haven't seen him for months. He twirls his thumbs around and around each other as he stares down at his hands.

"How long?"

I've never seen Julie so quiet as she watches on. This must be seriously strange for her. I don't know whether she's watched Kieren from a distance anywhere near as much as she's admitted to watching me over the years, but this is the first time she'll have been so close to him. And to both of us at the same time. As well as that, on some level, she's waiting for us to make all the decisions about what comes next – for instance, what will happen to her. Although I've agreed that we're in this together, Julie was the one who actually killed Hugh. However, I can't lose sight of the fact that without her shifting her allegiance, it could easily be me lying in that cellar.

"A month or so before Mum died," Kieren finally replies. "I think she wanted to make peace with herself."

"That was good of her," I say. "She wanted to be at peace herself, but burden us. And it's something we should have been told years ago." It's the first time I've felt anger towards Mum.- And I cannot believe they just left Julie to rot. Especially knowing she'd been taken into care. It's not as if they didn't have the means to support her. However, one of Mum's biggest faults was always that she cared too much about what other people might think. "What did she say to you?"

239

"Just that Dad had an affair when we were younger, that the woman had been quite young herself, had a daughter, then committed suicide."

"Kieren." Claire and I echo each other. He can be so blunt, and this is Julie's mum he's referring to.

"It's alright," Julie says. "I know the score. Though it sounds like it should have been *you* I hated more than Nicola." She glares at Kieren, her brow furrowed. "You're the one who kept quiet even after your mum told you about me." She points at him now, her voice rising. "Which means you're the one who got in the way of me receiving any inheritance. Whilst the two of you..." She slaps the heel of her hand on the table. "Have you any idea at all how hard life has been for me?" Her words echo around the kitchen. "Have you?"

"To be fair," Claire says gently. "Kieren firstly had his mum's death to cope with, and then the aftermath of his dad's suicide. If circumstances had been different..."

"Dad's death wasn't even a suicide." I can be blunt as well. Kieren needs to know, and the best way is just to come out with it.

"*What?*" It's Claire and Kieren's turn to echo each other. They both stare at me as I search for the right words to impart what I've found out. I still haven't got my own head around it. As I struggle to bring the words to the surface, Julie steps in, evidently calmer than a moment ago.

"They got wind that he was selling his campervan." She fiddles with the edge of the tablecloth.

"Who did?" Kieren lifts his glasses and rubs under his eyes. He looks knackered. I wonder if he came back from his course late last night or first thing this morning. Either way, he doesn't look to have slept much. *Last night.* It's almost eerie to recall it. Hugh was still alive, and we weren't potentially facing being locked in a cell, followed by a prison sentence.

"Hugh and my partner Gary, who I believe you've met. They're brothers. Twins. I think your dad went to where Hugh worked. He worked at a dealership."

I notice she uses the past tense when she talks about Hugh.- However, no one seems to pick up on that.

"Met? You've actually *met* Gary?" Claire turns to Kieren. "When?"

"I'll come back to that." He looks at Julie. "And?"

"Hugh and Gary locked your dad in the campervan in his garage. They locked the garage too. They'd snapped the key in the ignition then made it look like he'd rigged the hose himself."

Kieren's face seems to narrow as he surveys Julie. I wonder if he's about to lose his temper. "And you knew about this?"

"Of course I didn't." Her voice is small, but her words are fast. "I knew about Gary coming to see you after your dad's, our dad's death, but I had no idea they were to blame for it all. Not until last night. There's no way I'd have ever kept quiet about something like that."

"She's telling the truth," I tell him. "I was there last night when Hugh told us."

Everyone falls silent for a couple of moments.

"They've got away with killing my father for all these months." Kieren's face is grey now. "I should have known Dad wouldn't..." His voice trails off. "And then the bastard had the brass neck to turn up at my door. Thank God you weren't here when he came." Kieren turns to Claire. "The man's obviously mental. I couldn't bear it if it had been you having to face him."

"What did he say to you?"

"He told us he was here on Julie's behalf." Kieren nods in her direction. "Wanting her share of the estate. He was making all sorts of threats. Nasty piece of work, isn't he?"

"You don't need to convince me," I say. "I've experienced him first hand."

"If you'd come to us directly." Kieren looks at Julie properly for the first time since we arrived. He's very good at avoiding eye contact, especially in times of stress. "Things could have been different. But as far as I could tell, you'd sent your henchman and I would never have dealt with him, or you, after that."

"I'd had enough rejection in my life." Julie stares into her cup. "I couldn't take any more. That's why I let Gary come here. Besides, I hated the two of you, especially Nicola. As far as I was concerned, she had everything I should have had. Parents who loved her, a brother, a great house, a good life." She gulps in a breath of air, as though she's run out of it. "Obviously, things have changed now."

"Have they? How?" Kieren's voice is marble-hard towards her.

"We've got to know each other more," I reply. "And Julie's told me the full story Kieren. She didn't have to, but she finally felt she could trust me."

"You've always been a crap judge of character..."

"Look. Give it a rest. I need to tell you about something else that has happened." The words are out before I plan to say them. I have to ask my brother for help. Where else can I turn?

"What?" Kieren jerks his head up.

However, the expression on Claire's face conveys that she's heard quite enough already.

"Look. It's terrible. Really terrible. We really don't know what to do."

"Just tell me Nicola." Kieren sounds like Dad now.

I look at Claire, debating whether I should subject her to this conversation with her being pregnant and all. It might be too much. Perhaps I should have spoken to Kieren privately.

"I said tell me."

Julie and I look at each other.

"Hugh's dead." Julie's voice is flat and she once more looks down at the floor.

"What? Dead? How?" Kieren's words pump out, one after the other. I haven't seen him look this shocked for a long time.

"I thought he'd killed her." Julie slowly raises her gaze from the tiles towards me. "Show them your head Nicola."

I peel the headband away, flinching as it sticks to the dried blood. I haven't even tried to get a hairbrush through it.

"Oh my God." Claire clutches Kieren's arm. "I told you not to go back there Nicola. Why the hell didn't you listen to me?"

"And he was going to kill me too." Julie inches her arm from the sleeve of her cardigan, then tugs the sleeve of her t-shirt back to reveal the full extent of her injuries. "But I managed to get the spade off him."

"The spade! Bloody hell." Kieren stands from his seat and walks over to the sink.

"It was either him or us. I had no choice."

"What do you mean? You killed him?" Claire gasps as she puts her cup down. "You've got to be joking."

Julie both shakes her head and hangs her head at the same time. "I had to."

"So - where is he now?" Kieren grips the edge of the sink as he twists back around to look at us. "Do the police know?" He drops his cup into the washing up bowl. "God, I think I need something stronger than this."

"We-we got him into the cellar." Julie looks towards the cabinet in the corner of the kitchen. "I know it's early," she directs her question to Claire. "But I could do with something stronger too."

"And he's definitely...?"

Kieren nods at Claire who rises and heads in the direction of the cabinet.

"Yes. He's definitely dead."

"Are you absolutely sure?" Claire slides three glasses onto the table and sets the bottle of brandy down. I bet she feels like one herself right now. "Did you check his pulse, his breathing?"

"We didn't need to," Julie replies.

"We don't know what to do." I echo my earlier comment, looking at my brother. He's got to help me with this. I can't do it on my own anymore.

"It was self defence." Claire slops brandy into the glasses and wrinkles her nose. "God, this stuff stinks. You can prove it was."

"Maybe, but it happened last night, didn't it? We panicked. We even cleaned the kitchen in case anyone got in. His brother's been hanging around."

"Why on earth did you clean the kitchen?" Claire looks from me to Julie, wide-eyed. "Like I said, it was self defence. Why didn't you call the police? Straight away?"

"I don't know. It was my idea. I just panicked." Tears I didn't realise I was crying drip onto the table. "I wanted the whole thing to go away. And I wasn't thinking straight. All those tablets have really messed me up."

"Shit. Shit Shit. Claire's right. Why didn't you just call the bloody police?" Kieren strides back towards the table and grabs his drink. "It's utter madness."

I take a large swig of the brandy which burns the back of my throat. "After the time I've had with Hugh since we got married, I honestly don't know what I'm doing anymore." The heat of the brandy as it slides into my stomach is comforting. "And I was scared of Julie going to prison. She's spent her life in children's homes, as it is Kieren. We owe her."

He closes his eyes. "Well. What a fucking mess."

"It's not too late to report it." Claire wraps her fingers around her mug. I'd do anything to swap places with her. To have a happy marriage, to be expecting a baby, and to drink tea in the kitchen without all this going on. How the hell did my life get to this?

"I'd have more chance of getting off with it than Julie," I say.- "Or getting a more lenient sentence. I'm the one with the motive against him, and with that, the more mitigating circumstances."

"You can get those thoughts out of your head," Kieren snaps.- Julie seconds his opinion.

"Like I said Kieren. We owe her. Perhaps it's the right thing to do?"

"There must be another way through this." Kieren drums the side of his glass with his fingers. "And we'll find it."

"I think we should get some advice." Claire stares out of the window as a bird lands on the birdbath outside. "See a solicitor or something?"

"They can't do that Claire." Kieren seems calmer now he's got a brandy in his hand. "Solicitors are legally bound to report a crime that's unknown to the police. Especially one like a murder."

"So don't admit to anything then. Just get some advice." Claire continues to stare out of the window as though it's preferable to looking at us. I feel guilty dumping this on them both, but I've nowhere else to turn.

"But how can we do that without admitting to anything?" My voice rises several octaves. I can't see a way out.

No one says anything.

"We can't." I answer my own question. "Perhaps we should just take ourselves abroad or something. Before someone finds him in the cellar. Or maybe they might never find him."

"Sounds good to me." Julie sniffs.

"Great, so we're having a baby and you're on about buggering off abroad." Kieren slams his glass on the table. "Well, thanks a lot Nicola."

"Look, there's a way here. We've just got to find it." Claire brings her gaze back into the room. "Is anyone likely to report him missing?"

"Well, Gary, his brother, came looking for him at my house last night. He's probably the main reason I panicked so much. He'll probably report him missing at some point. Or his work will."

"Gary." Kieren looks at Julie as though he blames her. Maybe he's right to. I just can't think straight.

"Gary who helped murder our dad and then came around demanding money and threatening us before Dad was even cold in the ground?"

"He's totally got away with everything so far, hasn't he?" I shoo the dog away with my foot. In the scheme of things, the last thing I feel like doing is playing with the dog.

"When you tell the police what Hugh admitted to before he died – well, that adds to the self-defence – it builds a stronger case." Claire looks as though she'd prefer us to take our chances with the police instead of considering any sort of Plan B.

"They've no proof of anything. Hugh's dead. It's their word against Gary's. However..." Kieren rests his chin on his hand, looking like he might be concocting something.

"Have Gary and Hugh ever had any issues with one another?" He directs the question at Julie. I suppose she knows them far better than I do.

She shrugs. "I guess so. They're twins, and are always competing against one another. Well, they always have as far as I can gather. There was lots of jealousy, mostly about material things and especially money."

"Gary hated me," I add. "He's even threatened me a couple of times."

"Right, so from that, we could give Gary a motive." Kieren necks the last of his brandy.

246

"What are you on about?" Claire's forehead lines appear to deepen even further.

"Did you say Gary turned up at your house last night?" Kieren sits up straighter in his chair. The dog retreats to her basket, clearly accepting that no one will play with her.

"Ye-es... Why?"

My brother has got the same look on his face as when he was cooking up some master plan to get away with something when we were kids.

"And he was only *outside* your house? You didn't let him in?"

"Of course not. How could we with his brother sprawled dead across the kitchen floor? And yeah, he was hanging around for quite a while."

"It was definitely him? You're absolutely sure?" Kieren's expression is difficult to read, but I'm hopeful. He's clearly got something in mind.

"Yes, he was shouting and banging. And then he went to my house," replies Julie. "It adjoins the back of Nicola's. We heard his footsteps go up and down the staircase."

"He was probably in there for at least ten minutes," I add. "Why? What are you thinking?"

CHAPTER TWENTY SEVEN

Between us, we've got to get a move on with this before anyone can change their mind. Yes, Nicola and Julie could go to the police and tell them everything. It's commendable that Nicola is willing to take the blame and yes, there would be mitigating circumstances. But the fact that Nicola and Julie cleaned the whole place with bleach, concealed Hugh's body and then locked the house up for the night will not go in their favour. Panic or no panic. It will come across as premeditated. Even I can see that and I only work with computers.

I keep coming back to the same conclusion. Gary needs to atone for what he did to our father. Hugh's had his comeuppance, but there's no way I can allow Gary just to walk away from what he's done. And I'll never forget when he turned up at our door last year.

"Kieren Donnelly?" He'd looked like someone who might be selling double glazing as I opened the door to him. I nearly said *no thank you* and closed it again, but there was something in his tone that intrigued me.

"Who's asking?"

"I was sorry to hear about your dad," he continued. "It must be pretty shit, him dying in those circumstances. And so soon after your mum as well."

"What the hell do you know about that?" I stepped out of the door onto the garden path, closing the gap between us. Something about him warned me that he might try to force his way in. "Who are you?"

"A friend of a friend. Well, a friend of your sister actually."

"Nicola?" I stared at him. Stocky and blonde, he wasn't her usual type. Jason had been lanky and dark-haired.

"Wrong. Try again."

"I know of a half-sister. But I don't actually know her."

"Oh, you will be knowing her. Julie. That's her name. Juuuleee." The way he'd elongated the syllables had really irritated me.

"She's been well and truly shafted by your family, in my opinion. And I think it's about time she was recompensed."

"What are you on about?"

"You and Nicola are sitting pretty with your bulging bank accounts, so what about her?"

"What about who?"

"Julie. She's grown up with jack shit. Are you going to see her right out of your old man's estate, or what?"

"My parent's money is being divided between me and Nicola." I couldn't believe I was even having this conversation with a complete stranger on my own doorstep. With his scuffed shoes and stains on his trousers, I don't know how I'd mistaken him for a salesman.

"This is your chance to do the right thing then, isn't it?"

"Don't you come round here, telling me what I should or shouldn't do. This is none of your business."

"Actually, that's where you're wrong. Julie's my partner."

I stared at him, resisting the urge to tell him that Julie was really scraping the bottom of the barrel with him. "That doesn't mean you can turn up at my house and start making demands on my parents' estate. Tell her to go through the proper channels if she believes she's entitled."

"She can't afford to go through the proper channels. She hasn't got a pot to piss in."

I saw something in his face then. Desperation for money, combined with determination and greed.

"Lovely way with words, haven't you? Look, I'm not having this conversation. Not with you, anyway."

"You bloody well are." He stepped closer to me so our faces were almost touching. I stepped back and looked at him. He clearly meant business. I'm not a violent man, but I could have happily wrapped my hands around his fat neck at that moment.

"I want you off my property. Now. Or I'm calling the police."

If his visit had descended into violence in front of the neighbours, I'd have never heard the end of it from Claire.- Thank God this arsehole had turned up whilst she was visiting her mother.

"Your property," he echoed. "We'll be seeing about property.- You haven't heard the last of me. Or of Julie."

"She'll not get a penny out of me," I shouted after him, thankful beyond belief that he was leaving. He must have sensed that he wasn't going to get anywhere with me.

"She'll be getting half that estate." He turned back from the garden wall. "You watch this space."

And then, nothing. I couldn't regret anything more than not warning Nicola, or even telling her about Julie, but at the time she was only just hanging in there. She was already reeling from Mum's death. Then Dad's supposed suicide had totally floored her.

You could have scraped me off the floor when next, bloody Jason walked out on her. Right when she needed him the most. He could have hung in there until she was over the worst of it all. Or at the very least, he could have ensured she didn't find out the truth about his affair and bloody baby until she was stronger.

So, if I'd have laid the news of a half-sister and a potential claim on our estate, coupled with the threats Julie's loser boyfriend was making, I'd have possibly been responsible for pushing Nicola right over the edge. I didn't even tell Claire as I couldn't be certain that she'd keep it to herself. She and Nicola have always been close.

But it turned out to be Hugh that sent Nicola over the edge. Now I know I should have been more insistent about seeing her on the occasions I turned up there – forced my way in, if that's what it took. I hate myself now for being such a wimp and swallowing the lies Hugh was telling me. Nicola wouldn't just cut me off and block me from contacting her.

Instead, I not only got wrapped up in my own shit, but I positively buried my head in it. I didn't protect Nicola, so now I owe her more than ever. And the more I've spoken to Julie today, the more I feel like I owe her too. We can pull this off – I know we can. And if this is what I've got to do to make up for my lack of action so far, then so be it.

When I arrive at Nicola's house, I'm unable to recall the journey, apart from when I pulled over to have a check in with myself. I've gone over and over in my mind what I've got to do here. I've given myself plenty of opportunity to back out, but no, it has to be done. And it has to be today, before anyone thinks to report Hugh missing. It needs to be sooner rather than later, anyway. I've been told how nasty a decomposing body can smell and I'd rather encounter this one whilst it's only a day after the death.

The parallel streets where Julie and Nicola's houses sit back-to-back at the end, so I drive up and down them both, checking for CCTV. When I'm satisfied there is none, I park several doors up from Nicola's and slide my hands into gloves. It's early afternoon and thankfully, there doesn't seem to be a soul around. There will be in an hour or so though, when it gets to school pick up time. I need to get a move on.

No one will be looking for my car on any of the surrounding CCTV, and scrutiny of cameras should be concentrated around last night anyway – the time of his death. They can usually tell how long someone's been dead for nowadays.

I slip from my car around the corner to Julie's house and let myself in, after checking all around me that the street is still empty, and no one is watching me from surrounding windows.

Julie has told me where I can find a pair of Gary's trainers and a shirt, which he's left hanging in her wardrobe. She says he wore it last time they were out together. I take a deep breath, and as I ascend the unfamiliar stairs, my heart pumps harder with each rise. I hope to God I don't get seen. Or caught. Even I know that the chance of pulling this off is slim, but I've got to try.

Julie also suggested I look inside the toiletry bag in the bathroom. There could be a hair left in his comb or something else with his DNA.

And there is. There are several blonde hairs dangling from a comb in the bag. There's also what looks like a chewed fingernail wedged in the top of a set of nail clippers. That may well be enough.

I open the front door a crack, checking the street again before I dare to leave. I lock up and head around to Nicola's front door. So far, so good. But this part of my plan is the part I'm dreading the most. I slide my feet from my shoes and socks and leave them on Nicola's doormat. Next, I slide my feet into clean socks and Gary's trainers, which are a size larger than mine. I hurry towards the cellar door in the corner of the kitchen, scattering the hair and dropping the chewed up nails onto the lino as I go.

My breath comes in sharp rasps as I glance around the kitchen. No one would ever suspect that someone had been killed in this room last night. I feel certain that forensic searches will show up blood traces somewhere, but to the naked eye, it looks as though they'd need to do a damn good search for it.

My eyes fall onto the photo of my parents. Normally, misery would swell within me, but after all this, anger has replaced it. "This is all your fault." I point at the picture. My voice sounds hollow in the silence of my sister's kitchen. She'll probably never be able to live here again after this. I don't suppose she'd want to anyway.

In the distance I hear the nearby school, the sound of a playground collective. It reminds me of the child that will soon be in my world. I can't get this wrong. Any of it.

Wrapping my scarf around my mouth and nose, I steel myself to enter the cellar. I open the door as slowly as when I'd have crept downstairs for biscuits as a kid. Hugh's outline is visible before I even flick the light on, arms and legs stuck out at odd angles from the heap at the bottom of the stairs, which is sprawled in a pool of what looks like blood. Or who knows what else? My stomach gurgles. What if I'm sick? I can't be. It's all over for me if my DNA gets found down here. I take a deep breath. Mind over matter. Mind over matter. Thankfully, I can't smell anything because of my thick scarf, but I'm holding my breath just in case. I creep down the stone staircase, as though wary of waking him.

I trample around at the side of Hugh's body like a child splashing in a muddy puddle, ensuring the soles of Gary's trainers are completely coated with Hugh's blood. So far, so good.

I peer over at the other side of his head which reveals where his skull has been stoved in. After how he has treated my sister and what he did to my father, he had this coming to him. Bastard.

I really hope I can pull this off. I rub Gary's shirt over Hugh's blooded head. It's brushed cotton so should leave some fibres behind. The spade is lying alongside him – exactly where Julie said it would be.

"I didn't wipe it. I didn't wipe the handle!" She had become hysterical when I had got them both to take me through the entire story, beginning to end, and then back over it again, so I knew exactly what I would be dealing with.

"There'll be no sign of your prints by the time I've finished with it," I assured her. It was down to me now. They were both looking to me to sort this out. I had to stay in the moment – there could be no looking ahead or considering what might go wrong with the plan that was unfolding as they relayed the whole sorry story.

"But we used all the bleach." Nicola seemed calmer than Julie somehow, but then I guess she wasn't the one who'd actually killed someone, even though she was considering taking the blame for it. Plus, she still seemed somewhat dazed, which might be expected after weeks of being drugged up. What sort of deranged arsehole would do that to a woman? Someone who'd placed all her love and trust in him as well.

"There's some bleach under the sink." Claire had reached for Nicola's hand and squeezed it. That was enough to convince me she was on board with us. We'd spoken privately upstairs, and she'd been forced to accept that she couldn't talk me out of what I was planning to do.

"I don't know why you don't just go to the police," she had pleaded to start with. "Don't do this Kieren. Please! What if you get caught?"

"I won't get caught."

"What about me and the baby?"

"He killed my dad." I'd replied. If I'm honest, that was my main driver. But protecting my sisters from prison was a close second.

I stuff the bloodied shirt and shoes into a carrier bag before heading back up the cellar steps. I soak a cloth with the bleach from our house over the sink and wipe the spade's handle with it. Then I return to the doormat and slide my feet back into my own shoes. Once again, I steel myself, this time to leave. I'm trembling from head to foot as I check both ways from the front door before locking up. There's no concealing this spade as I stride back to the car, so I have to make sure no one sees me. I'm pretty sure I wouldn't be able to contain my anxiety either if anyone was to speak to me.

I lay the spade on top of a refuse sack in front of the back seats and dump the carrier bag on top of it. Part one done. Part two done. Now for the riskiest bit.

Julie was right. It's a shithole around here. No wonder Hugh and Gary were in league to get their hands on what they undoubtedly thought was easy money from our estate. It's probably stupid, carrying this out in broad daylight. However, it seems to be the only time I can do it. Before I set off, Julie made sure Gary was definitely at work, so I hope I'm in the clear on that front. I can't double check anything, as I've left my phone at home. I can't risk that being picked up and giving me away.

255

It's whether anyone sees me that I've got to be most wary of. Particularly since judging by the state of this neighbourhood, there'll be a lot of people at home. Looking at the disrepair of the houses and their gardens, people who live on this street wouldn't know a day's work if it bit them on the arse.

I need to put the bag and spade where neither Gary nor anyone else will find them for at least a few days. Julie and Nicola are going to stay with us long enough for their injuries to heal, and then Nicola's going to go home and 'find' Hugh.

When the police speak to both her and Julie, they are going to tell of the so-called 'hostilities' that existed between the brothers, and Julie's going to make a statement to verify that Gary has confessed what he's 'done' to Hugh.

Ultimately, it will probably be down to a jury to convict him, but I'm hopeful that we've got everything straight enough. Then a lot of it will hinge on Nicola and Julie keeping their cool and sticking to their stories.

There's no car outside the house next door to Gary's. A sign, Julie assured me, that the neighbour will be out. Apparently, he goes nowhere on foot, not even to the local shop.

Again, I glance around for CCTV – but as I suspected, none of the houses appear to have it, so I step from the car which I've parked a few houses away.

I've done nothing like this before. As clean as a whistle, that's me. Which was probably why Claire was so shocked and distressed when I told them all what I was planning.

My heart is pumping like the bass in a nightclub as I slide the bag and spade from the back of the car before heading up the tunnel that runs between Gary's terrace and his neighbour's. My footsteps reverberate around the concrete as I head into the overgrown yard at the back. I'm pleased to spot a dilapidated shed in the corner. Julie couldn't remember whether it was still here. Its door is hanging off and both its windows are smashed, which convinces me it isn't a place Gary would frequent. Perfect – at least I hope so. I shove the items behind the wreckage of a fridge and prepare to make a run for it.

Until I hear the slam of a car door close by. Too close by. I freeze against the wall of the shed. There's an echoey voice which sounds as though it's coming from the tunnel from which I've just emerged. "Yeah. It's me. You're really pissing me off now Hugh. Call me back, will you? Straight away."

Shit. Gary's literally yards from me. And he's looking for Hugh. I stand as still as a gravestone, praying that he heads straight into his house through the back door. He doesn't. Instead, he's pacing around the yard. If he looks in here, I don't know what I'm going to do. I could just pretend I've been lying in wait for him, having only just learned how he's treated my sister. But that wouldn't explain why I didn't jump out on him straight away. Shit. It could be all over.

Julie promised he was at work. I just hope we can trust her – I'm still not convinced. But there's no way I'm going to allow any of this shit to be pinned on Nicola.

I hold my breath. Gary's right at the side of the shed. There are just inches between us. I can't see him, but I can picture him – the plump piece of shit with a pathetic blonde cowlick. He could do with a good kicking after how he's behaved, but he's going to get much more than that. At least, I hope he is. That's if it all goes to plan.

"Where the fuck are you? I came to yours last night, and again this morning. You know I don't like being messed about like this Julie. Ring me back. I mean it. You'll regret it if you don't."

My breath seeps from me as Gary finally strides in the direction of the house, and I hear a key rattle in the lock.

For a couple of minutes, I'm unsure what to do. Continue to hide or get out of here? The adrenaline seems to ooze from me. Now I'm a shaking mess. I need to go. I need to get away. Finally, I dart back into the tunnel before nonchalantly striding away from Gary's house and back towards the safety of my car.

Epilogue

W e didn't attend court today. Verdict day. Claire only had
the baby last week and she's shattered with it all. I hold
my new niece against my shoulder as we wait together for the
news to break with the family liaison officer who's been sent
to support us. I'm not usually a fan of babies, but this time it's
different. I'm related to this one.

This life I've found is beyond anything I could ever have
hoped for. After a lifetime of nothing, absolutely nothing, I've
now got a brother, sister, sister-in-law and niece. Right on cue,
Nellie licks my leg, reminding me of her existence too.

I'm incredibly lucky that Nicola forgave me for my part in
trying to bring her down. She hasn't told Kieren and assures me
she never will. Perhaps I don't deserve her forgiveness, but I'll
spend my whole life making it up to her. I've told her everything
– even admitting to spiking her drink with a sleeping tablet, and
another time with an anti-depressant, after being coerced by
Hugh, but they were the only times. And only one extra tablet on
each occasion, not three like Hugh had demanded. Other than
that, I was only trying to persuade her to stay on her tablets. I
didn't actually do anything.

But I was reporting back to Hugh and Gary with absolutely everything she told me. And, of course, I was lying through my teeth to her the whole time. Even after my initial bitterness waned, I never told her who I really was. I regret it so much. Thank God I saw sense in the end before I ruined her life more than I had already. She's in counselling to talk about how an intelligent woman like she clearly is, could have been taken in with a man like Hugh in the first place. She's also having a phased return back into her job at the university. She's a different person to the one I saw dragging herself around last year.

I'm not sure what the future holds from here, but both mine and Nicola's houses are now on the market. Though who'll want to buy Nicola's after what happened in there is anyone's guess, even though its had specialist contract cleaners in to sort the cellar.

And we've all been able to come to an arrangement about money. Both Nicola and Kieren agreed I was as entitled to some of what our father left – after all, I didn't ask to be born and I certainly didn't ask to be abandoned by him.

No words pass between us all now. The only sound is the occasional vehicle passing by the house. From spending the day deliberating the ins and outs of all possible outcomes, we've been reduced to a periodic click of the mouse as Kieren keeps refreshing the news feed.

Nicola occasionally gets up, walks to the window, walks to the door, and then sits back down again. Claire is absently flicking through a magazine, though I'm sure she isn't actually reading it. I sit as still as a rock, just needing to know. We all keep looking at the family liaison officer – perhaps she'll know something before the media broadcast it.

According to the news reports, the jury finished their deliberations ages ago. There should be a verdict by now. None of us could bring ourselves to go back in to court to hear it.- Giving evidence a couple of days ago was traumatic enough.

Although nothing was as horrendous as making the statements in the first place. I was convinced the police could see straight through everything I was telling them. I was an absolute wreck, but we'd planned exactly what we were going to say, and we stuck to it.

Nicola had nightmares for some time afterwards, especially after going back to the house. We'd allowed enough time for our injuries from the battle with Hugh to heal, and then Nicola had returned there alone, pretending to have only discovered Hugh's body in that moment.

Gary hadn't reported him missing, which we understand will have gone hugely in our favour. I expect he believed that Hugh had buggered off somewhere with Nicola, with the house being all locked up. Even though Hugh and Nicola's entire relationship had been phony from the start, Gary drove himself mad with worry that something more genuine could have developed between them, leaving him out in the cold, as he saw it.

Eight days on, the body was apparently in a poor state and poor Nicola got a face full of flies as she opened the cellar door. But of course, she had to 'discover' him there, and call the police. There was no alternative other than for her to return to his body.

"It's here. It's here." Kieren's voice rings out from the corner of the room. The baby startles in my arms. I lay her in the pram in front of Claire's chair. Then, all at once, we rush across the lounge and gather around Kieren. There's a photograph of Gary, front and central, along with the headline, Killer Twin Caged. I grip the back of Kieren's chair. I can't bear to look at the picture. I feel sick.

"Read it out Kieren." Nicola clutches my arm. "I daren't look."

Even the family liaison officer looks nervous as she rests a hand on Nicola's shoulder.

"OK." He clears his throat. "Leeds Crown Court have today found Gary Anthony Wainwright, aged forty, of Ashfield in West Yorkshire, guilty of the murder of his twin brother Hugh John Wainwright, of Coveley in West Yorkshire, in March of this year.

Police were called to the home of Hugh Wainwright after the discovery of his body was made by his wife. She had been away with family, and it is thought the badly decomposed body lay in the cellar of their home for over a week."

"It still makes me feel sick to think of that." Nicola screws her face up. "I don't think I'll ever forget the stench in there."

"Forensic searches were able to place Gary Wainwright at the scene of his brother's death, and the murder weapon and bloodied items of clothing were discovered at Gary Wainwright's home.

The motive for the killing remains unclear, though it is known there were financial tensions and some jealousies between the two brothers. Gary Wainwright has maintained his innocence throughout the trial, despite having previous convictions for public disorder and violence."

"Well, I never knew that." I say. "I can't believe I ever got involved with either of them."

"You and me both," Nicola replies, though if it hadn't been for me spying on Nicola's night out last year, Hugh would never have known to target her through the dating site. Again, something else I need to forgive myself for.

"Carry on Kieren." Claire squeezes his shoulder.

"Right... The jury heard testimonies from the wife and brother-in-law of the deceased, the partner of the accused, the pathologist, and the chief investigating officer in the case. They also listened to several character statements. It took them less than two hours to unanimously find the defendant guilty of murder.

In his closing comments, his Honour Judge Boothroyd declared Gary Wainwright to be a jealous man, lacking in self-control and moral fibre. He had, he said, demonstrated a level of violence that was incomprehensible, especially since it was perpetrated against his own twin brother. He added that killing him was appalling enough, but to abandon him to his undignified decomposition made what he had done even more dreadful.

Gary Wainwright will be remanded to Yorkshire Prison and will be sentenced in the new year."

We all stare at the screen for a few moments. We've all got to be incredibly guarded in our reactions. After all, we've got someone from the police in our midst.

—— *eee* ——

"I thought she was never going to go." Claire returns to the room with the baby on her shoulder. "We did well not saying anything out of order."

"I know."

"Well, I never." Kieren eventually breaks the silence and looks towards the photograph of his parents. "We did it Dad. Justice." He punches the air. "I wasn't sure we could, you know. The judge and jury clearly found Gary as objectionable as I did when I met him last year. He didn't do himself any favours when he was cross examined, did he?"

"If it wasn't for his car having shown up on the cameras coming and going from your house on the night, we might not

263

have pulled it off." Claire nods at Nicola. "That was bloody lucky."

Nicola lets a long breath out. "It didn't feel lucky when he was hammering on the door and prowling around outside, but now – yes, we've been incredibly fortunate."

"I'm the lucky one here." And I am.

I sweep my gaze around the family who've taken me in, whilst waiting for the inevitable twinge of guilt I've been expecting.

After all, I've helped to ensure Gary ends up where he's now going. And I thought something of him once. I must have done. I wait and I wait. But the guilt doesn't come.

Before you go...

Join my 'keep in touch' list to receive a free book, and to be kept posted of other freebies, special offers and new releases. Being in touch with you, my reader, is one of the best things about being an author.

If you want to read my next psychological thriller, find out more about Frenemy on Amazon.

Book Discussion Group Questions

1. Discuss the factors that initially made Nicola vulnerable to Hugh.
2. Who could have helped Nicola more in her predicament and to what extent did they fail her?
3. Discuss the term gaslighting. What does it mean?
4. How does it manifest in the story?
5. Discuss the reasons Nicola and Kieren's parents might have turned their back on Julie in her childhood.
6. There are said to be seven forms of domestic abuse – what are they, and to what extent does Hugh inflict them on Nicola?
7. Explore the reasons a person might stay trapped in an abusive relationship.
8. The theme of suicide is recurrent. Discuss.
9. Which character elicited most of your sympathy?
10. The other goal of the initial plan was the incarceration of Nicola by sectioning. What might this have achieved for Hugh?

11. Discuss what Hugh and Gary's childhood might have been like.
12. Why might Gary have felt jealous and wary about Nicola?
13. Had Nicola and Julie gone straight to the police, how differently might the story have ended?
14. How do you see each character going forward from this?

FRENEMY - PROLOGUE

I stand back from the door, looking up at the house.- The upstairs is in darkness, but the flickering TV is visible between the cracks of the blind. Is she hiding in there? Ignoring the door? She would have had no idea I was coming tonight, so it can't be that.

I lift the flap of the letterbox and peer inside. Nothing. I check up and down the street. Deserted. I brush the beads of sweat from my brow, before creeping around the side of the house, picking my way through the bins and stepping over plant pots. The gate creaks as I push it open.

Curtains curl out of the open patio doors. As I start in that direction, my attention's diverted to a dark shape at the side of the shed.

It's... She's...

I reach down and take her hand in mine. As my fingers search her wrist, I notice the pool of liquid surrounding her head like a halo. Her hair fluttering in the breeze. Her glassy eyes staring back at me.

Dead.

Available from Amazon

WIN A YORKSHIRE 'GOODIE BAG'

To win a fabulous Yorkshire-themed reader goodie bag, see below to enter the prize draw. I will announce the winner on the 31st May 2022.

To enter:

If you are reading this in eBook - click <u>here</u> to enter, or
If you are reading this in paperback, send a message to:
maria@mariafrankland.co.uk with *Reader Goodie Bag* in the subject line.

BY THE SAME AUTHOR

Psychological Thrillers

Left Hanging

The Man Behind Closed Doors

The Last Cuckoo

Hit and Run

The Hen Party

In His Shadow

Frenemy

The Dark Water Series

The Yorkshire Dipper

Drowned Voices

270

Emergence

Memoir

Don't Call me Mum!

Poetry

Poetry for the Newly Married 40 Something

How-to Books for Writers

Write your Life Story in a Year

Write a Novel in a Year

Write a Collection of Poetry in a Year

Write a Collection of Short Stories in a Year

ABOUT THE AUTHOR

My domestic thrillers shine a light into the darkness that can exist within marital and family relationships. I'm no stranger to turbulent times which has provided some of the material for my novels.

I'm a born 'n' bred Yorkshirewoman, and mum to two grown up sons. In my forties, I've been able to pursue long-held ambitions of gaining an MA in Creative Writing and making writing my full time occupation. I've also married for the second time and found my happy ever after.

This isn't something you will find in my novels though! We thriller writers are amongst the nicest people you could meet because we pour all our darkness into books – it's the romance writers you've got to watch...

I plan to release four novels per year and if you'd like to be kept in the loop about new books and special offers, join my 'keep in touch list' or visit www.autonomypress.co.uk. You'll receive a free novella as a thank you for joining!

ACKNOWLEDGMENTS

Thank you, as always, to my amazing husband, Michael. He's my first reader, and is vital with my editing process for each of my novels. His belief in me means more than I can say.

The next big thank you goes to my brilliant book cover designer Darran Holmes, who always manages to capture the design I have in my head from a simple cover brief, and also to Sue Coates, the photographer who took my author photo.

A special acknowledgement goes to my wonderful advance reader team, who took the time and trouble to read an advance copy of In His Shadow and offer feedback. They are a vital part of my author business and I don't know what I would do without them.

I will always be grateful to Leeds Trinity University and my MA in Creative Writing Tutors there, Martyn, Amina and Oz. My Masters degree in 2015 was the springboard into being able to write as a profession.

And finally, to you, the reader. Thank you for taking the time to read this story. I really hope you enjoyed it.

Made in the USA
Las Vegas, NV
07 May 2022